The aliens have landed. But this time, we are the aliens . . .

Planet G889—humanity's last hope. Fueled by her passion to save her dying son, Devon Adair uses her own wealth and influence to fund the Eden Project—a mission to colonize a new world where children can grow and thrive in a healthy environment.

But a malfunction strands the crew thousands of miles from their destination of New Pacifica. Now, forced to travel through harsh terrain, Devon and her group discover that they are not alone . . .

Leather Wings

The journey continues . . .

And don't miss these other fantastic adventures . . .

and

Puzzle

Available from Ace Books

Earth 2 Novels from Ace Books

EARTH 2
PUZZLE
LEATHER WINGS

EARTH™ 2

LEATHER WINGS

A NOVEL BY

JOHN VORNHOLT

Based on the television series *Earth 2*
from Universal Television and Amblin Entertainment.
Created by Billy Ray
and Michael Duggan & Carol Flint & Mark Levin.

ACE BOOKS, NEW YORK

Earth 2: Leather Wings, a novel by John Vornholt, based on the television series *Earth 2* from Universal Television and Amblin Entertainment. Created by Billy Ray and Michael Duggan & Carol Flint & Mark Levin.

This book is an Ace original edition, and has never been previously published.

EARTH 2: LEATHER WINGS

An Ace Book / published by arrangement with MCA Publishing Rights, a Division of MCA, Inc.

PRINTING HISTORY
Ace edition / May 1995

ISBN: 0-441-00198-X

ACE®
Ace Books are published by The Berkley Publishing Group, 200 Madison Avenue, New York, NY 10016.
ACE and the "A" design are trademarks belonging to Charter Communications, Inc.

PRINTED IN THE UNITED STATES OF AMERICA

10 9 8 7 6 5 4 3 2 1

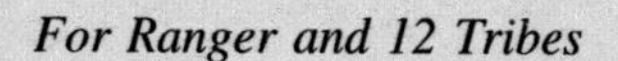

For Ranger and 12 Tribes

Chapter 1

Alonzo Solace was flying, which was not an easy thing to do for a man with a compound fracture in his right leg. But he couldn't think about that now, because canyon walls soared half a mile into the air on either side of him. The majestic ramparts were the color of sunset, and they stretched into jagged buttes that looked like the fingers of a giant. He could see the reddish sun peeping between monstrous archways that looked like rings for the giant's fingers. The rushing wind pounded in his ears and stung his face, but he could still hear the faint sound of rushing water far below him.

Alonzo looked down and caught his breath. Snaking through the wilderness a mile beneath him was a blue-green river, speckled with boulders. As he flew, he dipped lower, and he could see where two rivers collided and roiled into frothy rapids. In the rivers' path, an avalanche had left boulders the size of houses, and the flyer could feel the spray hitting his chest as the water smashed into the rocks, shooting gushers into the air. The danger of water made him angle his wings and glide higher, back toward the monstrous cliffs.

Now he heard more crashing water, and he swept around an outcrop of rock to see a glorious waterfall. The water poured from a hole in the rock and plunged so far and so fast that it turned into mist and rainbows halfway down. Alonzo could barely take his eyes off the waterfall, it was so beautiful. Then a sudden draft of cool air from the waterfall twisted his right wing around, sending him into a dangerous spiral.

Alonzo fought the momentary panic and decided not to save himself by ending his dream. Instead, he concentrated on leveling off and finding a thermal that would take him away from danger. He strained every muscle in his back, shoulders, and arms, but his right wing—or right arm—was in pain. He could feel himself plunging toward the frothy water half-a-mile beneath him.

Reluctantly, he opened his eyes to find two women leaning over his hammock, staring at him with concern. One was the auburn-haired and beautiful Devon Adair. She was intense, some might say obsessive, about the things that mattered to her, but Alonzo liked her. He liked take-charge types, and Devon was certainly that. She had amassed several fortunes before she was thirty, only to give up her privileged life to drag a bunch of strangers twenty-two light-years through space to this chunk of rock called G889. Now she was driving the bedraggled survivors thousands of miles across the wilderness to reach a communications dish. All she cared about was reaching that dish before a shipload of sick children arrived. Devon was tightly wound, but he could deal with people like her.

The other woman, Dr. Julia Heller, he wasn't too sure about. Sure, she was gorgeous—with that angelic face, and golden halo of hair—but she had been genetically enhanced to be beautiful. Julia had never done or said anything against him; in fact, he was her star patient, which galled him no end. He had arrived here the healthiest one of the lot. Maybe what Alonzo hated most about Julia was that she looked at him as a patient, not as the handsome man he knew he was.

By contrast, Devon's son, Uly, had arrived on the planet an invalid, and now he was healthy as a bull. It didn't figure.

Julia scrutinized him as a biologist looks at a microbe. "You were dreaming again, weren't you?" she asked.

"So what if I was?" he growled. "Everybody's got to have a hobby. With my leg broken, that's about all I can do."

As usual, Devon was more direct. "So what were you dreaming about? The dish and New Pacifica? Terrians or Grendlers? Any humans in your dream?"

Alonzo smiled wistfully. "Nobody at all—only this most incredible place. And I was flying." He lifted his arms to demonstrate, and he found that his right arm was still in pain.

"Flying," said Julia doubtfully. She turned to Devon. "Not all his dreams are going to represent contact with the Terrains. Maybe he was just having a pleasant dream."

"Yeah," said Alonzo thoughtfully, "but I never had dreams like that before I came here. In fact, I never had dreams at all. I don't know where that place is, but I hope we never see it."

"Why do you hope that," asked Devon, "if it's so beautiful?"

Alonzo chuckled. "If you ever see this place, you won't need to ask me that, believe me."

Devon granted him a rare smile. “All right, Solace, that’s enough time in dreamland. I’m going to help Danziger load the TransRover and get ready to break camp.” She strode off with her customary briskness.

However, Dr. Julia Heller remained at the side of his hammock. She gave him an encouraging smile and said, “I’m glad you’re having normal dreams. I’m not just worried about your leg, but also about your mental condition.”

“To hell with my mental condition,” grumbled Alonzo. “There’s nothing in my mind that wouldn’t be cured by getting some exercise.”

He sighed and slumped back into his hammock. Damn, he felt like a baby in diapers! And why the hell did he have to have this gorgeous doctor who *looked* at him like a baby in diapers?

“Do you promise to be good?” she asked.

“Yeah,” muttered Alonzo. “Whatever you say, Doc.”

She patted his shoulder. “I’ve got to pack up too. I’ll have somebody bring your breakfast.”

He watched Julia walk off toward the camp they had thrown together last night. He looked around, noting that everyone else was busy—fixing breakfast, packing up supplies, folding tents, or fine-tuning the solar-powered vehicles. Some were efficiently busy, such as John Danziger, and some were just going-through-the-motions busy, like Morgan Martin.

More than anything, Alonzo wanted to get off his back and give that useless bureaucrat what for! As much as he tried to put it behind him, he still blamed Morgan for his crippling accident.

The ex-pilot turned his attention away from the sight of a dozen healthy people, a robot, and Yale, to gaze in the other direction. As far as the eye could see, there was nothing but rolling hills and dense forest. Despite the unspoiled majesty of the landscape, he knew that Terrians could be poking out of the earth at every step, Kobas could be lurking to flick their quills at them, and Grendlers could be waiting to steal them blind.

Twelve miles a day their caravan tried to make, and that was just a few less than Alonzo used to *run* for his morning exercise. They barely made their twelve miles most days, what with the unforgiving terrain and weird animal life. Who knew what else stood between them and their goal of New Pacifica?

He hadn't told Devon and Julia, but the reddish sun that had frolicked among the archways in the canyon of his dream looked awfully similar to the one rising behind the trees right now. If he was going to have an unreal dream, wouldn't he instead dream of the double suns of Aurelia, one of his favorite space ports for rest and relaxation? Why that same red sun?

Alonzo decided not to mention it. No sense getting everyone upset.

"Alonzo," said a youthful voice. He turned to see True, John Danziger's tomboyish, ten-year-old daughter, a moon-faced kid with an attitude. He grinned at her, because she was his favorite member of this goofy band. She looked especially good holding a bowl of spirolina stew.

"Hi, True," he said, taking the bowl from her. "How's it going?"

True scowled. "Uly took off in your ATV again. But we've already called to get him back."

"It's not *my* ATV," he snapped. "I'd be very happy to walk."

The girl looked down, and Alonzo instantly regretted his churlishness. "I didn't mean to be grumpy," he said.

"I know. Dr. Heller told us that you might be feeling grumpy."

"Yeah, well," he muttered, "I wish she wouldn't think of me as such a burden."

"She doesn't," True countered. "Nobody does. After all, you're the only link we have with the Terrians."

Alonzo rapped his knuckles on his splint. "That's more of a burden than this bum leg, believe me. So, are we going to make our twelve miles today?"

True motioned toward the great unknown stretching before them. "That depends on what's out there."

"Yeah," mused Alonzo, thinking of the mile-deep canyon of his dreams. "Let's hope we get lucky. You don't need to hang around me—I think your dad could use some help."

"Hey, I like talking to you. You're like our guru, or something."

Alonzo rolled his eyes. "Oh, please. I'm just an idiot pilot with a broken leg. After all those jumps, the law of averages was bound to catch up with me."

True started off toward the truck-sized TransRover, then twirled around. "I'm looking forward to walking with you, Alonzo!"

"Me too!" He smiled and waved back. True joined her dad, and they walked across the camp, passing among Devon, Uly, Bess, Julia, and the other good people in this misbegotten crew. Despite being the blind leading the blind, this bunch gave Alonzo hope. Who knew? Maybe they could march across this continent and reach the beacon dish before the colony ship arrived.

Or not, thought Alonzo. Sometimes this starstruck caravan reminded him of the line from the old blues song: *If it wasn't for bad luck, we wouldn't have no luck at all.*

Good luck was with them for most of that day's journey. That was Yale's assessment at any rate. Yale was a cyborg with dark, leathery skin; he was part man, mostly machinery. Most of the bionics had been added during his thirty years of servitude to Devon Adair and her family, as they had spent goodly sums to update him and keep him in top repair. And keep him alive. Whenever Yale felt old, he reminded himself that he *was* old. Most people considered him to be an antique.

He could remember bits of his past, when he had been entirely human, but he tried not to. That human had been a criminal. His more recent memories, dating from his early tutorship of Devon, were much more pleasant, and he preferred to think of them as his real past.

Yale had plenty of time to think, as the DuneRail he was driving jostled over the uneven terrain, flattening scraggly bushes, swerving around trees. He was capable of taking control of the solar-powered dune buggy, but he didn't need to. He let Zero's podlike head drive most of the time. Zero was their all-purpose robot, the only robot to survive the looting of the cargo pod. It was just as well, thought Yale, because one Zero was enough.

Zero's head was affixed to a special port in the front of the DuneRail, and it was singing:

"Michael, row the boat ashore. Alleluya! Michael, row the boat ashore. Alleluya! The River Jordan is deep and cold. Alleluya! Chills the body but not the soul. Alleluya!"

Yale broke in. "My dear Zero, you have been singing that song for six miles now, and maybe there are two dozen words in it, most of which are 'Hallelujah.' Do you think you could sing a different song?"

"Do you know 'Kumbaya?' " asked Zero.

They careened over a bump, which jarred every servo in Yale's body. It was a few seconds before he could answer, "Yes, I know 'Kumbaya.' What is your fixation with campfire songs?"

"Devon Adair suggested that we are on a camping trip,"

answered Zero. "At least, she suggested that the others would feel more comfortable thinking we are on a camping trip."

Yale shook his head. "It may *seem* like a camping trip, but we can't fool anyone about what kind of trip this really is. It's a great trip of exploration and adventure, unseen since the ruthless *conquistadors* of Spain first set foot in the New World."

"*Conquistadors?*" asked Zero's head. "You know I'm not programmed to speak Spanish. Speak English, please."

"It means 'conquerors,'" answered Yale. "But we aren't conquerors. For one thing, there are far too few of us to conquer anything. For another thing, we have learned from all the ruthless conquerors of the past. Conquering for the sake of precious metals or a misguided sense of moral superiority only results in enslaved and downtrodden native peoples. Do we want that?"

"Some of us do," answered Zero. "Mr. Morgan Martin, for one. The mining companies, for another."

"Then they are misguided," said Yale. "The purpose of this mission is the health and continuation of the human race. Witness how young Uly has benefited from his contact with this planet and the Terrians. The Syndrome that has afflicted so many human children is in complete remission with Uly."

"That might be a coincidence," said Zero.

Yale shook his head. His bodiless companion had a singular lack of imagination. Of course, he reminded himself, Zero wasn't built for imagination, but for heavy construction, controlling machinery, and driving vehicles. Sometimes Yale despaired that anyone on this trek, including Devon, really understood the monumental importance of their mission. Other worlds had been colonized, but it was always in the name of profit and greed. G889 was the first chance to do it right—to change both history and humanity for the better.

"Kumbaya, my Lord, kumbaya!" sang Zero. "Ooooh, Lord, kumbaya!"

Yale rolled his eyes back in his head, just as they crested a ridge, so he didn't see the sharp decline and chasm until Zero slammed on the brakes. The tires of the DuneRail spun in reverse, knocking him forward into the windshield.

"What are you . . ." Yale's voice trailed off, and his aged eyes bugged out.

"Hang on!" warned Zero.

Zero kept the DuneRail in reverse, but they were on some kind of chalky surface that offered no traction and was crumbling beneath their wheels. Yale craned his neck slightly and could see the edge of the cliff dead ahead. The chasm had no end in sight! The other side of the canyon was so far away that it looked as if it were on another continent.

The wheels of the vehicle were spinning at full throttle in reverse, spewing up clouds of white dust, and they still kept slipping the wrong way—toward the edge of the cliff.

"Stop spinning!" ordered Yale. "It's not working! Go slow. Get some traction."

Zero obeyed, and the wheels slowed to a steady grind. Still, it didn't help much, and the DuneRail hung in a precarious state, not quite climbing off the decline but not slipping at its previous rate. They might have a full minute to act, thought Yale, instead of mere seconds. He wasn't as nimble as he used to be, but the cyborg clambered over the seat and jumped off the rear of the vehicle.

"Oh, fine!" moaned Zero. "Just leave my head attached to this thing, while you save yourself . . ."

"Don't give up!" snapped Yale. He dashed to the top of the rise and began yanking vines and bushes out of the soil as fast as he could. He hurled them toward the spinning tires, not bothering to look at how accurate his aim was. He kept throwing more and more stuff, hoping that something would catch under the wheels and give the vehicle some traction.

"It's working!" yelled Zero with delight. "I'm climbing up!"

Yale didn't pause to admire his handiwork. He just kept throwing brush into the path of the vehicle, until it abruptly rumbled toward him, and he had to scramble out of the way. The DuneRail shot over the rise and came to a dead stop. Zero killed the motor and just sat there.

Yale took several deep breaths, staggered back to the vehicle, and sank into his seat. "Well," he said, "now we know why they send *us* out in front of everybody else."

"Gosh!" exclaimed Zero. "We'd better report that thing. What is it?"

Yale shook his head in disbelief. "It is a gigantic, immense canyon. Miles across, perhaps miles deep. It's quite beautiful, I'm sure, if you could calmly admire it instead of nearly plunging into it. Let's not report this discovery until I have a chance to take a better look. By foot this time."

Yale stepped slowly out of the vehicle, his limbs aching from the effort of their escape, and trudged to the top of the rise. He took a sharp intake of breath. Stretching in both directions as far as he could see was a rift that was so huge it seemed to descend to the very core of the planet. Majestic plateaus of copper rock rose up on all sides, and some buttes rose in the middle of the canyon, like islands in the air. The sheer cliffs dropped to dizzying depths, yet there was a vertical carpet of lush vegetation clinging to the canyon walls. Waterfalls poured like giant faucets from the far wall, tumbling to the bottom in misty elegance.

There were immense stretches of metamorphic rock,

polished into weird shapes and colors by eons of rushing water. Millions of years ago, thought Yale, there must have been a river flowing here that would have made the Mississippi River look like a mud puddle. Perhaps it still flowed, somewhere in the depths of this awesome spectacle.

He heard Zero's voice. "Haven't you seen enough? When are we going to tell them?"

Yale sighed. "They're over a mile behind us," he said. "I'm in no hurry to tell them that our journey may be ending right here."

The TransRover chewed up the terrain with its balloon tires, keeping a steady if unspectacular pace. Still, eight-year-old Uly Adair had no problem walking beside it. The vehicle looked like a big dune buggy, piled high with supplies and equipment. In the cockpit rode the driver, John Danziger, and half-a-dozen passengers were scrunched down among the sleeping bags and rolled-up tents. The colonists traded off walking and riding, just like settlers on the old wagon trains in the American West. But riding wasn't Uly's style anymore. He loved to walk, to feel his muscles expanding, getting stronger. He loved the raw feeling of air in his lungs and dirt on his face.

Uly had never imagined that the mere act of walking could bring such joy. The others, especially his mom, Dr. Heller, and True, often looked at him as if they expected him to keel over. But he was going to surprise them!

He had spent the first eight years of his life as a weakling in an immuno-suit, and he wasn't going back to that life. Not ever. He'd die first; it was that simple. This is what he had dreamed about all his young life—a big adventure, and a body strong enough to live it. When the Terrians had pulled him into the ground, they had given him a rebirth. He couldn't explain it—no one could. Maybe Alonzo came closest to understanding what had happened to him, but the change in Alonzo was small compared to his. Uly was G889's first guinea pig, and as far as he was concerned, the experiment was a grand success.

Bess and Morgan Martin were riding on the TransRover, as usual, and Bess looked down at Uly with a kind smile. "Hey, Uly, do you want to ride for a while? Morgan could use some exercise."

"Now, Bess," protested the fussy Morgan, "the boy needs the exercise more than I do. Besides, I've got a cramp in my legs from this lousy heat."

Bess smiled sweetly. "Maybe you need the Terrians to kidnap you, too, honey."

"No, thanks," answered Morgan, taking her joke seriously. "All I need is a little rest, some decent food, a vacation on a nice space station. Civilization—that's all I need." He leaned back on a sleeping bag and pulled his hat over his eyes, as if to end this unpleasant discussion with a quick nap.

Bess shrugged at Uly, and he grinned back at her. He wasn't about to complain. No matter what hardships lay ahead of them, they had to be better than a life of wheezing helplessness. He slowed his brisk walk to a stroll and let the TransRover rumble ahead of him. A handful of settlers trudged past him, including Zero's headless body, jerking along as if it were perfectly normal not to have a head.

A few seconds later, Alonzo cruised past in the ATV, giving him a jaunty salute. Alonzo was the one who needed to go underground with the Terrians, Uly thought. But the pilot had his own special relationship with them, and it apparently didn't include any quick healing.

"Uly," said a familiar voice, and he turned to see his mother, Devon, striding toward him.

"Yeah, Mom?"

"We could find you a spot on the TransRover," she said with concern.

"No, thanks, Mom. When I'm tired, I'll let you know."

"Will you?" she asked doubtfully.

He laughed and looked up at the reddish sun riding high in the sky. "How could I be tired on a beautiful day like this? I feel like I could *fly* to New Pacifica!"

She shook her head. "You and Alonzo are both into flying today. I think we're all starting to feel the loss of the hovercraft."

"Believe me," said Uly, "even if we had a hovercraft, I would rather walk. It's the greatest feeling. The only thing I would rather do than walk is . . . *run*!"

He dashed away from her toward the back of the strange caravan. He could see True, bringing up the rear as usual. She liked to walk in the back, because she had a secret in her backpack.

At Uly's approach, something squirmed in the canvas bag, and the flap lifted up. A scaly little arm poked out.

"How's your friend?" asked Uly.

True looked at him warily. Even though he hadn't given away her secret yet, he knew that she didn't trust him to keep quiet. Uly couldn't exactly say that he and True were friends, but she was the only one in the group who was even close to his own age. When one of them got into trouble, the other one usually did too.

Now the Koba poked his scaly head out of the bag. Uly gave him a little wave, and the alien creature gave him one right back. Expert mimics they were, thought Uly. Too bad those quills they tossed off with a flick of the wrist were so dangerous. This very same Koba had put Commander O'Neill into a deathlike coma—gotten him buried alive. The adults hadn't stopped thinking about that terrible incident. They would go bananas if they knew that True had made friends with the Koba and was bringing him along on their trek.

"He seems fine," said Uly when she didn't answer.

"Yeah," she admitted. "I don't know if I could get rid of him now, even if I wanted to."

"Then don't," said the boy. "I've made up my mind that Terrians and Kobas are friendly. At least, the ones I've met are. I don't know about those Grendlers."

They had pretty much figured out that the toadlike Grendlers had stolen their supplies and equipment from the cargo pod. The Terrians seemed to be afraid of Grendlers, and that was enough to make Uly leery of them too. He kept wondering if someday he would see a bunch of Grendlers flying around in their hovercraft.

"You know," said Uly, "this is going to be a pretty long hike. You might as well be friendly to me."

True blinked at him in surprise. "I thought I was being friendly to you."

"Oh, yeah?" asked Uly. "When we first met, you acted like I was a freak. You called me all kinds of names. And you blamed me for getting you and your dad stranded here. Did I leave anything out?"

True smiled shyly. "When we first met, you *were* a freak. I had never seen a kid with The Syndrome before."

"Well, better get used to it. You're going to see hundreds of them when the colony ship gets here."

True stared ahead of them. "When the colony ship gets here, my dad and I can leave."

In shock, Uly asked, "You'd leave this place?"

The Koba gave them a matching look of shock that made both of the children laugh. True finally shook her head.

"I don't know what we're going to do," she admitted. "Nobody planned on us being here. My dad counted on making enough money from this job to buy a little place somewhere and settle down."

Uly motioned around at the pristine wilderness. "Now you've got a whole planet where you can settle down."

"After what happened to you, it's normal that you want to stay here," said True. "You got what you came for. But we're still trying to figure out what we want, if you know what I mean."

"Your dad is great with machines," offered Uly. "I would think he could do whatever he wanted to."

True snorted a laugh. "You don't know much about the job opportunities for mechanics these days. But I guess you wouldn't—you were born rich."

"Hey!" said Uly in protest. "I can tell you a thing or two about having problems . . ."

But True had stopped in her tracks and was staring at the vehicles ahead of them. "Something's wrong."

Uly looked too, and he could see that both the Trans-Rover and the ATV had stopped in their tracks. True's dad leapt off the TransRover and was jogging toward Uly's mom and the others. Sure enough, something must be up.

"I'll race you there!" said Uly.

They were both off in a flash. Much to Uly's chagrin, True was soon ahead of him, even with her backpack and passenger bouncing along behind her. Of course, he tried to tell himself, she was two years older than he was, and she had been healthy all her life. Still, it burned him when she reached the knot of settlers first.

John Danziger stood looking into the distance, his hands on his hips. He was square-jawed, and there was a quiet presence about him, as if he knew more than he ever said.

"I just got a call from Yale," he reported. "There's something about half-a-mile ahead of us. He says it's big."

"Big?" asked Devon. "Is that all he said? What does he mean by that?"

Danziger shrugged. "I don't know. He said he couldn't describe it, that we had to see it with our eyes. He said that we should proceed on foot, bringing up the vehicles slowly."

"Quicksand?" asked Morgan Martin with abject terror. "I *hate* quicksand."

Devon scowled at him. "Yale knows how to describe quicksand. If it was something we'd seen before, he would just tell us. Let's do exactly as he says. All of us will walk ahead, and Danziger and Solace will bring up the vehicles at half speed. Okay with you?"

"Sure," said Danziger.

Alonzo Solace didn't say anything. He was just leaning on the steering wheel of his ATV, staring into the distance.

"Did you hear me, Solace?" asked Devon, louder.

He turned to her, a weary look on his face. "I heard you. There's something big ahead of us. We can get there at half speed or full speed—it doesn't make any difference. If it's what I think it is, this thing is not going anywhere."

Chapter 2

"Good Lord," muttered Devon Adair, as she climbed the rise and came face-to-face with infinity. That's what the canyon looked like to her—a series of deep gashes in the crust of the planet that seemed to extend forever in either direction, and to descend forever into limbo. There was no way to fathom the forces that had created this divide, and it made her feel small and helpless just to look at it.

Devon was in the lead, and there were gasps all around her as the others caught up.

"Awesome!" said Uly, and for once it was exactly the right word.

"Gee," said Bess, "you could fit two or three Grand Canyons in there."

"How are we—" Julia Heller began, but she cut herself off.

"Wow!" exclaimed Morgan. "I want to claim the mineral rights! And the tourist rights! And hologram reproduction rights!"

Bess patted him on the shoulder. "You can't own this, honey."

Devon couldn't take her eyes off the majestic gorge, even as she heard the vehicles stop behind her and their motors cut off. The setting sun deepened the shadows and made the jutting buttes seem higher than mountains peaks, and the plunging depths were deeper than oceans. The crevasse was ageless, unfathomable, unconquerable . . .

Uncrossable.

"Damn!" yelled Devon, throwing her cap to the ground.

"Careful," said John Danziger as he strode up behind her. "You throw that cap over the edge, and you may never see it again."

She stared at him. "I'll tell you what I'll never see again—the communications dish! New Pacifica! Those sick children! How the hell are we going to get across this?"

Danziger gave her a wry smile. "Not much for appreciating nature, are you?"

"I'd appreciate it just fine," scowled Devon, "from a hovercraft!"

From deep in the canyon, some bird made a cawing sound that reverberated up the canyon wall. Devon grunted and scooped up her cap. She slapped it against her thigh to get the chalky dirt off.

"Sorry, Danziger," she muttered. "There's no reason I should be mad at you. This canyon is gorgeous all right, but it stands between us and New Pacifica. Unless my eyes are playing tricks on me, it goes for hundreds of miles in either direction."

"Probably *thousands* of miles," said a cultured voice. She turned to see Yale walking toward them, holding Zero's head in his hands. He carefully set the head onto Zero's body and twisted it into place.

"Thank you," said the rejoined robot.

"You've looked around?" asked Devon.

"I don't need to look around," answered the cyborg. "It takes billions of years to get erosion like this. The course of this river has probably changed little since the first single-cell organism evolved on this planet. We know that we're approximately in the center of a huge continent, so we can assume this is approximately the middle of the river. This is no isolated formation—this is what it looks like for thousands of miles."

"Great," muttered Devon. Something caught her eye, and she shrieked, "Uly!"

The boy was hanging over the lip of the chasm, with only his skinny legs and butt in view. With several quick strides she reached him, grabbed the waistband of his pants, and yanked him back to safety.

"What's the matter with you!"

"Mom," he protested, "I was just trying to get a better look. I was holding on." He showed her the stub of a branch in his hand. It had been ripped out by the roots.

"So what did you see?" asked Devon, trying to calm herself.

"It's pretty far down," he answered, "but I think I see water down there! If there's a river, couldn't we build rafts or something, and float to the coast?"

"No way," said a voice behind them. Devon turned to see Alonzo, leaning on the steering wheel of his ATV.

"The river has rapids like you wouldn't believe," he said. "Taking a raft down there would be suicide. I've rafted rough waters before, but nothing like that."

"You dreamed about this place, didn't you?" asked Devon.

"Yep," he admitted. "I hoped it was only a dream. As you can see, it wasn't."

"Did you dream of a way down?" asked Julia.

Alonzo shook his head. "I was falling to my death when I woke up."

This somber pronouncement was followed by several moments of reflective silence. There was no point in them speaking their minds, as everyone shared the same thought. They were finished. At best, thought Devon, they could hike along the rim of the canyon until the river turned into a delta, but that could take them thousands of miles out of their way. It would delay them a year or more from their goal, and maybe cause the breakup of the band.

Trying to cheer up the others, Yale stepped forward and declared, "We should take heart in the fact that we have made an amazing discovery! This canyon may be the most remarkable natural phenomenon on the entire planet!"

"Yeah," muttered Julia, "but it won't get us any closer to New Pacifica."

Devon slammed her fist into her palm and vowed, "We're not going to give up! There's got to be a way across, and we're going to find it."

No one argued with her, but the argument was staring them all in the face. It was miles deep and miles wide, and it was carved out of sheer rock.

"It would be nice," said Alonzo, "if the rest of my dream was true."

"What was that?" asked Julia.

He smiled wistfully. "In my dream, I could *fly* across this canyon." He touched the splint on his leg. "I know it sounds crazy, but it seemed so real in my dream."

"It's getting dark," said Danziger. "Time to make camp. It looks like there's plenty of firewood around here—"

"Excuse me," Yale interrupted. "This area has a considerable amount of sediment and volcanic material that can crumble easily. My advice is to establish our camp about a hundred yards to the east, where there is solid granite and limestone underfoot."

"Lead on," said Danziger.

Out of habit, Devon nearly asked Yale how many miles they had traveled that day. But she stopped herself, thinking that this could be the last mile the band of survivors traveled together. How many of them would follow her down a river of no return?

Devon gazed again into the canyon. The fading sunlight tried to pierce its depths but failed, leaving only a few streaks of gold on the rusty buttes. It was so ironic that their ambitious dreams for G889 could be thwarted by the most spectacular natural wonder on the planet.

"Confidentially," said John Danziger to Yale as they strode ahead of the others, "even a scouting trip down the canyon could take several days. So let's find a place we can call home for a while."

Danziger looked thoughtfully at the canyon. "It may be a long while."

"The sooner we find out what to expect, the better," answered Yale. "It will be a disaster if we can't go on."

"By the looks of that chasm," said Danziger, surveying a sheer cliff on the other side, "it's going to take a lot of determination to go on."

"That should still be our goal, don't you think?" Yale asked with alarm.

"Yep, until we've figured out that it's too risky. Getting to New Pacifica isn't worth losing lives."

"Agreed," said Yale solemnly. He stopped and pointed to a clearing amid the trees about fifty meters away from the crevice. "May I suggest this spot? It's on bedrock, but it's close enough to the canyon to monitor temperature changes and weather conditions."

Danziger cupped his hands and yelled to the rest of the weary, still-in-shock band of survivors, "We'll camp in the clearing! Follow Yale. Firewood detail, get to work! Tent detail, pound those stakes in hard—we may be here a few days."

He didn't need to expand on that possibility.

Collecting the firewood was supposed to be the job of the children, Baines, Magus, Bess, and Morgan. Bess Martin was good at it. As the only one of them born and raised in the polluted wilds of Earth, the friendly brunette had a feel for the land. She never tried to collect growing branches with green leaves on them, and she had an eye for picking out fallen timber that was dry enough to burn. Bess wasn't so good at picking men, in Danziger's opinion, but there was no denying, or explaining, her devotion to Morgan Martin.

He could see the two of them in the fading light. Bess was lugging a sack twice her size and bulging with wood, and she was headed toward a tree that had been split by lightning. Morgan, on the other hand, was tugging uselessly at a bunch of living roots that would never burn. But they happened to be nearby.

Danziger finished pounding in a tent stake and hefted his combination axe/hammer onto his shoulder. Morgan apparently didn't have the good sense to follow his wife's example, and maybe he would need a gentle reminder just to follow her and do what she did.

He strode toward the struggling bureaucrat. "Morgan, that won't ever burn. Bess has the right idea—why don't you follow her?"

"Why don't you mind your own business?" scowled Morgan. As if to show his manliness, he gripped the root for all he was worth and yanked. But his hands slipped, and he tumbled back onto his butt.

Danziger couldn't help his laughter. "Sorry," he said. "The idea is to *gather* firewood, not create it."

Morgan glared up at him. "Now I'm being bossed around by a dumb mechanic."

Danziger's face darkened, but he tried to remember that it wasn't personal. Morgan was a jerk to everyone. He extended his hand and helped him to his feet.

"This is all pointless," muttered Morgan, brushing off his pants. "We've reached the end of the line, and you know it."

"That remains to be seen," said Danziger, sounding angry. He had to remind himself that he had voiced a similar sentiment a few minutes ago.

"Anyway, Morgan, you seemed happy enough to see the canyon. You claimed it for everything it was worth."

"Yes," Morgan admitted, "and I intend to stay here and *guard* my claim to Martin Canyon."

"Martin Canyon?" asked the mechanic with a smile.

"Martin River too," said Morgan. "And, Danziger, there's no sense pretending with me. You know damn well that we'll never cross that monster without a fleet of aircraft. I say we make camp permanently here and send for some mining equipment. It may take a few years to get Martin Mining off the ground, but we can all be rich!"

Danziger lifted his strong jaw and stared into the gloom that was quickly engulfing the horizon. "Mining companies, get-rich-quick schemes—that life is all behind us. You're the one who's fooling himself. This is reality for us, not corporate boardrooms and mining contracts. Maybe mining ships will follow us someday, but I sorta doubt it. This planet is too far away from Earth to make it practical. That's why Devon chose it."

"Damn her," growled Morgan. "She won't listen to any kind of reason. I hate idealists."

"Listen," said Danziger, "Bess has got a big bag of wood, and the sooner you get it back to camp, the sooner we can start dinner."

The mention of food got his attention. "Okay," said Morgan. "It's not like I don't want to cooperate. It's just that all of this is new to me."

"Right."

The bureaucrat started off. "Remember what I said about getting rich. I could use a can-do partner like you!"

Danziger nodded glumly. He was "can-do" all right. Look what all his doing had gotten him so far—no money in the bank and a primitive life on an alien planet fraught with danger. What every parent dreamt of for his young daughter. He sighed and trudged back to camp, wondering if, indeed, this would be their home for a long time to come.

The campfire was sputtering its last spark, and a chill was seeping from the dark canyon beyond its circle of light. Uly pulled the blanket tighter around his shoulders and crept a few inches closer to the fire. He could get off his rear end, he supposed, and find some more sticks to throw on the fire, but he was afraid somebody would see him. He was supposed to be asleep. Everyone else was, as far as he could tell, except for Zero, who kept watch in the woods, about fifty yards away from the camp.

Uly was too excited to sleep, but he didn't know why. He should've been upset about this giant obstacle, like his mom and everyone else was. But there was something fascinating about it, something that beckoned him to explore its amazing depths. From the moment he had first seen the canyon, he had wanted to lean over the edge and look deeper into it. Even now, in the dark, he was tempted to grab a flashlight to steal a look. Was it the danger of those sheer cliffs? The grandeur of its soaring peaks? Or maybe, he thought, it was the way it cut deep into the center of this planet, into a place where he felt he belonged.

At any rate, he didn't fear the canyon, and he was anxious for first light, when he could go exploring. That is, if his mother would let him. He sighed, wondering if she would ever consider him anything but an invalid. When he felt like that, he just wanted to crawl back into his tent.

Suddenly Uly saw a small figure dart across the circle of firelight and disappear. A second later, a slightly larger figure followed the same path, and this figure was holding a flashlight.

Uly was on his feet in an instant, casting off the blanket. He thought he recognized both figures, but he wasn't entirely sure. He was sure of one thing, though: Both of them were headed straight toward the canyon.

"True!" he whispered. "Be careful!"

The flashlight stopped. "Ssshhh!" Her voice hissed. "Don't wake anyone."

He stepped cautiously toward her and whispered, "You're the one who's running around and causing a commotion."

"It's the Koba," she explained. "He was snuggling with me in my sleeping bag, when we heard a little twittering sound. Then he was off like a shot—that way."

True ran her flashlight beam along the ground until it got swallowed up in the utter blackness of the ravine.

"Well," said Uly, "it probably heard some other Kobas and decided to join them. You know, it wasn't likely that it would stay with you forever."

"No," True said firmly. "It didn't come all this way just to leave me now."

Something rustled in the dark bushes at the lip of the canyon, and True followed the sound with the flashlight.

Suddenly the Koba jumped out, the scales of its lithe body gleaming in the spotlight. It chattered and shielded its eyes from the beam, and True pointed the light elsewhere to spare it. Then she got worried and tried to find the Koba again with the beam, but it was gone.

"This is a great place to play hide-and-seek," muttered Uly.

"He wants us to follow him."

"Yeah," said Uly, "a mile or two straight down."

The girl smiled mischievously. "I saw you looking over the edge. You want to see what's down there, don't you?"

"Yeah," admitted Uly, "but not in the dark."

There came a twittering sound several yards to their left, and True again aimed the flashlight. This time they were astounded to see several lithe figures scampering among the bushes. They disappeared almost as soon as the flashlight beam caught them.

"Come on," whispered True.

She shuffled cautiously to the lip of the blackness, keeping the flashlight beam on the ground a few inches ahead of her feet. Uly felt like a fool, but he followed her. They had pitched their camp about a hundred yards away from the place where they had first discovered the canyon. Because of the hurried relocation, there hadn't been time to inspect the rim of the canyon here. Uly would have preferred to explore it by daylight, but there was no guarantee his mother would let him.

Suddenly the little Koba, or one just like it, poked his head above some scrubby bushes and waved. When True turned the light in its direction, it popped out of sight, but another one leapt across the beam. Unless the Kobas were committing suicide, thought Uly, there had to be something beyond the bushes for them to stand on.

True got down on her hands and knees to creep closer to the edge. "Hold onto my belt," she whispered.

It reminded Uly of the rude way in which his mother had snatched him from the rim of the canyon, but Uly grabbed the back of her pants as instructed. By the wavering flashlight beam, he could see that the cliff didn't drop straight off here, as it did other places. The slope was steep but more gradual, and it was covered with shrubs and deformed-looking pod plants.

"Look!" gasped True. "A path!"

Sure enough, saw Uly, there was a well-worn trail of smooth dirt winding down between the bushes and out of sight. Being a Koba path, it was only about eight inches wide. But a person could travel it, thought Uly, if he were very brave. Of course, there were no handrails, and one false step would mean a quick, one-way trip to the bottom of the chasm.

"Let's go tell my mom," Uly suggested.

"But what about my Koba?" asked True. "I want to find him before we bring everyone over here. You know what they would do to him. If you're afraid, you can go back."

"I'm not afraid," the boy grumbled.

"Kitty, Kitty!" whispered True. "Come on back."

She stuck the flashlight in her mouth, like a single headlight, and crept down the path on her hands and knees. That at least gave her a low center of gravity, thought Uly. He got down on his hands and knees and followed close behind, ready to grab her at a moment's notice. Although he wasn't real fond of True, he wouldn't want to see her plunge thousands of feet to her death. A death on the heels of what happened to Commander O'Neill would probably cause a mutiny against his mom.

"Whoa!" True gasped as her left hand came down into open space.

He instantly grabbed her calves. "This is crazy," he breathed.

True shined her flashlight off to the left and found nothing but blackness. She shined it to the right, and Uly could see where the path meandered upward, around the outcrop of boulder on which they were crawling. He could also see the little Koba, down on its hands and knees, inching along in perfect mimicry of them.

They both laughed with relief, but Uly could feel his arms and legs shaking. A blast of cool air struck them, as if the canyon were yawning.

"I want to go back," moaned Uly. "But I'm not sure how."

He and True were hemmed in by rock and thickets on one side and certain death on the other. There was no room on the path to turn around, without standing up, and he for sure didn't want to do that. Nor did he want to try to negotiate the narrow path in reverse.

True seemed to read his mind. "We have to keep going . . . until we can find a place to turn around."

Uly gulped. "Okay."

He took courage in the fact that the path meandered upward, even if it was just for a few feet. True put the flashlight back into her mouth and started crawling, with Uly on her tail. It seemed like an eternity that they inched forward, scraping their hands on nettles and bushes. Uly was almost relieved that it was so dark, because he didn't want to see the gaping gorge below them. Nor did he want to see that they had spent an hour traveling ten feet, but that's what it felt like.

They journeyed in silence, except for the wind, which picked up a lonesome moan as it whistled through the darkness. As for their progress, thought Uly, it didn't feel as if they were going either up or down, just sideways.

Suddenly the beam of light wavered, and he thought True was falling! But she was just stopping to take the flashlight out of her mouth.

"Uh-oh," she said.

"What? What?"

"I've hit a stone wall." She moved her hand along the cold granite. "The path continues, but it's like the ledge on a skyscraper."

"And the wind is picking up," Uly added with a shiver. "Where's the Koba?"

True shook her head glumly. "I think he's ahead of us, but I don't know for sure. We'll have to figure out a way to turn around."

"Great," muttered Uly. "It's even narrower here than it was back there!"

"You didn't have to come," said True. Then she softened her tone. "Your mom will kiss us when we show her this path."

"If she doesn't kill us first."

True shone the light a few feet behind them, up the sheer canyon wall. There didn't seem to be any footholds or handholds, nothing but unforgiving rock and a few scraggly bushes. They weren't going to climb out, that was for sure. A deep, howling sound assaulted their ears.

"What's that?" asked Uly, scared.

True looked back at him and shook her head. "I don't know. Listen, maybe we should just plan on staying here until it's daylight."

"Can't we call for help?" asked Uly.

"Do you want our parents to go diving off that cliff looking for us? They will, you know, if we start yelling our heads off. This was dumb to come out here in the dark, I admit it."

Uly snorted a laugh. "You, the great True Danziger,

wrong about something? Excuse me, while I alert the universe."

True frowned. "There's no sense being nasty about it. I thought I could get the Koba to come back to bed. Guess I'm not a Koba."

"Well, you can't climb rocks like one, that's for sure. Do you think there's enough room to sit down here? Maybe if we swung our legs off the edge . . ."

"Yeah!" True exclaimed. "Maybe if we swung our legs out, we could turn around. It's worth a try!"

"I was thinking about just sitting."

But True had already taken the initiative. She set the flashlight on the ledge and pressed herself against the rock wall. With the flashlight shining out into space, Uly couldn't see exactly what True was doing, so he backed off a few inches to give her more room. Again they heard the strange howl, and it distracted her for a moment.

True gasped as her rear end slid off the rock! Uly could see her losing her balance, clawing the air, pitching forward. He reached out for her, but he had moved himself too far away! His strangled cry mingled with hers as the ten-year-old tumbled off the ledge.

"True!"

In the blink of an eye, she was gone.

The flashlight rolled after her, and he saw it bounce off a rock and disappear. Then all was darkness.

Chapter 3

• • • • • • • •

Yale was leaning against a tree trunk, dozing, when Zero shook him awake.

"Master Yale," said the stocky robot, "I must speak with you."

The aged cyborg blinked his eyes and looked around. The night was still pitch black and much colder than before. "Are there intruders?" he asked.

"No," answered Zero.

"Then can it wait until morning?"

Zero considered the question for a moment. "I suppose." He turned and clanked away.

But Yale was already awake. He straightened his bionic limbs and heaved himself to his feet. "Zero," he whispered, "wait!"

The robot stopped obediently and waited for him to catch up. "Yes?"

The cyborg yawned. "What is it? What did you want to tell me?"

The robot shrugged. "Only that the children are missing."

"What?"

"Missing," repeated Zero. "You know that it is part of my security program to check the supplies and personnel every two hours. We wouldn't want any more abductions or robberies."

"Yes, yes," said Yale immediately, "go on."

"When I ran a visual check, I found neither Uly Adair nor True Danziger in their sleeping bags. A subsequent check confirmed that they are not in camp at all."

Yale looked around at the sleepy camp, with its smoldering fire, neat rows of tents, and slumbering vehicles, drawn around the sleeping settlers like the covered wagons of old Earth. Nothing whatsoever seemed out of the ordinary except, of course, for the immense canyon looming nearby in the darkness.

"You're sure there were no intruders?" asked the cyborg.

"Positive," answered Zero. "Of course, the Terrians can appear suddenly from underground, but I detected no vibrations. Should we wake the others?"

Yale twisted his wizened face in thought. "Not quite yet," he answered. "Perhaps they took a walk. You check the forest, and I'll get a lantern and check the canyon."

The robot cocked his head in a puzzled manner. "They wouldn't go walking in the canyon, would they?"

Yale sighed. "One thing you learn about human children is that they are capable of anything."

Uly didn't know how long he sat there, stiff as the spires of rocks all around him. He was afraid to move, afraid to breathe, afraid to think. True was dead! Well, he told himself, he didn't know that for sure. He didn't know anything for sure, sitting there on the edge of a cliff in almost total darkness.

He wanted to scream, to holler as loud as he could for help. But True had been right about one thing: causing a panic out here in the darkness would probably result in more deaths. He had to stay calm. If he fell off the ledge too, then no one could report what had happened. It would be like both of them had dropped off the face of G889.

Trying to make his way back up the narrow path in the dark was out of the question. Morning would come soon enough, and with it the cold realization of what had happened. The group would most certainly climb down the canyon now, if only to recover True's body. What would her father do without her? Uly didn't want to think about it. It had been her love for animals that had killed her. In a strange way, he thought, she wouldn't have wanted it any other way.

The weird howling noise sounded again, but it didn't frighten him anymore. Uly had determined that the howling was the wind, because it was always accompanied by a blast of cold air. He tried to keep from shivering, but he couldn't help himself. This was the worst night of his life, the kind of night that couldn't have happened if he had still been cloaked in his immuno-suit and tubes. He knew now that freedom demanded responsibility. Or at least common sense. He hadn't shown much of either one so far, but he was determined to start acting sensibly, even if it meant waiting here in the shivering cold all night.

Then Uly saw something that made his heart thump against his rib cage. *A light! A light below him in the canyon. But how could that be?*

"True!" he rasped. In his excitement, he moved a bit too

much on the narrow ledge, and he felt himself slipping. He held his breath and stiffened his back against the rock wall, waiting either to die or breathe again.

After a moment, he wasn't dead, and he peered again over the edge into the chasm. There was no mistaking the fact that a light was moving down below him, but it seemed ghostly, unreal. It weaved in and out of view, revealing nothing.

"True!" he croaked again.

This time, he was answered by a high-pitched chattering. It was the Koba!

"Bring it up here!" he called. "Bring me the light."

Sure enough, the light was headed slowly his way. There must not have been a path down there, because even the Koba was making slow time up the rock face, dragging the light behind it. Several times, Uly caught his breath when the light disappeared, but each time it reappeared, swaying in the wind. The Koba must have been climbing from root to root, thought Uly, dragging itself along.

He finally closed his eyes, because he couldn't bear to see the Koba die too. But wait a minute, thought Uly, if the flashlight had only fallen a few yards, maybe True had only fallen a few yards.

It gave him hope, and he cheered the little animal on. "That's it! Come on, you can make it!"

The last few feet were the hardest, because Uly wanted to reach out to help the Koba—but he couldn't. He dared not move, except to mouth his encouragement.

"You can make it! Come on!"

Now he could see the little Koba, struggling up the cliff, hampered by having to carry the flashlight. With a burst of strength, the Koba finally hurled itself into Uly's lap. The sudden action made Uly yelp with surprise, but he kept his balance and grabbed the flashlight before it could tumble off again. He hugged the scaly creature, and the Koba gripped him around the neck with its clammy claws.

"I'm glad to see you too!" said Uly. "Where is True? Did you see True?"

The Koba made a sleeping motion, putting its hands to the side of its head and closing its eyes. Uly hoped that it meant that True was only unconscious. But would a Koba know the difference between unconscious and dead?

Taking a deep breath, he shone the light down, but the beam wasn't strong enough to illuminate more than a few yards before it was swallowed up by darkness. He heard the low howl of the wind again, and he suddenly wondered where it came from. So he shone the flashlight straight up. This time the beam wasn't completely swallowed by darkness—it glinted off what looked like a stone roof!

As he explored with the light, Uly realized that he and the Koba were in some kind of archway carved in solid rock by erosion. It was like a giant doughnut! That was why the wind howled so fiercely through here. With mounting excitement, Uly realized that True couldn't have fallen all the way to the bottom of the canyon—she had only fallen to the bottom of the archway!

Now he knew he had to get help. He turned to the Koba, thinking he could send it back to the camp. No, he decided, the Koba wasn't cute and adorable like a typical pet. Morgan or some other trigger-happy adult would probably shoot it. He would have to go himself.

His legs were already hanging off the ledge, so he could try the same maneuver that True had tried to make. For once, it was good that he was smaller than her. Screwing up his courage, Uly put the flashlight into his mouth. He waited until the wind died down, then he leaned forward onto his hands and swung his legs up behind him.

So far, so good! He was on all fours again, and the path

was going up. The Koba moved ahead of him, also on its hands and knees, but Uly was too tired and scared to laugh at its antics. The boy was surprised to remember every rock and thornbush that he had passed before. They were like old friends. Only once did he try to put his hands into space, and he quickly grabbed a bush, not caring how much it scratched his hands. He went slowly, but he was making progress.

Then he saw something even more amazing—another light at the top of the canyon! The Koba chirped and dashed off, but Uly took the flashlight out of his mouth and waved it.

"Down here!" he called.

Yale's familiar voice asked, "Is that you, Uly?"

"Yes," he breathed with relief. "There's a path, but be careful."

Yale made a motion with his arm, and Zero joined him at the summit of the canyon. "Get lots of rope," ordered the cyborg.

As Zero walked off, Yale moved cautiously down the slope. Uly found that he didn't have enough strength to move or even stand up, so he just waited until his tutor wrapped a strong arm around his waist and carried him to safety.

"Where is True?" asked Yale.

Uly pointed back down the path. "She fell, but I think she's okay."

"You *think*?" asked Yale with disapproval. "You couldn't have been thinking when you went down there. What were you doing?"

Uly decided to tell the truth, or at least most of it. "True and I saw a bunch of Kobas. We followed them, and we found this path. We thought it would solve our problems, you know, help us get down the canyon. But after we started down, it got so narrow that we couldn't turn around. That's when True fell off." Uly started to cry. "I'm sorry."

Zero showed up with several coils of rope, a winch, a pulley, and another lantern. "Ready," he said.

A somber Yale asked, "If True fell off, what makes you think that she's still alive?"

"There's a natural archway," said the boy. "It's like a giant doughnut. That's where we were when she fell. I'm pretty sure she's at the bottom of it."

"Stay here," ordered Yale. "Better yet, go back to bed."

True felt a slimy kiss on her face and tried to brush it off. "No, Uly," she muttered groggily. The goofy boy was trying to kiss her! Then she realized that the back of her head was throbbing with pain, and her arms and legs didn't feel much better. She opened her eyes, but that didn't help at all—everything was still dark and painful.

Something crawled onto her chest, and she could see the vague silhouette of the Koba.

"Kitty," she breathed happily. "Where are we?"

The sudden howling of the wind and the sharp sensation of a rock poking her in the back brought her entirely back to her senses. When she tried to move, she heard a rock clattering down—a long way down. She straightened her left leg, but there was nothing to rest her foot on—nothing but empty blackness.

"Whoa!" True groaned. Her hands were pinned under her legs, and she was afraid to move them.

Hold still, she told herself. Hold very still. She remembered now—trying to turn around on the rocky ledge, and tumbling straight off. By all rights, she should be dead.

"This isn't Heaven, is it?" she asked the Koba.

The reptilian creature seemed to chuckle, then it gave her another slimy kiss. Well, she thought, there wasn't any point in trying to figure out where she was. She was somewhere in a very deep, very dark canyon. Alive, but in a lot of trouble. True remembered her flashlight, and she twisted her neck to look for it. When she didn't see it immediately, she knew she would have to get along without it. She wasn't about to go looking for a broken flashlight in the darkness.

Was Uly still up there, somewhere? She couldn't see a light above her; in fact, she couldn't see the stars or anything. When they had first gotten stuck on the path, she hadn't wanted to cause a panic by screaming for help, but now she had no choice. She didn't know how long she could hold out in this one position—with pain in every limb and her head throbbing. This wasn't Heaven, but the slightest wrong move could send her there.

"Uly!" she screamed. "Uly!"

Only her companions, the wind and the Koba, answered.

"Help!" True screamed again. "Anybody! Help!"

Her screaming turned into blubbering, and she couldn't stop her tears. The Koba lay down on her chest and stroked her cheek.

"It's okay, Kitty," she assured him. "You go away—you save yourself."

The Koba tittered softly, trying to comfort her. She took a chance on yanking her right hand out from under her leg and reaching up to hug him. When she moved her hand, a rock clattered down, and she froze. When nothing else happened, she completed her maneuver. True's chest was heaving with fear, but she felt a lot better with her arm wrapped around the Koba's tiny rib cage.

"I still think you should go," she insisted. "If I fall, I don't want you to go too."

The Koba abruptly sat up, and with one leap he was gone.

"Hey!" she called after him. "You don't have to do everything I say!"

Then she saw what had frightened him—two strong lantern beams crisscrossed above her head on what looked like a bridge made out of stone.

"Help!" she screamed. "Down here!"

"True!" called Yale's voice. "Hold still! Don't move!"

You don't need to tell me that, she thought to herself. A moment later, their lantern beams found her and blinded her. She couldn't see who was up there, but she heard the voices of Yale and Zero.

"The archway looks strong enough to support a rope," said Zero.

"Throw it over," answered Yale. "I'll tie it around my waist. Do you have a place to secure it?"

"Yes," answered Zero.

Yale called down, "Are you badly injured?"

"I don't think so!" answered the girl. "My head hurts, but I don't think anything is broken!"

"Don't move until after I grab you!" ordered the cyborg.

True held her breath as the two rescuers worked. She was relieved about one thing—her dad didn't seem to be with them. If she was going to start blubbering and begging forgiveness, she wanted to be standing on her own feet, on level ground.

More rocks clattered down the cliff as Zero threw the rope over the archway and secured it. Several minutes later, True screamed when she saw Yale fly unexpectedly over her head. Yale swayed in the wind for several seconds before stabilizing enough for Zero to begin lowering him. When he started to descend toward her, his gangly body looked like some kind of giant, high-tech spider.

Gosh, she thought, I've been kissed by a Koba, and now I'm going to kiss a robot and a cyborg!

"You're awfully damn lucky, young lady," said Yale as he came closer.

"I know," she breathed.

Soon his arms were around her, and she arose from the uncomfortable bed of rocks. True didn't mind any of the aches and pains now, because they all meant that she was alive!

Dr. Julia Heller removed the medical scope from True's eye. "A concussion," she pronounced, "plus several cuts and contusions. I suggest bed rest and observation for at least twenty-four hours."

"Plus a good chewing-out," scowled John Danziger.

"The chewing-out can wait," said Julia, giving Danziger a stern look. She turned to True. "Get lots of water to drink, young lady, then go lie down in your sleeping bag."

The ten-year-old nodded, stealing a quick glance at her irate father. Then she shuffled out.

The mechanic turned his anger on Yale. "Why didn't you come and get me?"

"Yes, why didn't you?" seconded Devon Adair, crossing her arms angrily.

The cyborg smiled. This was the thanks he got for saving their children, a chewing-out for not making it more complicated and dangerous.

"Uly returned on his own," he reported, "and his exhausted condition demanded rest rather than prolonged explanations. I also felt it best not to waste time. After evaluating the situation, I decided that myself and Zero were capable of rescuing True. Our immediate concern was to determine whether a rescue was possible, or necessary."

Yale looked Danziger in the eye. "Would you have preferred to be the first one to discover her dead body?"

Danziger's lips thinned, and he looked down. "No," he muttered. "Thanks. You did well."

"You're welcome, sir!" chirped Zero. "All in a day's work!"

Devon sighed and looked back toward the tent where Uly was still sleeping. "Sometimes I could almost get nostalgic for the days when Uly couldn't go anywhere or do anything."

"At his age," said Yale with a smile, "you were even more rambunctious. I daresay, you would have investigated too, after seeing a band of Kobas apparently leap over a cliff."

"Did they really find a trail down the canyon?" asked Devon.

The cyborg nodded. "Yes, they did. Being a Koba trail, it's narrow and dangerous, but I feel we could manage it. By daylight, of course, with the proper safeguards."

"What about the vehicles?" asked Danziger.

Yale shook his head. "This is definitely a footpath, no more."

Devon looked up at the sky, which was whitening into a creamy slate-gray from the abject black of a few moments ago. "It'll be morning soon," she said. "I don't want to do it, but it looks like we're going to have to split up our party. Some of us will have to go down into the canyon, and some of us will have to stay with the vehicles until we find a way to get them down. Or we decide we have to abandon them."

Danziger frowned. "That's a little drastic, isn't it?"

Devon stared at him. "With or without vehicles, we have to keep going to New Pacifica. Maybe we should decide how to split up the group now, while everyone else is asleep."

"Some assignments are obvious," said Julia. "I should go down the canyon, in case there are any accidents. But Alonzo can't do any mountain-climbing. He'll have to stay with the ATV."

"I don't like this," growled Danziger, staring back at

Devon. "These people have their own free will. We can't make decisions for them. If you abandon the vehicles, you also abandon most of our supplies and protection. Maybe a few of them would like to keep eating regularly and sleeping in a tent."

Yale cleared his throat, hoping to break the tension. "Can't we pause for a moment to celebrate the fact that the children are safe? And that there may be a way across this canyon."

"And another thing," said Julia, "True can't go anywhere for at least twenty-four hours."

Devon clenched her jaw and looked intently from the doctor to the mechanic. "We can't afford to waste twenty-four hours. If it makes you feel better, Danziger, I'll ask for *volunteers* to scout the trail down the canyon. There must be somebody here who's not afraid to go without a tent for a few days."

She stalked off, her hands balled into fists.

Danziger just shook his head and watched her go. "She's a hard case, isn't she?"

Yale chuckled nervously. "Oh, this is nothing. You should have seen her with the board of directors of her first corporation. Devon Adair does not like to be told that she can't do something."

"Whether she likes it or not," said Danziger, "we're not board members of one of her fancy corporations. We're free people with our own ideas, our own dreams, and some of us are here by accident. This planet has its own sun—it doesn't need to revolve around Devon Adair. She needs to figure that out."

He stalked off in the opposite direction.

Julia Heller turned to Yale and smiled. "They're made for each other."

• • •

After breakfast, the settlers and stranded crew members just stood around, gazing into the canyon, unsure what to do next. Normally, they would have broken camp, loaded the vehicles, and plowed ahead for twelve more miles. That was the routine, although it was hardly ever routine. This morning, the immense gorge yawned at them, promising that this wouldn't be a routine day either.

John Danziger checked on True and found her fast asleep in her sleeping bag. He was beginning to realize that he had nearly lost her the night before, and that terrible thought had melted his anger and stubbornness. As long as they were both alive and kicking, they would find a way to endure. Who led, who followed, who was on the top or the bottom of the pecking order—it didn't really matter. He had lived in worse places than this and had endured worse bosses than Devon Adair, that was certain. He had survived. As long as True was safe and protected, nothing else in the universe mattered.

He brushed her hair away from the scratch on her cheek and kissed it.

When Danziger left True's tent, he wasn't surprised to find Devon Adair standing on a stump, summoning the others to hear a speech. She cast a wary glance in his direction, but he simply folded his arms and gave her a peaceable smile. Maybe it was a trick of the morning light, but for a second it looked as if she smiled back.

"Can I have your attention, please!" She waved her arms. "Those of you by the canyon—come on over! Soon you'll see enough of that canyon to last you a lifetime."

Slowly, they formed a semicircle around her, all except for Alonzo, who listened from his hammock. There were Bess and Morgan, Yale and Zero, Julia, Walman, Baines,

Magus, and a handful of others. Everyone was present, except for True and Uly, who needed their rest.

Devon smiled at them, just like a confident politician. "We got a break!" she claimed. "Last night, the children found a Koba trail that leads, we think, to the bottom of the canyon."

There were some murmurs, and Devon held up her hands to quiet them. "But it's only a footpath, which means, for the time being, that we have to leave the vehicles up here."

She glanced at Danziger, then went on. "I'm looking for volunteers to follow the trail down and make sure it leads to the bottom of the canyon. I don't know how long this will take, but I think I can promise you some excitement. Every step of the way, the advance party will be in Gear contact with the base camp here on the rim."

"I'll go!" yelled Alonzo.

There were a few sympathetic chuckles, but Devon shook her head. "Sorry, Alonzo. At a minimum, you, Yale, Zero, and the children will stay up here with the vehicles. Actually, you'll drive along the rim of the canyon and try to find a way to get them down. I don't know if you'll find it, but we have to try. Okay, do I have any serious volunteers?"

Danziger stepped forward. "I'll go."

Devon stared at him, an expression of gratitude and surprise on her lovely face. "Don't you want to stay here with True?"

"No," he said. "Yale has proven that he can look after the children." At those words, the venerable cyborg puffed his chest with pride.

"All right," said Devon. "I'll go with Danziger. The two of us are probably enough. None of the rest of you have to go."

"I want to go," announced Bess.

"Are you crazy!" Morgan screamed at her. "That's

straight down! We don't know what's down there! Or how far it is!" He stamped his foot. "You can't go without me."

She patted him on the back. "Good, honey, you volunteer too!"

Morgan sputtered for a moment, trying to find a way to back out. With Bess smiling serenely at him, and the others watching expectantly, he finally slumped his shoulders and nodded.

After Morgan unexpectedly volunteered, the others sheepishly raised their hands.

"I've already volunteered," said Julia, "but Yale has to keep me informed on True's condition."

"Of course," said the cyborg.

For the first time in recent memory, Devon Adair was beaming. "You're all very brave, and I want you to know that I appreciate this vote of confidence in our mission. Packing up should be a simple affair—only the water, food, and clothing we can pack in our backpacks. Only as much as you can comfortably carry. And plenty of rope. In fact, we'll be roped together at the waist at fifteen-foot intervals." She clapped her hands. "Let's get moving!"

Danziger wanted to say good-bye to True, but he didn't want to waken her. Julia checked her first and said she was sleeping normally, not in any sort of coma. True's respiration, temperature, and vital signs were all normal, and Julia expected a full recovery from the concussion in a day or two. So the mechanic slipped into the tent and kissed his daughter good-bye, before he joined the others.

The novelty of packing only backpacks brought the group together in a strange way, he noted, and tying the ropes around their waists brought them together in a very physical sense. In less than an hour, they were a team. Not exactly a crack team, but a team nevertheless. It was all for one and one for all, as they traipsed toward the rim of the canyon, with Devon in the lead.

The sun had crept over the monumental buttes, bathing the crevasse in a clear, copper sheen. They could plainly see the giant archway ahead of them, through which the path wandered ever downward. The archway seemed like a doorway to some mysterious place, because there was nothing visible beyond it except blue sky.

Chapter 4

• • • • • • • •

"I'm scared of heights!" wailed Morgan.

"Now's a fine time to tell us," Devon replied dryly.

The fussy bureaucrat was right behind her on the narrow path. She had placed him there personally, because she wanted to keep an eye on him from the lead position. In some respects, she was using Morgan as the old coal miners used to use canaries to test for dangerous, underground gases. As the leader, it was her job to determine if the way was safe; it was Morgan's job to tell her if anyone might freak out. Because if anyone would freak out, it would be Morgan.

"I tell you, I can't look down!" he shrieked.

"Then don't look down," his wife, Bess, suggested from the position behind him.

As at a fancy dinner party, Devon had assigned a

boy-girl-boy-girl order to the string of climbers. First her, then Morgan, then Bess, Baines, Julia, and so on until Danziger brought up the rear. She had positioned Danziger there as a reserve in case the rest of them started to fall. He might only have a few seconds to react, but she hoped that he would somehow have time to secure his end of the rope.

"Yeeeee!" whined Morgan as he shuffled along the ledge.

Baines scowled. "If he don't shut up, I say we cut him loose."

"No, no!" gasped Morgan. "I'll be all right, I swear!"

"It looks like a long way down," said Devon, "but this path has obviously seen plenty of use."

"Not by people!" Morgan protested.

"How do you know?" asked Devon.

The leader looked down, and she had to admit that the view was terrifying, or at least sobering. There was nothing for hundreds of yards but jagged boulders and buttes, most of them striated by the elements into a colorful pattern of stripes and ridges. Growing like fur on the cliffs were clumps of green and brown vegetation. The weird perspective, looking straight down, made it hard to judge distances, and Devon couldn't tell if the plants were stumpy shrubs or towering evergreens. At the bottom, there was a cool, turquoise strip of water, and it made for an inviting goal. Devon wondered how long it would take them to reach it, and whether they would all make it.

The trail was everything they could hope for, she thought. It was narrow and treacherous, but it wasn't haphazard. Eons of use had worn the path level, even where it crossed over sheer rock. So far, there were no steep slopes or missing sections, as she had feared. They occasionally had to take a step down a foot or two, especially where the trail wound back in the opposite direction. They took their time, and the person in front always helped the next one down.

The climbers spent most of the time with their backs against the cliff, sharp rocks gouging them, just inching along. Other places, the path wandered over ledges that were three or four feet wide, and they could walk normally, or as normally as people walked with a deadly abyss staring them in the face. Devon was thankful that they had a clear day, with little wind, lots of sunshine, and no precipitation. She certainly wouldn't have wanted to be doing this when the path was slick and wet. That thought made her look up in the sky to check the clouds.

While Devon gazed upward, her foot came down in empty space! She recovered quickly by throwing her weight on the other foot and slumping against the rock wall.

Morgan screamed, "She's trying to kill us!"

The caravan ground to a halt and peered at her with concern. "It's all right," muttered Devon. "My fault."

But Morgan was hyperventilating. "Ah! Ah! Ah! Ah!"

Bess reached around and slapped him in the face, and Morgan recoiled in horror. "What was that for?"

She shrugged. "I saw it in a movie once. Did it work?"

Morgan massaged his cheek. "If you wanted to break my jaw, yes."

Devon looked back up the canyon wall. Despite hours of nerve-wracking descent, she could plainly see the rim of the ravine. They had made disappointingly slow progress, and it looked as if they would continue to do so. This brought home the very real possibility that they would have to spend the night in the canyon, clinging to a narrow ledge. That meant no sleep, cold winds, and raw nerves. It wasn't a prospect she looked forward to.

Maybe she should have descended with Danziger alone, or with a smaller party. Should she send some of them back? While there was still time. No, Devon decided instantly. If they didn't cross this canyon—with her and right now—they were as good as lost to the colony. She needed every one of them, even Morgan. Once she got them to the bottom, they would have no choice but to climb up the other side, and then they might as well continue on their way. The ascent on the other side would give her enough time to go back and get the children, Alonzo, Yale, Zero, and the vehicles, she hoped.

"How is everyone holding up?" she yelled down the line.

Several of them waved wearily. A few of them tightened the ropes around their waists. Almost everyone slumped against the rocks, looking for a place to sit down where there was one.

Danziger shouted back, "Can we bring some jetpacks next time?"

Devon chuckled and motioned for them to follow her.

Uly sat up in his sleeping bag, feeling tired and confused. He'd been having a weird dream—about hanging on a ledge in the dark, watching ghostly flashlights and a troop of Kobas leaping around. Then he felt a prickling on his hands, and he turned his palms upward to see dozens of tiny scratches and bruises.

It hadn't been a dream! True was in danger!

He dashed out of the tent and was nearly blinded by the bright sunlight. "True! True!" he screamed.

"Whoa, pardner," said a calm voice. "True is just fine."

Uly blinked his eyes and peered in the direction of the voice to find Alonzo, lying in his hammock, whittling a piece of wood with his pocketknife. It was midday, the tents were still up, and the big TransRover was parked and silent, all of which was very odd. But the strangest thing was that he and Alonzo seemed to be the only ones in camp.

“True is okay?” he asked dazedly.

Alonzo nodded. “Yeah, she’s in her tent, sleeping. But let’s let her sleep, because she got a pretty bad bump on the head.”

“Where is everyone else?”

“Ah,” said the pilot, “Yale and Zero took the ATV and the DuneRail and went in opposite directions along the rim. Your mom and the others went down the trail you discovered.”

“Without me?” gasped the eight-year-old.

“Hey, without me, too,” said Alonzo with a shrug. “They asked for volunteers for the important job of guarding the vehicles, and I volunteered you, me, and True. Hope you don’t mind.”

The boy looked doubtful about all of this. “What if Grendlers, or somebody, attack us?”

Alonzo fumbled in his hammock and held up his Gear and a rifle. “We’re covered. We’re in Gear contact with everyone. Hey, would you like to go check on True for me? Don’t wake her up, but make sure she’s breathing regularly. Feel her head, and make sure she doesn’t have a temperature. You know, the usual stuff parents do.”

Uly managed a smile. “Sure, okay.”

The trail down the canyon had stopped doubling back and forth, like a winding mountain road, and had sloped in one direction for about an hour. The trail wound between a staggering array of silver spires, like giant stalagmites, which made Devon feel as if they were traveling through a forest of stone trees. Even though the trail was still narrow, at least there was rock on both sides and less chance of falling, which gave everyone a break.

Devon made a mental note of the place, thinking they could return to it if they didn’t find a more congenial place for sleeping. She had given up hope that they would reach the bottom of the canyon before sunset.

In the forest of spires, they began to hear a strange noise. At first, Devon thought it was thunder; she planted her feet firmly before gazing up into the sky. But there wasn't a cloud, at least in the window of sky between the immense spires; there was nothing but crystalline blue. Morgan gave her a worried look, and she pressed on.

The roar increased, and Devon was prepared to find something big on the trail ahead of them. However, nothing she had seen in her entire life prepared her for the spectacle that greeted her when she rounded the last spire. Spraying her in the face was a towering wall of turquoise water and mist! It plummeted from somewhere unseen overhead to somewhere unseen below, and it looked as wide as the canyon itself.

Morgan bumped into her and staggered back, his jaw hanging open. He tried to say something.

"What?" she shouted. The roar was deafening.

Again he tried to speak—to express his awe—but it was no use. Devon knew what he was feeling. She waved for him to follow her behind the waterfall, for that was apparently where the trail led. She couldn't tell for sure, because the trail was obscured by the mist. She plunged ahead, anyway. Before she even reached the waterfall, Devon was drenched and shivering, and she had to breathe through her wide-open mouth instead of her nose. She hoped that it wasn't going to be too slippery inside there, wherever they were going.

One by one, the hardy band vanished into a curtain of mist, with a sheet of water arcing over their heads.

After her eyes got used to the darkness, Devon breathed a sigh of relief. She was in a cavern filled with real stalactites and stalagmites, caused by the mist condensing and dripping though cracks in the rock. She could see the immense waterfall beyond the columns of mineral; it looked like a shimmering turquoise curtain, not tons of plunging water. The noise was such that she still could barely hear herself thinking, as she moved with baby steps over the slippery rock.

If it hadn't been so damp and cold in the cavern, she thought, it would have been a perfect place to stop for the night. But they would have to keep going, shivering and wet as they were.

Devon emerged into the sunlight and got another soaking. She turned to see how Morgan had fared behind her. Even the jaded bureaucrat looked awestruck and humbled by his stroll behind the waterfall. Devon forged on through a thicket of podlike plants that thrived on the dense mist. It was almost half an hour before her hearing returned to normal.

True and Uly sat patiently in front of Alonzo's hammock, watching him watch his watch. The pilot had tried to keep True in bed, per Julia's orders, but the girl had insisted on sitting quietly with them. Since Alonzo was often guilty of ignoring doctor's orders, he decided not to force the issue. Besides, she seemed okay, and that was the important thing. He knew that kids, with their flexible bones, could often survive stuff that would kill adults.

"Is it time yet?" asked True.

"Almost," said Alonzo. "I've got one minute to go." He smiled at Uly. "And you know how punctual your mom is."

"Yeah," he said. "Where are Yale and Zero now?"

"Don't know. I don't expect to see them back before sundown. They wanted to cover as much ground as they could."

Suddenly, the Gear crackled. "Scout party to base camp," said a tinny voice.

"Base camp here," answered Alonzo. "Your signal is weak."

"I'm not surprised," answered Devon. "There's not much distance between us, but lots of rock. How are the children?"

"Both fine."

"Is True resting in bed?"

The little girl smiled and put her finger to her lips.

Alonzo smiled back. "Of course. Although she was awake, and she seemed fine."

"Yale and Zero?"

"They took the ATV and the DuneRail to scout in both directions. They reported in at midday. Nothing to write home about. How are you doing?"

"We're drying out," answered Devon.

"Drying out?"

She sighed. "We had a brush with a waterfall. Pretty amazing. I couldn't tell you how far down we are in the canyon, but we haven't had any mishaps, except for a few scratches and stubbed toes. When you see them, tell the children that they found a great trail."

Alonzo nodded, and both children beamed with pride. "They've been asking me when you're coming back to get them."

"Well," said Devon, "the plan is to reach the bottom and take stock then. While the others scout for a trail that goes up the other side, Danziger and I will probably come back for them."

Alonzo swallowed hard. He didn't want to ask this next question. "Is there any way to get *me* down there?"

"You're a top priority," answered Devon diplomatically.

The pilot chose not to push her for an answer. "Okay. Well, I don't know about you, but we're dry and comfortable up here."

"We'll check back at twenty hundred hours," said Devon. "We should be squared away by then, wherever we spend the night. Kiss the kids for us."

"Will do. Over and out."

"Out."

Alonzo pushed back the feeder on his Gear. He looked at True and Uly and shrugged. "Never a dull moment."

True frowned. "I'm sure they'll find a way to get you down."

"Maybe," said Alonzo. He pointed a thumb at the big TransRover. "What about that thing? It might just be me and the Transy, bombing around the planet."

"We'll go with you," vowed Uly seriously.

Alonzo chuckled. "Thanks, kid. You would be good company. I appreciate it. I wonder how Yale and Zero are doing out there on the rim."

At that moment, Yale sat leaning on the wheel of his ATV, staring off a sheer cliff into the immense gorge. The aged cyborg had reached the allotted distance and knew it was time to turn back to camp, but he was feeling intensely disappointed. He realized that in this stretch of the canyon there was no way down, unless you were a Koba, a human on foot, or a mountain goat. Driving down in four-wheeled vehicles was just plain out of the question. He realized the canyon had to end somewhere, but that could be thousands of miles away.

The cyborg got out of the ATV and strolled to the very lip of the abyss, thinking that he had certainly taken the wrong fork in the road. He hoped that Zero had had better luck in his scouting expedition. Here, and for at least two miles before it, there was a straight drop—not even a twig to break your fall. No creature could go down this way, except a lemming on a suicide mission. Because of the drastic erosion in this part of the canyon, it was very wide at the bottom, and there appeared to be a lovely white-sand beach on both sides of the river. Although, Yale thought glumly, a lot of good a beach would do them.

He heard a cawing sound, and peered into the distance to see a bird drifting lazily on the thermal air currents of the canyon. Okay, he admitted to himself, a bird was the one creature who could negotiate this stretch of the canyon. And even the bird would have no place to land except the bottom.

He suddenly got a very crazy idea, but he dismissed it immediately. After all, they weren't birds or lemmings.

With a sigh, the venerable cyborg climbed into his vehicle, started the engine, and made a U-turn.

Devon's muscles were aching by the time she reached the top of the plateau. It was like a little island in a sea of rarified air, she thought to herself. On a hunch, she had left the others on the trail to climb up six feet or so to reach this plateau, and she was elated with her discovery. It was not entirely level, offered no protection from the elements, and was only about a hundred square feet, or about the size of a small bedroom, but it looked like heaven to her.

Devon glanced down at Morgan, who now looked like he was about to have a heart attack. His chest was heaving, his legs were wobbly, his eyes were glazed, and he was soaked in sweat. The rest of them didn't look much better. Maybe Danziger could've gone on for another hundred yards, but that was about it. There were probably a couple hours of daylight left, but Devon knew the shadows down here in the canyon would darken quickly once the sun slipped behind the rim. She didn't want to be stuck on a narrow ledge when that happened.

"This is it!" she called down. "We're camping here."

A weary cheer went up, and Devon continued. "Danziger, take your rope off and climb up. The rest of you, leave your ropes on and climb up one by one. We'll help you up."

When the lanky Danziger joined her atop the plateau, he looked around and smiled. "No firewood, wet clothes, nothing to shelter us from the cold—I'd say we're going to be doing a lot of snuggling tonight."

Devon glared at him. "Maybe, but it will just be for warmth. Remember that."

He nodded, but he still looked as if he were enjoying himself entirely too much for her taste.

"Let's get them up," she ordered.

Yale and Zero arrived back at the base camp as the sun departed. There were long shadows and long faces as they delivered their similar reports to Alonzo.

"Nowhere to cross," said Yale simply.

"That about sums it up," Zero added.

"It can't be worse than this," said Alonzo, pointing toward the lip of the canyon.

"Oh, yes, it can," answered Yale. "I see now why the Kobas picked this place to begin their trail. It's the most accessible spot I've seen. For three miles, I saw nothing but absolute, sheer drop-off. Not even a butte or an archway—it was like the side of a skyscraper."

"I see," muttered Alonzo with disappointment.

Zero reported, "In the other direction, not only is there no way to drive down, but the soil at the rim is dangerous and tends to crumble. You can't even park there."

"Great," groaned Alonzo. The pilot leaned back in his

hammock, and he suddenly became aware that the others were staring at him. Waiting. Nobody had elected him leader of this ragtag outfit, but among two children, a robot, and an antique cyborg, the cripple would have to be in charge, he supposed.

He sat up and tried to look as dignified as a man with a broken leg can look. "All right, I'll tell you what I know. As soon as the others reach the bottom, True and Uly's parents are coming back to get them."

Alonzo motioned toward the vehicles circled around them. "We'll need three drivers. So, gentlemen," he looked at Yale and Zero and frowned, "let's accept the fact that we're going to have to drive these vehicles as far as it takes to find a crossing. We should just head out in the direction the current is traveling, figuring the river will branch into a delta sometime."

He jerked a thumb at the TransRover. "As the TransRover is much more valuable than the other two, we don't want to abandon it. We may find a way across for the ATV and DuneRail, but I'll stay with the TransRover, regardless."

"Regardless of what?" asked True.

"Regardless of this stupid leg!" snapped Alonzo. He instantly regretted his harshness and smiled at the girl. "You know, True, I'm ticked off about my leg, but I can't complain too much. Did you know that I'm older than Yale here by a long shot—thanks to all those interstellar jumps I've made in cold sleep. I've known a lot of space jockeys younger than me who never woke up, or ended up as space dust."

The handsome pilot held his hand out to True, and she took it. "What I'm trying to say, I've had a lot of good luck in my life. Especially in love. I guess it was bound to happen that the bad luck caught up with me. So don't feel sorry for me—I'll do whatever has to be done."

"Excuse me, sir," said Yale, "but you cannot possibly protect the TransRover by yourself. As soon as you fall asleep, the Grendlers will be after it, or someone else. I shall volunteer to go with you."

"Me too, sir," said Zero.

"Me too!" shouted Uly with a sob in his throat. He rushed forward to hug Alonzo.

"Me too!" exclaimed True, wrapping her arms around his neck.

Alonzo hugged the two children and felt his own eyes tearing up. "I imagine your parents will have something to say about that, but I appreciate the offer, I really do. I'm going to miss you guys."

As the pilot hugged the two children, Yale tapped Zero in the chest and said, "Let's collect firewood, shall we?"

Devon Adair was certain that she must have been colder at some other instance in her life, but she really couldn't remember when. Night fell like a cold rain on their tiny plateau in the middle of the canyon, and the wind howled around them like a ferocious banshee. They had packed mostly food and water in their lightweight backpacks, along with a few thin blankets. As the night wore on, many of the climbers began to wish for a warm sleeping bag instead of a full stomach. But even if they'd had sleeping bags, there was no place to stretch out on the tiny plateau.

Devon felt better after calling the base camp at the top of the canyon and finding that everyone up there was safe and warm, each with a choice of numerous tents and sleeping bags, and a roaring fire to boot. Once again, she began to wonder whether it had been a good idea to bring so many of the party down on the first attempt. But what difference would it have made? They wouldn't have been able to carry more supplies than this on a trip later, and it wouldn't have been any warmer at night either. The only real shelter they had seen was under a leaky waterfall.

Face it, she told herself, this was a grueling trip. It wasn't supposed to be fun and games. They were doing all of this for the sake of hundreds of sick children, and Uly's remarkable recovery had shown that they were on the right path. "No struggle, no progress," was an African saying she often thought about. It had guided her many times when she faced terrible obstacles, both professional and personal. Uly's illness, an apathetic government, even public ridicule—they had all been overcome. She could do anything she set her mind to, even get through this night.

But, damn, it was cold!

"Get closer together," John Danziger was telling people. Clouds of condensation shot out of his mouth. "Come on, huddle up, conserve your body heat—it's all we've got. Huddling up will keep you away from the edge too. You can rest your head on someone else's shoulder. Come on, huddle up."

Bess and Morgan already looked like one lump of quivering flesh, and they were quickly joined by Julia, Baines, and the others. After a few seconds, only Devon sat apart—an island on top of another island.

Danziger hunkered down into the pile of people, and he looked expectantly at Devon. She didn't budge. Finally, he held out his long arm and smiled. That smile alone was enough to melt her, and she scooted over to nestle under his brawny arm, against his hard chest. She wouldn't look at him or tell him how good it felt, but he must've known.

He hugged her tighter, and the chill and the aches began to go away. It had been a long time since a man had held her, Devon realized with a start. It felt disturbingly good. He was just a mechanic, she told herself, and it was by pure accident that John Danziger was such a large part of her life. But tonight his embrace felt like life itself. Tomorrow she would put him in his place. Tomorrow.

Wrapped in the cocoon of his arms, Devon drifted off to sleep.

Alonzo and True were also fast asleep, so for once they were obeying doctor's orders. Yale and Uly sat quietly by the campfire, tossing on twigs and watching the sparks shoot into the sky.

Zero was out in the darkness somewhere, making his nightly rounds, although Yale had some doubts as to how accomplished a guard Zero really was. The robot never slept, which was a plus, but he wasn't a combat robot by any means. His night sight was only average, with no infrared vision, and his hearing was limited, restricted mainly to interpreting human commands. He had no sense of smell or special sensors. In other words, a German shepherd would've been a lot better.

Yale didn't know why, but he was feeling uneasy tonight. That was one reason why he didn't insist that Uly crawl into his sleeping bag. That, and the fact that he enjoyed the boy's company.

No doubt Uly was still disappointed at not finding a way to get the vehicles down the canyon. Despite Alonzo's agony over having to remain behind, there was no alternative to the plan he had outlined: They would simply have to drive the vehicles until the canyon eroded to a manageable ditch.

Yale twisted his head and found Uly looking at him. "You looked worried," said the boy.

"Just thoughtful," answered the cyborg. "I don't like the idea of splitting up our party, but I have no alternative to suggest. Well, there is one . . ."

"What is it?" asked the boy eagerly.

The aged cyborg smiled and shook his head. "If I proposed what I am thinking, your mother would have my head replaced, probably with Zero's."

The eight-year-old laughed, a musical sound. "You'd looked funny," he agreed.

Yale put his hand on Uly's scrawny shoulder. "Come now, I have let you stay up way past your bedtime."

"No," the boy protested. "I slept all morning! Please, I like sitting by the fire."

"But that's how you got into trouble last night," Yale reminded him.

"I promise not to chase any Kobas tonight. Please, let me stay up a little bit. I haven't had any studies in a long time—how about a history lesson?"

Smart, thought Yale, just like his mother. When losing an argument, divert your opponent onto another argument—one you can win.

"All right," said the cyborg, "let me get away from the fire, so that you can see better."

Yale stood up and turned his back to the fire. As Uly watched eagerly, he projected a holographic image a few feet in front of his chest. It was a canyon, not quite as deep as the one in front of them but more varied and complex, with many smaller canyons running into it. Overlooking the canyon were soldiers in strange metallic uniforms, with crested helmets and staffs. One man wore a brown robe and a wide-brimmed hat, and another man sat atop a hairy, four-legged beast.

"That's not history," said the boy, "that's our canyon. But who are those weird creatures? Aliens?"

"This is not our canyon," answered Yale, "but the Grand Canyon of North America. The year is 1540, five centuries before mining companies leveled it. Spanish conquistadors and missionaries, led by Garcia Lopez de Cardenas, were the first Europeans to see the Grand Canyon. *They* were the aliens, as *we* are the aliens in this strange place. We must never forget that, Uly. Although Cardenas reported that he had 'discovered' the canyon, Native Americans had been living in it for a thousand years."

Eagerly Uly asked, "Do you think anybody lives at the bottom of our canyon?"

"I wouldn't be surprised," answered Yale. "We already know that Kobas move freely in the canyon. They might have a thriving colony down there, for all we know. We must never make the mistake that Cardenas made—we have discovered *knowledge* of the canyon, not the canyon itself. Despite what Mr. Martin espoused, we can make no claims here. At the very least, this canyon belongs to the Kobas, who were here first."

Uly looked confused. "But what's wrong with Mr. Martin claiming mineral rights and stuff like that?"

Yale shook his head sadly. "There is a wise saying: 'Those who ignore history are condemned to repeat it.' That is how the natural resources and native people of Earth were plundered, for what turned out to be a disaster. Believe me, I would welcome the opportunity to give Mr. Martin a history lesson too."

Suddenly they heard a shrill whistling sound, and Yale shut off the projection and whirled around. Nothing seemed out of place. The three vehicles stood like stark sculptures on the rugged landscape. The campfire smoldered, and Alonzo snored peacefully in his hammock. All but two of the tents had been packed away, and True was sleeping in one of them. Yet the cyborg felt ill at ease, as he had all evening.

Plus, there was an acrid smell in the air.

"Mrrrf-mrrrf," something muttered, and a bizarre apparition burst through the trees.

It was Zero, with three toadlike creatures hanging on his back! One of them was trying to pull his head off! A troop of the weird, gangly reptiles hopped out of the forest and headed straight for the vehicles.

"Grendlers!" Shrieked Uly.

Chapter 5

As the Grendlers overran the camp, Yale scooped up Uly and dashed toward True's tent. He got there just a second before the Grendlers descended upon it, and he yanked True out of her sleeping bag as the thieves made off with the sleeping bag, canvas, and tent poles. A Grendler attack was less an attack than it was a daring robbery, a raid. The unsightly creatures had no stomach for fighting—they were merely trying to grab everything they could find and run with it!

Four of them had actually grabbed the bumper of the ATV and were dragging it off! Alonzo bolted upright in his hammock, put the rifle to his shoulder, and squeezed off a shot in their direction. He didn't hit them, but they dropped the ATV and loped off, screeching. Zero was still staggering around with three lumpy attackers on his back, but Alonzo couldn't get a clear shot.

"Hang on!" shouted Yale. He rushed to the TransRover and lifted the children onto it. "Climb to the top!" he ordered them. True and Uly scampered up the truck like frightened Kobas.

Zero continued to run around, tormented by a mass of misshapen limbs that were clinging to him and trying to rip his head off.

"The fire!" shouted Yale.

The robot nodded and in desperation dove headfirst into the campfire. At once, the Grendlers squealed horribly and rolled out of the flames, their ragged hoods on fire. The gang of little fireballs bounced around in the dirt.

But there were dozens more, dragging off the tents, the supplies, everything that wasn't nailed down. A handful of them started after the children, and Alonzo sent them scurrying with another rifle shot. It was a losing battle, Yale could see. The surprise attack had been well planned, and they were vastly outnumbered.

The cyborg pulled Zero out the fire and helped him to his feet. Since his head was half-off, Yale removed it the rest of the way and ran toward the DuneRail. Grendlers were trying to strip it, but Yale and the headless robot beat them off with their fists. The Grendlers scampered away, howling. Yale was finally able to screw Zero's head into place on the DuneRail, and the robot's torso jumped into the seat behind his head.

"Drive two miles east and stop," ordered Yale.

"Yes, sir!" snapped Zero. He started the engine, turned on the headlights, and roared off. An unlucky Grendler squealed as the tires bounced over it.

Yale rushed back to the TransRover, with half a dozen misshapen attackers loping after him. Alonzo's rifle spit enough rounds to scare them off, but they didn't go far. Yale could see their yellowish eyes glowing in the darkness at the edge of the forest. They were waiting, regrouping—they weren't going away.

While there was a lull, the cyborg lifted Alonzo from his hammock and took him to his specially equipped ATV. He gave him the same order he had given Zero. "Two miles east!"

"Gotcha!" the pilot said with a salute. He turned on his motor and lights and rumbled off, the band of Grendlers loping after him.

With the rifleman gone, they were coming en masse! Yale barely had time to leap up into the cockpit and get the big TransRover moving. He wanted to check on the children, but there was no time even to look their way.

"Hang on!" he yelled at the top of his lungs.

"Don't worry!" True screamed back. *"Go!"*

The whistling and the squeals were almost overwhelming as the Grendlers descended upon the camp, scooping up everything that was left. Yale peered over his shoulder and could see the celebratory chaos in the distance. At least they weren't coming after the vehicles . . . yet.

The cyborg slumped back in his seat and debated whether to report this unseemly retreat to Devon and her party down in the canyon. But it was the middle of the night, and there was absolutely nothing that either group could do to help the other. The last thing he wanted to do was to bring Devon running back in the dark to a camp that had been overrun by Grendlers. Best let them attend to their own problems, he finally decided.

He did stop briefly to make sure that the children were ensconced in safe places in the TransRover. They were, and he carefully drove the two miles to the rendezvous point.

Zero and Alonzo were waiting for him in their vehicles.

Alonzo looked extremely grim; his knuckles were white around his rifle stock. Zero's head wasn't capable of showing emotion, but the robot's body sat slumped in his seat, his body language unmistakable. The Grendlers had figured out that they were vulnerable, and the vehicles were a big prize. They would return. And return.

Alonzo muttered, "That was close. Anybody got any ideas?"

"Not me," said Zero's head.

"Well," admitted Yale, "I have an idea, but it's a very *bad* idea."

"Bad ideas are better than no ideas," said Alonzo. "Spill it."

Yale climbed out of the cockpit, and he could see True and Uly peering at him from the top of the TransRover. Alonzo and Zero were also staring at him with interest.

"I would like to show you a history lesson first," said the cyborg.

Alonzo looked doubtful. "There's something in history that's going to help us?"

Yale nodded. "You might find it instructive."

"He's a good teacher!" Uly piped in.

"Fine," grumbled Alonzo, "give us the lesson."

Yale activated his holographic projector for the second time that night, and he showed them some grainy black-and-white war scenes.

"That's very entertaining," said Alonzo. "Are you suggesting we find some tanks somewhere and blow up the Grendlers?"

"Not exactly," said Yale. "Here is the part I want you to see."

He projected scenes of soldiers jumping out of primitive prop-driven airplanes. Their tiny white parachutes blossomed like flowers captured in stop-motion photography, and they floated safely to the ground. There were not just human paratroopers in the scenes—jeeps, half-tracks, crates, and other objects were pushed out of airplanes to float to the ground on gossamer wings.

Yale explained, "In the ground wars of the twentieth century, it was common to drop military vehicles by parachute into combat zones. I merely felt that if you had seen it done, you might not consider my idea to be so bad."

Alonzo's eyes widened in amazement. "You want to drive the vehicles off the cliff—with parachutes on them!"

Yale turned off the hologram and frowned. "*Want* is not the correct word. I don't have a burning desire to drive off a cliff; I'm just saying it could be done. The TransRover already has a rear parachute for emergency braking, and we could take the extra nylon tents we have and glue them together with molecular bonding material. With the extra harnesses, we could make parachutes for the smaller vehicles."

"Yeah, but . . ." Alonzo motioned toward the immense chasm in front of them.

"I scouted this area today," said Yale, "and there are no obstacles in the canyon. From what I could tell, the bottom of the canyon has a wide, sandy beach. Of course, there are dangers, mainly that your parachute wouldn't open, or you would land in the water. Landing in the water might not be fatal. The parachute refusing to open would be."

Alonzo rubbed his square jaw, considering the plan. "That's a bad idea, all right, but it's the only idea we've got. We're too shorthanded to fight a retreat from the Grendlers for hundreds of miles, that's for sure. If they come after us again, we'd better be prepared to go for it. What do we have to do?"

"In the case of the TransRover," said Yale, "we only have to find a way to secure the driver and any passengers. The rear parachute can be operated manually, so the driver would simply drive off the cliff and open the chute, as if the brakes had failed."

He studied the vehicles. "With the harnesses and the extra tents, we can make some sort of parachutes for the small vehicles. To be on the safe side, perhaps they should be sent over the cliff unmanned. I believe we can find room in the TransRover for all of us. Plus, Alonzo needs to be in the TransRover to lower the possibility of reinjuring his leg."

Alonzo gave Yale a devil-may-care smile. "Don't worry about me—I wouldn't miss a ride like you're talking about for anything! The question is, do we tell the kids' parents about it?"

"No!" said True and Uly in unison. They looked at each other and grinned.

Yale added, "I don't believe their parents would care to see them captured."

Alonzo squinted down the dark rim of the canyon and cocked his rifle. "All right," he said, "I'll keep guard while the rest of you start making those parachutes."

True and Uly spent most of the night strapped inside their seats on the TransRover, watching Yale and Zero working methodically by flashlight to glue together four small tents to make one huge parachute. They did this twice, to accommodate the DuneRail and ATV. Following Alonzo's directions, they fastened the extra harnesses they had scavenged from the escape pods to the tent grommets, then they rigged one of the ersatz chutes to each of the vehicles. These were not the kind of parachutes you would trust your life to, thought True, but nobody was trusting their lives to them, unless you considered Zero to be alive.

When it was Alonzo's turn to get strapped in, the injured pilot was firmly secured at the back of the TransRover, facing rear. From back there, he would have no idea where they were going, but he would have a dandy view of the parachute when it opened. True craned her neck to watch Yale tightening the belts and ropes around Alonzo's torso.

"This way," explained Yale, "your back will absorb the impact instead of your legs."

"Sounds good to me," said Alonzo with a grin. He hefted his rifle. "And if they come at us, I can get off a few shots from here. True and Uly, how are you guys doing?"

"Fine!" they shouted. Like Alonzo, they were roped in, but directly in the center of the craft. They were cushioned considerably by sleeping bags, but True figured they would still have a good view of the free-fall.

Zero's head was attached to the front of the DuneRail, several yards away, but the robot's body was strapped onto the TransRover in a prone position, like a stack of lumber. Yale draped the homemade parachute over the frame of Zero's DuneRail, and it looked like a poorly fitting convertible top. Zero's head was to be the guinea pig, the first one over the rim if the Grendlers attacked. If he made it, the rest of them were going too.

The ATV was stationed midway between Zero's DuneRail and the TransRover. It looked like a lumpy couch that someone had thrown a sheet over. The plan was for Yale to start it up and send it over, unmanned, then run like hell to the TransRover and jump into the cockpit, to drive it over the cliff.

Content with the job he had done tying them all into their vehicles, Yale waved to the passengers on the TransRover. Then he strode to his ATV.

"Are you scared?" Uly whispered to True.

"Yeah," she admitted. "I'm scared I'll have to go to the bathroom."

"That's all you're scared about?"

True shook her head, looking somber. "No, I'm scared that I'll never see my dad again. What about you?"

Uly nodded, and his lower lip began to tremble. "Maybe this isn't such a good idea."

"We're all waiting to hear a better one," said True.

When Uly could think of no better idea, the girl added, "I wonder if I'll ever see my Koba again."

"I'm sure he's okay," said Uly. "You know, he saved both of our lives when he brought me back the flashlight last night."

True beamed with pride. "Yeah, he's a good Kitty."

She looked up in the sky and could see the first slivers of dawn playing across the billowy black clouds that had rolled in overnight. She was glad to see the sunlight, although it really didn't matter when they made the leap, according to Yale. As they had no way to steer the plummeting vehicles, with parachutes or without, it didn't matter if they could see where they were going or not. Somehow, that thought did not bring her a lot of comfort.

"What if we just tied ourselves up for no reason?" asked Uly. "What if they never come?"

At that moment, the far-off DuneRail roared to life, and True, Uly, and Alonzo twisted their necks against their bindings in order to get a better look. It had been no accident that Zero was the guinea pig, the first in line, because they knew that a robot wouldn't hesitate to carry out orders. Want somebody to drive a buggy over a cliff, dropping a mile or two straight down in the process—just get a robot like Zero. To him, it was the same as digging a ditch.

True heard Alonzo shout, "The Grendlers are coming!"

"And we're going," answered Uly. He gave True a brave smile, but his lip was still quivering.

As if it were the most natural thing in the world, the far DuneRail suddenly launched itself toward the vast canyon and shot out into space. True could see Yale rush to the rim and kneel down to watch Zero's progress, as they all held their collective breath.

Suddenly the cyborg threw his arms into the air and cheered. But it could barely be heard over the angry whistling and screeching of the Grendlers, as they poured out of the woods. Even at a distance, True could see that the toadlike creatures were hopping mad over losing their prize.

"This is no time for celebrating!" yelled Alonzo. He squeezed off several shots, although it was highly doubtful that he came close to hitting anything in the dim light.

The shots at least got Yale's attention, and he stopped peering over the cliff long enough to start the ATV. The attackers were almost upon him before he shoved the vehicle into drive and stumbled backward. The Grendlers stopped and stared in amazement as the unmanned ATV rumbled toward the rim of the canyon and drove off into nothingness.

Yale had no time to check if the ATV's chute opened—he was running for his life, with dozens of nimble Grendlers in pursuit. Alonzo muttered something, and squeezed off as many shots as he could, but it looked like a stampede of giant frogs. After seeing two vehicles go off the cliff, the Grendlers must've realized that they were in danger of losing all the loot. They weren't going to get any more chances after this, and they weren't going to be frightened off by a few loud noises and bullets.

Yale ran for all he was worth, but he was old, and not so nimble. He stumbled, and the Grendlers were upon him.

"Damn! Damn!" cursed Alonzo, struggling against his bindings. "Why did I let myself be tied down?"

Using a different tact, Alonzo took no more rifle shots. Instead, he screamed at the top of his lungs, "Hey, you! *This* is what you want! We're over *here*!"

Bullets were ineffective, anyway, thought True, against this rampaging horde. One thing in their favor was that the Grendlers never seemed to be well organized. They could band together for attacks such as this, but they reacted as individuals, with little discipline or teamwork.

"Scream with me, kids!" Alonzo shouted.

As requests went, it was an easy one, and True and Uly screamed for all they were worth.

"Help! Help! Aaaaah! Aaaah!"

As they had hoped, the front wave of Grendlers decided to ignore the meager prize of a cyborg in favor of a bunch of screaming captives and a huge, high-tech vehicle. The hordes were soon leaping toward them, and Yale was able to stagger to his feet. He must've decided to blend in, because he crouched down and began loping toward the TransRover, like just another misshapen creature in the darkness.

A second later, it was total bedlam as the band of Gendlers descended upon them, shrieking and whistling. True saw them scampering up the sides of the TransRover, and she closed her eyes as a scaly foot stepped near her face. The beasts began to pull and yank stuff off, with little interest in the humans . . . yet. She could see Alonzo wielding his rifle like a club, smashing all those who got too close to the precious parachute at the rear of the vehicle.

"No!" screamed Uly, as a Grendler gripped his brown hair and tried to pull it out by the roots. True stared at the grotesque creature, and its hood fell away from its slimy face. It burped at her, and True screamed so loudly that the Grendler actually leapt off the vehicle.

Without warning, the TransRover groaned and shook itself, like a woolly mammoth waking up from a nap. Yale had made it to the cockpit! True could see the cyborg battling off a horde of hunchbacked reptiles, and the TransRover suddenly lurched, causing several of them to lose their balance. There were still a dozen or so Grendlers clinging to the vehicle as it made its inevitable run toward the rim of the deadly chasm.

Now True and Uly really screamed, and they were joined by several startled Grendlers. True saw the beasts leap off at the last moment, and her instincts were to do the same. Unlike them, however, she was tied down. She could do nothing but shriek as the TransRover lumbered up to the rim and careened off.

Headfirst, they plummeted into the dark abyss, and True's stomach rose up and tried to climb out of her mouth. Her lips were so dry that her scream went silent, and the wind and gravity stretched her face into a tight mask.

Uly wailed beside her, and she could hear Alonzo cut loose with a wild "Yahooooo!"

Suddenly there was a jerk, like they were on a giant rubber band, and True's chin bumped against her chest. She craned her neck backward, and she could just barely see the edge of the dark parachute as it blossomed above them. This was a braking parachute, and she wondered whether it would hold against the full force of gravity. The air roared in protest as the parachute enslaved it, and there were eerie whistling noises as the wind tore through the baffles.

True was afraid to look down, but where else was there to look? She took a deep breath and peered over the edge of the sleeping bag in front of her. From her weird vantage point, it looked as if the ground were a giant hand reaching up to slap her. She could see the lines and fingers in the hand, and it was with a start she realized that it was really water, sand, and plants that were rushing toward her! A mile went by fast, she thought, when gravity had you in its grip.

Now there was no more screaming, just the sober certainty that they were going to hit.

"Brace yourself!" she told Uly.

"Okay," the boy murmured.

True kept waiting to be whisked away to safety at the last second, like on a roller coaster. But no, instead they plowed into the sand like a runaway freight train! She bounced forward, and some of her ropes sprang loose, as a ripple effect shook the great TransRover. Then everything went dark.

"No!" shouted Uly. "I'm blind!"

True was worried too, then she howled with laughter and stuck her hands out. "No!" she shouted, "it's the *parachute*! It fell all around us and covered us up!"

"All right!" hollered Uly. "We're alive! We're alive!"

"Wow," sighed Alonzo from somewhere above them. "Yale, are you all right? Yale!"

It was so dark with the parachute draped around them that nobody could see anything.

"Yale! Yale!" shouted Alonzo, sounding worried.

"Pooh, piff, paah," came some strangled spitting sounds. "I'm okay," croaked a voice. "Just got sand in my mouth."

Alonzo, Uly, and True all screamed, "Yahooo!"

They heard Yale laugh heartily. "I can truthfully say that sand never tasted so good!"

A few seconds later the sound of an engine came, and the glimmer of headlights shone through their silvery cocoon like twin ghosts.

"Hello!" called the unmistakable voice of Zero. "Is anybody home?"

"Yes, yes!" cried Yale. "We're all present and accounted for. Please, see what you can do about getting the parachute off us."

"Be careful you don't tear it!" ordered Alonzo. "It's the most glorious parachute in the universe!"

At that, True laughed again. "It sure is!"

• • •

Atop a cold and exposed plateau in the middle of a foreboding canyon, Morgan Martin was having a very strange and wonderful dream. In real life, Morgan was barely thirty years old, but in this dream he was ancient—and rich! He was hundreds of years old, living in a Greek villa on a planet with glassy lakes and shimmering, snow-capped peaks. Despite his advanced age, he felt great, and he had the best of everything—servants, a private space yacht, a sleek ocean yacht, gourmet food, fine wines, and Bess, right at his side. He could see it all from the veranda of his classic villa.

Bess was hundreds of years old too, although she didn't look a day past fifty. And she still looked good for fifty. A young French maid brought him his favorite book—a priceless copy of *Swimming with the Sharks,* a first edition from the late twentieth century. He and Bess took seats on their elaborate wrought-iron furniture to enjoy a breakfast of crumpets, beluga caviar, and Mumm champagne.

Morgan lifted his fluted glass to propose a toast. "To youth, forever," he said.

"To youth," echoed Bess with a grin. "And for making all of this possible."

They drained their fluted glasses. "Ah," said Morgan with satisfaction. "It was worth rerouting a convoy to bring us this champagne."

"I don't want to think how much it cost," added Bess. The jovial tone in her voice made it clear that she didn't care.

Morgan nodded his solemn agreement. "To think, that dismal planet, G889, made all of this possible. Who would have guessed?" He chuckled at the absurdity of it.

"Don't forget the Terrians," Bess remarked.

"The Terrians," Morgan echoed, trying to remember them. What was it about the Terrians that deserved a toast?

"No matter," he said, refilling his glass. He held it up again for another toast. "To the Terrians!"

As he lifted the fine crystal to his lips, an arm rudely bumped him.

"Hey!" he muttered groggily.

The arm bumped him again. In fact, it shook him.

"Wake up," said John Danziger.

"Oh, no!" groaned Morgan. He blinked his eyes at the dreary plateau, surrounded by walls of gray rock. The sun filtered down from above, but it did nothing to dispel the gloom. "Why did you have to wake me up? I was having the most wonderful dream."

"Well, I'm glad somebody got some sleep," muttered Danziger. "Watch your step when you get up."

"Come on, sweetie," said Bess, struggling to her feet. She helped him up.

"Bess," he whispered, "I was having the most wonderful dream. We were growing old together . . ."

"Well, I hope so."

"No, I mean, *really* old. Like centuries old. It was incredible—we were rich!"

She cocked an eyebrow at him. "I thought you only had those dreams when you were awake."

"I know I think big," said Morgan, "but this was so *real*. Something had made us extremely rich, beyond my usual greed and avarice. And we were toasting the fact that we could live forever!"

Bess grimaced as she massaged the small of her back. "I'll take living through the next few days." She started to search through her backpack. "Let's see what's for breakfast." She held up a brown box of prepackaged rations and read the label. "What is pemmican?"

"It's a comedown from Beluga caviar, I can tell you that much," grumbled Morgan. He looked around at the dark, forbidding canyon and smiled. "There's something down here that's going to make us rich."

Suddenly Devon Adair was in his face, staring at him with interest. "Were you dreaming about this canyon?" she asked.

"Not exactly," said Morgan secretively. "Just a pleasant dream, that's all."

"You know," said Devon, "the Terrians have been communicating with Alonzo Solace through *his* dreams. If you were dreaming about Terrians, I want to know."

"Terrians?" echoed Morgan, remembering what Bess had said in his dream. The Terrians deserved a toast for something they had done. But what? He looked at Bess, but she was busy opening her pemmican.

"I was dreaming of civilization," Morgan said to Devon. "Can you blame me?"

"No," muttered Devon as she gazed around the rugged canyon. "Not at all. And you keep dreaming of that, Morgan, because we're going to build a civilization here. Not one like you know, but one where everybody has a chance at good health, where we don't rape the land or exploit the people. It'll be better than any civilization you've ever seen."

Morgan smiled. "It would be hard put to match the one in my dream."

Devon leveled him with a gaze from her dark eyes. "I don't think our dreams are the same, but I'd be interested in hearing about yours. Especially if there are Terrians involved."

"Some other time," offered Morgan.

Devon nodded and clapped her hands. "Eat up, folks! We want to get an early start. I don't think any of us want to spend another night clinging to this canyon."

There were murmured words of agreement, and Danziger

came up to her. "Devon, do you think we should contact the base camp?"

She smiled fondly. "No. They've probably had a relaxed night and are sleeping in this morning. Let's let them rest. I figure, with an early start, we can reach the bottom by mid-afternoon. Then we'll contact them."

"Yes!" said Morgan exuberantly. "Let's get going!"

Devon cast a suspicious glance at him, then shook her head. She picked up the rope and began to tie it around her waist, as Morgan eagerly measured off ten feet and knotted the rope around his waist.

"Are you feeling all right?" asked Devon.

He grinned. "Never felt better!"

Chapter 6

• • • • • • • •

As the tiny band descended deeper into the immense chasm, Devon began to get the feeling that they were transcending the usual three dimensions and going on to the fourth: Time. The eons that it had taken to form this rock cathedral were etched in every stone and every striated layer. It was a panoramic snapshot of hundreds of billions of years.

Devon was reminded of the faraway galaxies she had viewed from orbital telescopes. Due to the immense distances that light had to travel, those galaxies existed in two different time frames: the observer's present and the moment when the image had begun its journey across space, billions of years in the past. The ancient canyon worked the same kind of magic, bridging billions of years in a single moment and affording the observer a rare glimpse into a time beyond reckoning.

Adding to the eerie sensation was the silence. It was so profound as to seem holy, as if noise were forbidden in this vast tomb. It *was* a tomb, Devon decided, a place where each year was marked by a nick in the canyon wall, as if the canyon were a vertical field of tombstones. She kicked a stone off the path and heard it clatter down hundreds of feet to the bottom. It had taken that stone a billion years to reach this place, she thought, and now she had kicked it a billion years into the future.

The journey of that rock reminded Devon of her own incredible journey through space and time to reach this point. Twenty-two years she had lost, or gained, in cold sleep. As with the walls of this canyon, her life seemed condensed and laid bare, one part of it no more important than another. The child, the student, the engineer, the explorer—all just so many stripes on a small boulder. What am I really after? she wondered.

The answer came as Devon glanced down to see the turquoise river, weaving through the sand and thistle at the bottom of the canyon. She wanted to continue to grind away year after year, like that river, carving the canyon ever deeper.

She thought of little Uly. Why would anyone go through the pain and sacrifice of having children? The answer was again the river. A child was a way to leave something behind, to flow onward. The same instincts drove people to build buildings, found companies, write books, and create colonies on distant planets. It wasn't just ego, Devon decided, but a natural instinct to leave something behind. If you didn't leave something behind, you were just a nick in the rock, not the river itself.

She looked behind her, and it seemed as if everyone, even Morgan, had been lulled into a state of silent awe by the grandeur of the canyon. As they descended, the slope had leveled somewhat, and there were more and more copper-colored buttes rising all around them. The path wound its way between the spires as a cobblestone lane might wind its way through the old part of a European city. At times, the majestic buttes looked like skyscrapers that had been left out in the sun to melt.

Devon suddenly felt a tug on her rope, and she turned around to find Morgan, chipping away at the base of a silvery boulder with his pocketknife. Everyone slowed behind him.

"What are you doing?" asked Devon.

Morgan smiled and folded his pocketknife. "Just taking samples."

"You would be able to identify the composition of these rocks?" she asked doubtfully.

"You never know," he answered, still smiling, still unaccountably cheerful.

A few spaces behind him, Julia Heller wiped her brow with her bandanna and leaned into a narrow spire. It crumbled away at her touch, and she tumbled over the stump of the rock and dropped twenty feet in a second!

The scream of panic were immediate, as Baines, Bess, and Walman nearly tumbled after her. Devon immediately ran behind the nearest spire, wrapping as much rope as she could spare around it. That yanked Morgan off his feet, and he began to scream.

"Brace yourselves with your legs!" Devon shouted at Morgan.

She followed her own advice and inched her feet up into a cranny in the rock, where she braced herself with her muscular legs. She could see Danziger in the distance, doing the same, but everyone else had been jerked off their feet by Julia's fall and were clawing the ground and scraggly bushes, trying to find something to hang onto. Devon gripped the rope and tried to pull it back, but the dead weight of several bodies made it just too heavy to budge.

Bess and Baines continued to slip toward the edge, Baines being dragged by Julia and Bess being dragged by Baines. There was just no place for them to hang on.

"Cut me loose!" cried a pathetic voice. "Save yourselves!" Julia was swaying in midair, nowhere to go but straight down hundreds of feet to certain death.

"No!" yelled Devon. "First thing, let's stop this fall!"

Morgan was still in a netherworld, neither falling nor stopping the fall of the others. He was scrambling along the ground in a panic.

"Morgan!" she shouted. "Plant yourself on your butt, grab the rope, and use your feet to back toward me. I need your help!"

He stared at her, panic-stricken.

"Do it, baby!" screamed Bess, as her legs slid over the edge. Baines's entire body had fallen off, and only his arms, shoulders, and head remained above the ledge. He groaned with the effort of hanging on.

Bess's cry galvanized Morgan into action, and he sat down and got a firm grip on the rope. Then he used his legs to push himself back slowly toward Devon's foothold. The rope in his hands tightened, and he had to strain muscles he never knew he had.

"Pull!" yelled Devon. "You can do it! Pull your wife up!"

Morgan gulped with determination, then found an even stronger foothold of his own between two spires. He planted his feet and tried to pull Bess to safety. Bess helped by getting a leg up over the ledge. Devon fought the temptation to leave her cranny and help Morgan; she knew that if he lost his grip on the rope while she wasn't firmly planted, all of them would go sailing over.

"That's it!" Danziger shouted in encouragement. "Keep pulling!"

But it was no use. Alone, Morgan didn't have the strength. Bess began to slip back, and Baines hollered with panic as Julia's body yanked the rope off his waist.

"The rope is slipping!" cried Baines.

Devon and Danziger looked at each other, and Danziger swiftly untied the rope around his waist. His side of the line was holding, although all of them were frozen with fear. He knotted the rope around a vine and strode across the supine bodies to reach Baines. With total disregard for his own safety, he dived to his stomach and reached over to retrieve the rope that had slipped from Baines's waist to his thighs.

"Okay," Danziger muttered through gritted teeth. "Get up!"

Freed from the weight of Julia's rope, Baines was able to climb up and stagger to his feet. He grabbed Danziger's waist just as the mechanic was about to go over, and both untethered men held desperately to Julia's rope.

"Pull!" yelled Devon. "Everyone! Pull!"

She yanked on her rope, dragging Morgan a few inches toward her. Given some slack in the rope at long last, he scrambled to his feet and joined Devon at her cranny, and the two of them were able to yank Bess back over the ledge.

Morgan grinned at her. "Keep pulling!" she snarled.

Panic had been replaced by purpose, and everyone pulled as if it were a tug-of-war contest for their very lives. Danziger and Baines hauled in handfuls of rope, and Julia finally began to move up instead of down. That gave the others even more rope to grab, and they pulled for all they were worth.

Julia's hands clawed for the ledge, and Danziger and Baines each grabbed a hand and pulled her up. Then all three of them sank onto their backs and panted. Devon finally took time to breathe, and she found that her legs were cramped with pain when she set them on the ground. Morgan rushed to hug Bess, and nobody seemed able to talk or do any more than take in great gobs of air.

Julia gulped and tried to wave to all of them, but her arm just flopped to her chest. "Thanks," she breathed.

"You're welcome," said Danziger from his back. He gave her a weary smile. "Good thing for you, we're short of doctors."

"Are you okay?" asked Devon.

Julia shook her head. "I'll tell you when we get to the bottom."

"That was everyone's fault," Devon said angrily. "I don't know about the rest of you, but I was just walking along, daydreaming. We all got careless, like this is some stroll in the park. We can't do that again."

"I don't plan to do it again," muttered Julia.

Danziger rose slowly to his feet and glared at Devon. "Don't be too hard on us. If you had wanted mountain climbers, you should have hired some. None of us signed on for *this*." His sweeping motion took in the endless miles of rock and buttes, rising straight up to a summit that was almost invisible.

"Yeah," said Baines, "it's a miracle we made it this far!"

Devon took a deep breath, trying to control her temper. They had indeed been careless, no matter what anyone cared to believe, but perhaps this wasn't the time or place to chew them out for it.

"Okay," she sighed. "It's about midday, I guess. Let's break for lunch."

There was a collective sigh of gratitude, and they began to reach for their canteens and backpacks. Julia rolled over and sat up, and Devon knelt beside her. She helped Julia take off her backpack.

"I know you weren't thinking about this when you were hanging off the edge," said Devon, "but did you happen to see how much farther we have to go?"

The shaken doctor shook her head. "It looked like a long way down to me, but I would guess it was only about a quarter of a mile."

Devon gave Julia a smile and patted her on the back. "That's good. I don't mean to drive everybody, but the sooner we're down, the sooner we're safe."

"Don't you mean," said Julia, "the sooner we start up the other side?"

Devon looked down and rubbed the sweat away from her eyes.

"And you *do* mean to push everybody," Julia insisted. "John is right—we aren't mountain climbers. We aren't any of the things we need to be to cross three thousand miles of wilderness."

Devon scowled. "We've got to be. If the Colony ship arrives, and we aren't there—"

"They'll get along without us," Julia cut in. "You trust in Dr. Vasquez's abilities, don't you? I mean, you made it very clear that you trusted him a great deal more than me to be the lead physician on this project. You got stuck with me on the Advance ship, but maybe it will work out for the best, with Vasquez on the Colony ship."

Devon muttered, "I don't feel like I got stuck with you. Not anymore. Come on! We need to have a positive attitude."

Julia shook her head wearily. "We also need to have a realistic attitude. How do we know that over the next rise there aren't ten more canyons like this? Or creatures much more dangerous than we've met so far? You've got to accept the fact that we're outnumbered and short on supplies. And we're only human. If we have to abandon the vehicles . . ." The doctor didn't need to finish the sentence.

"Okay," muttered Devon, "you've made your point."

Morgan suddenly knelt down beside them and thrust an opened package into each of their laps. "Come on, ladies, eat up! Have to keep your strength up! Bess says this pemmican isn't so bad, like fruitcake, only not so sweet. It'll keep you going!"

"Why are you so bloody cheerful?" asked Devon suspiciously.

He grinned. "I've found that I enjoy all this exercise. I may take up canyon climbing as a hobby."

Devon took a nibble of pemmican and made a sour face. "As soon as we build a kitchen, I'm going to take up cooking."

"You could open up the first restaurant on G889!" said Morgan excitedly. "Sounds like a solid investment."

He stood and walked away, humming. Watching him go, Devon folded up her package of food and stuck it in her shirt pocket. "He's up to something, but I haven't got time to figure out what it is."

The dark-haired woman stood and took a long drink of water from her canteen. "Let's get going!" she called out. With a glance at Julia, she announced to the others, "If we make it down to the bottom this afternoon, I've decided we're going to take tomorrow off. Just a little incentive."

A weary cheer went up. John Danziger grinned and peered over the ledge at the river below. "Do you suppose there's any fishing down there?"

A big, ugly fish with a barbed mouth and jagged fins all over its misshapen body leapt out of the river. It snapped its enormous mouth and shook like a trout before disappearing back into the swirling turquoise water.

"Wow!" said Alonzo, sitting up on the sand. "Did you guys see that sucker? Must've been four feet long! It looked like a cross between a barracuda and a catfish."

Uly and True looked up from the creation they were building in the cream-colored sand. "Didn't see it," said True, shaking her head.

"Me either," replied Uly.

"To me," said a voice, "it looked more like a *Coelacanth latimeria*." Alonzo turned to see Yale shuffling toward them, wiping his hands on a rag.

"And what does one of those taste like," asked Alonzo, "fried up in a little olive oil and garlic?"

"Hard to say," answered the cyborg. "They've been extinct for quite a while. Considering the distances between bodies of water on this planet, I wouldn't be surprised if some of the native fish have rudimentary lungs, in addition to gills."

"That still doesn't explain how they'll taste," said Alonzo. "On a more practical subject, how are the vehicles coming?"

"The TransRover has a few more dents, of course, but nothing major. Your ATV has a leak in the lubrication pan, but I think we've patched it. I wouldn't say they're as good as new—they haven't been as good as new for weeks—but we can leave whenever you're ready."

"Yale?" asked Uly, "what makes the water turquoise?"

"You see," answered the cyborg, pointing upward, "the water picks up a lot of minerals as it filters down the canyon. Calcium carbonate, magnesium carbonate, calcium sulphate, and magnesium chloride—those compounds would give it that color."

"Is it safe for drinking?" asked Alonzo.

"We should boil it first to kill parasites," answered Yale, "but I don't see why not. It's an experiment we should try."

Alonzo leaned back on his elbows and stared up at a

stripe of blue sky that appeared to be painted across the ceiling of the canyon. It was strange, but from above, the canyon had seemed foreboding and deadly. Now, deep within its protective walls, the canyon felt peaceful and benign, as if they were being cradled in the bosom of the planet. There was a soft breeze, which rustled plants and trees at the water's edge and coaxed some pleasant scents from a patch of bright red flowers. The sight and sound of flowing water seemed to tap into some kind of primal relaxation center inside Alonzo's brain.

He lay back on the sand and yawned. "Do we have to leave?"

"We're not actually leaving," Yale pointed out. "We're just driving a couple of miles to see if we can rendezvous with the others."

"We could use the Gear," Alonzo suggested.

Yale crossed his arms and peered off into the distance. "They may be having a less pleasant time of it than we are. I hate to disturb them if they are inching their way down the side of a cliff."

Alonzo grinned and closed his eyes. "They should've taken the express, like we did."

Yale bent down to study the children's handiwork. "My, that is a very nice . . . Uh, what is it?"

"Space dock!" both Uly and True answered at once.

True added, "It's hard to make one when it's on the ground. You have to imagine it in orbit."

The cyborg smiled. "Of course, I see it now. Maybe, one day, you children will learn what it's like to make buildings that are supposed to be on the ground."

"I'd like that," Uly said and beamed.

"But right now," said Yale, standing, "we're still in transit. Alonzo, shall I drive your ATV over to you?"

"Sure," muttered the pilot, his eyes still closed. "How about a fifteen-minute nap first?"

"All right," conceded the cyborg. "Fifteen minutes."

At long last, the treacherous ledges of the canyon gave way to a steep hillside, festooned with red flowers and small rust-colored boulders. To everyone's relief, there were no more sudden drops to terrifying depths, and they could see their goal shimmering at the bottom of the hill. The blue-green river looked like a mirage, thought Devon, it was so beautiful.

She couldn't find the Koba path any longer, but she didn't think it was necessary to follow it. After slipping on her butt and sliding several feet, she had decided that a strong rear end was all that was needed from here on down. She was the first person to untie the rope around her waist.

"Take off your ropes!" she ordered. "It's everybody for himself! But take it easy—slide on your butts if you have to!"

With relief and happy chattering, the others untied their ropes and became individuals again. Each person studied the slope and decided how best to tackle it. Danziger got down on his hands and feet, with his head pointed toward the summit, and worked his way down backward. Morgan and Bess slid on their rear ends, until Morgan bounced over a rock and howled with pain. Then he slid on his stomach. Julia got down in a crouch and took baby steps, and the others performed some combination of these antics.

Devon just sat for a few moments, admiring the view of the river and the monumental buttes on the far side of it. They had made it! She sniffed with a puzzled expression, wondering what smelled so fragrant, then she realized that the tiny red flowers dotting the hillside were giving off a scent. *Devon Adair actually stopped to smell the flowers!*

she thought with amazement. A lot of people didn't think that was possible.

Sitting on the hillside, watching her comrades slide comically past her, Devon felt a sense of peace and accomplishment that she hadn't thought she would feel until they reached New Pacifica. It really was a gorgeous planet, she told herself, well worth all the sacrifices and struggle. And these were good people she had brought with her, even if they weren't mountain climbers and some of them were here by accident.

Devon thought about the night before, when she had slept nestled in John Danziger's arms. She didn't know how much sleep Danziger had gotten—as the tallest member of the party, there had been no one to shelter him from the cold—but she wouldn't forget the camaraderie and warmth he had offered her, or the way he had cajoled the others into doing the same. If she could stop to smell flowers, thought Devon, maybe someday she could stop to enjoy a man's embrace again.

Lying there in a field of flowers, watching a turquoise river weave through a lush valley that had been undisturbed for millions of years, anything seemed possible.

"Hey!" screamed Bess. "The vehicles!"

Devon bolted to her feet and nearly rolled headfirst down the hill. "Take it slow!" she cautioned everyone, including herself. "They're not going anywhere!"

She shielded her eyes from the sun and shook her head with amazement. The two smaller vehicles were rumbling along the riverbank, followed by the TransRover. They looked as if they were barely crawling through the sand and sediment, but they had obviously made great time down the canyon. How did they get down first? she wondered.

The only explanation was that they had found an extremely easy way down, meaning all the danger and misery she had put the others through over the last two days had been for nothing. Only her impatience had made it necessary, thought Devon glumly.

Danziger set off a flare, probably thinking that they looked like just a dozen specks on a very tall hill. At once, the small caravan of vehicles stopped, and the TransRover blew its airhorn. Well, thought Devon, anyone who didn't know they had arrived in the canyon certainly knew it now.

She was still troubled as she picked her way down the pebble-strewn hill, partially sliding and partially running. She had risked everyone's life for nothing, it seemed, if the presence of the vehicles made any sense. But the presence of the vehicles didn't make any sense!

When she had talked to the base camp the night before, they were all getting ready for bed, after having scouted for miles in both directions and reporting no easy route down. When did they have time to find some mysterious highway to the bottom of this monstrous crevasse? Well, the proof was right before her eyes—find it, they had.

Devon tried to cheer herself with the realization that they wouldn't have to abandon the vehicles. Plus, she wouldn't have to spend time trekking back up the canyon to fetch the children. They were down too. She could see Uly waving from the TransRover.

Baines gave her a funny look as she scooted past him. Okay, she had nearly cost him his life for apparently nothing, she thought. She couldn't make it up to him now—she would try to later. Only Morgan, still in his unaccountably blissful state, smiled at her.

At least a cute eight-year-old boy was glad to see her. Yale was just lifting Uly off the TransRover as Devon reached the sandy bottom. He ran to her, and she enveloped him in her arms and smothered him with kisses.

"Oh, Uly," she breathed, "I'm so glad to see you."

"Me too, Mom."

True climbed out on her own and ran to her father. "Oh, Dad, you should've seen what *we* did!"

Danziger glanced at Devon. "I was going to ask you how you got down here so quickly."

True, Uly, and Yale all began to talk at once: "We drove off the cliff! We parachuted! Straight down!"

"We took the express!" Alonzo shouted from his ATV.

As the others in the party began to gather around them, Devon held up her hands. "Let's have Yale tell it first." She smiled at Uly. "Then the rest of you can tell it."

The cyborg looked worried for a moment, as if he had some explaining to do. "You must realize, we were driven to desperate measures by two determined attacks on us—by a large force of Grendlers."

Devon crossed her arms angrily. "Grendlers! Why didn't you call us?"

"This was late last night," Yale replied, "and it didn't sound as if you were in much position to help us."

"Okay," Devon conceded. "Go on."

"There were hundreds of 'em!" Uly interjected.

"He's not far from wrong," said Yale. The cyborg went on to describe their battle and motorized retreat from the camp, only to find themselves at a sheer cliff, expecting another attack. He explained how they reviewed a hologram of heavy military equipment parachuting to the ground, followed by a discussion in which they decided that they could do the same, if need be.

"The TransRover had its parachute for emergency braking," said Yale, "and it wasn't too difficult to rig up some tents to make parachutes for the smaller vehicles. We tied Uly, True, and Alonzo into the TransRover, while I drove it, and Zero manned the DuneRail. The ATV went over unmanned."

Devon and Danziger exchanged horrified parental glances. "Remind me never to let you baby-sit again," muttered Danziger.

Alonzo cut in. "We didn't have much choice, John. Honest. Even diving off a cliff, we barely got away from the Grendlers."

Uly was jumping up and down, and Yale smiled at the boy. "Perhaps Uly would like to finish the story."

"It was cool!" said the boy. "We drove right off the cliff—right into space! The parachute went up, just like Yale said it would. I wasn't even scared." True cocked an eyebrow at him. "Well, maybe a little."

"The landing was scary," True admitted. "With that ground rising up . . ."

Devon shivered and shook her head. "Don't tell me any more. I'm just glad you're all safe."

Julia went to True, bent down, and looked closely into her eyes. "Do you feel all right?" asked the doctor. "No headaches, or anything?"

"I feel fine," said True. "Maybe a little tired."

"We didn't have any sleep last night," said Alonzo. "If somebody will get me out of here, I can tell you that lying in that sand is awfully comfortable."

Morgan slumped down into the sand and stretched out luxuriously. "Yeah, I see what you mean."

As most of the others collapsed gratefully into the sand, Devon, Danziger, and Julia strode over to Alonzo and helped him out of his ATV.

"How do *you* feel?" Julia asked.

"Oh, never better," claimed the pilot. "Yale strapped me in so that my back took the impact." He yawned. "But there's something about that river that makes you sleepy. You'll see."

Danziger nodded and looked around at the fertile valley,

nestled within the silent walls of the canyon. "This is a pretty peaceful spot, once you take the trouble to get down here."

"And there's fish in that river," added Alonzo.

Danziger smiled. "No kidding? But that water is moving along at a pretty good clip."

"Yes," said Devon with a frown. "That's our next task, to figure out how to get across it."

"Remember," said Julia, "you gave us the day off."

"That's tomorrow," said Devon. "We still have a few hours left today."

She strode over to the TransRover, where Yale and Zero were making an inspection. Devon felt much better knowing that she hadn't endangered anyone's life unnecessarily, and she intended to keep working toward that goal. However, it didn't change the fact that they were only one-third of the way across the canyon. Crossing was another third, and climbing up the other side was the last third. They had to keep moving.

She smiled at the cyborg and the robot. "So, you've turned into skydivers?"

"Yes!" said Zero with a jerk of his podlike head. "It was quite exhilarating."

"Well, now you can be scuba divers." Devon wrapped her knuckles on the TransRover. "If you can get this thing to fly, maybe you can get it to swim. Any idea how deep the river is?"

"No," admitted Yale. "We haven't taken a sounding yet."

"Can we use the sonar in the TransRover?"

"That should give us an approximate depth." The cyborg motioned to Zero. "Climb in."

Devon turned to survey the river, and something caught her eye on a distant plateau. It was just a bird, sweeping in for a landing—but what a bird! Its wingspan had to be at least twelve feet. Before she could get a really good look, it had disappeared behind the plateau.

"Is there something wrong?" asked Yale.

"No," said Devon, shaking her head. "Did you see some giant birds in the canyon?"

"No," answered Yale. "We saw two birds and a fish. The fish was rather large, but the birds were medium-sized, somewhat like hawks. There is considerable indication of Koba activity, but we haven't—"

"That's all right," Devon assured him. "We don't want to disrupt the life down here—we're just passing through."

She glanced back at the plateau but couldn't see any movement. Perhaps the huge bird had been an illusion, a trick of the distances and the clarity of the air in this vast wonder. Her eyes drifted down to the riverbank, where most of her intrepid band were sacked out, dozing like a bunch of tourists on holiday at the beach.

Devon sighed and said to herself, "At least I *hope* we're just passing through."

Chapter 7

“Reverse! Reverse!” yelled Danziger from the bank. He waved his arms like a windmill caught in a storm. The TransRover was mired in mud and water, and it was starting to tip over into the swirling river.

He glared at Devon. “It’s not working!”

Devon glared back at him, then at the TransRover. “Reverse!” she echoed.

It was doubtful whether Yale, in the cockpit of the TransRover, could hear either one of them over the roar of the water. But his sense of balance was still apparently working; he must’ve known that the only place the Trans-Rover was going was under, not across. He threw the ungainly vehicle into reverse, and its huge tires spun, coating Danziger and Devon with globules of mud and sand. But they stood there, shouting encouragement. They were joined by several others, who tried with shouts and body language to coax the TransRover out of the muck.

The giant vehicle shuddered and righted itself for a second, then it sank helplessly into the soft mud, listing in the other direction. Danziger was reminded of paintings he had seen of mastodons trying to extricate themselves from the La Brea tar pit.

Yale turned the wheel sharply, pointing the nose of the craft into the onrushing water. The new angle not only gave the tires some added traction, but the force of the water actually propelled the vehicle into reverse. It slid a few feet, and Yale spun the wheel the other way. The rover's momentum carried it up over the bank, and it lumbered to safety, dripping mud from the river bottom. With a jerk, the vehicle stopped, and Yale cut the engine. He removed his mud-splattered goggles and looked forlornly at Danziger and Devon as they jogged toward him.

"Whew!" breathed Danziger. "That was close."

Devon looked crestfallen. "I thought it would make it across. Sorry."

"It's shallow enough," said Yale. "But that's a bad combination—swift current and soft mud."

"So we aren't going to drive over," said Devon thoughtfully. "What about a raft? Once we get to the other side, we can rig up a pulley system to get the others across. Like a ferry."

"We could build a raft," said Danziger, "but it would take us days. And I don't think we could control a raft in that current."

"I agree," said Yale. "It would be too dangerous. If the raft broke up, even the strongest swimmer would be swept away."

Devon slammed her fist into her palm and looked up in

frustration. As if fate were continuing to spit on her, a big raindrop landed between her eyes.

Danziger chuckled. "Sorry," he said.

A second later, they were all pelted by gigantic raindrops. True, Uly, and most of the people who had been lounging in the sand bolted for cover under the vehicles, but Danziger lifted his face into the natural shower. He noticed that Devon did the same, slicking back her wet hair and opening the collar of her shirt.

"What are you looking at?" she asked accusingly.

He smiled. "You. You're attractive, when you relax a little bit."

"Well, I'm not relaxed," she countered, "I'm just dirty."

Danziger surveyed the turquoise river, now misty with a scrim of raindrops. "You know, if we look for a place where the river is wider than this, the current isn't likely to be as strong."

"How do you know that?" she asked.

"It just stands to reason. The same amount of water flows down the river. Where it's narrow, it's got to be deeper and faster. Where it's wide, it'll be slower and probably more shallow."

She smiled at him. "That's good thinking. Which way should we go to look for this shallow crossing?"

Danziger pointed upriver. "I would go toward the head-waters. Just a hunch."

Devon nodded. "That's the way I saw the giant bird."

"Giant bird?"

She shook her head and laughed. "Maybe I was dreaming, like Alonzo. Don't worry about it. In the morning, while the rest of you enjoy your day off, Yale and I will take a look upstream."

Devon pushed her sleek hair away from her lovely face

and turned to go. "Oh," she said, "you were very brave today, the way you rescued Julia."

He shrugged. "Well, it was a one-for-all, all-for-one sort of thing."

She gave him a rare look of frank appreciation. "Not really. I owe you dinner sometime."

Danziger frowned and watched her stride toward the Trans-Rover. What did that invitation mean, exactly? Everything she did was too intense, too unforgiving. There would be no casual affairs with Devon Adair. In love, as in everything else, he doubted if she took prisoners. It would be all or nothing with Devon Adair, and nothing was a lot safer at the moment.

He glanced toward the riverbank and saw Alonzo sitting alone. The rain had let up a bit, but not enough to see clearly what the pilot was doing. Maybe he wanted some help getting to shelter. Danziger jogged over to ask him.

As he got closer, he saw that Alonzo had a long, metal gear antenna, and he was tying a spool of filament to the end of it.

"A fishing pole!" said Danziger with delight.

Alonzo grinned. "We only need to catch one of those suckers to have dinner for everybody. I'm using the spool for a weight, and a tent stake for the hook, but I'm not sure what to use for bait."

"I remember that tent stake," said Danziger. "I was the one who pounded it the wrong way and bent it."

"And a good job you did," said the pilot. "My mother taught me never to throw anything away. But without bait or a lure, it's no good. Now what would an old leathery fish like to eat?"

"Here," said a feminine voice. The men turned to see Devon removing a soggy package from her shirt pocket. "I bet they would love pemmican." She tossed it into Alonzo's lap.

"Thanks." He removed the paper and wrapped the soggy mass around the hook. "Perfect! Since I can't stand up, I can't get much of a cast."

"Let me do it," offered Danziger. He took the makeshift pole and hefted it with satisfaction. Then he strode to the water's edge.

By now, everyone was braving the rain to see what they were up to.

"Daddy, I didn't know you knew how to fish!" marveled True.

"I haven't been fishing since I was your age," admitted Danziger. "Of course, it's a lost art on Earth. No fish left. But we used to give it a try every now and then in my uncle's pond. Once we caught a grizzled old bluegill, but we wouldn't eat it."

"They used to say that rainy weather was good for fishing," offered Bess.

Danziger looked around to make sure that nobody was in the way. "Stand back," he cautioned.

The others moved back as if he were about to set off a stick of dynamite, and the mechanic sent the hook, line, and sinker sailing over the blue-green water. It landed with a pleasing plop, and the swift current took it even farther out.

With some effort, Alonzo crawled closer to the water, and Danziger handed him the pole. "You should do the honors," he remarked.

The pilot beamed. "Thanks."

For a couple of minutes, nothing happened, and Morgan complained. "What's taking so long?"

"This is fishing," said Bess. "Patience is the name of the game."

Devon smiled at Morgan. "That lets us out."

Yale stepped forward with a look of concern on his face. "If you hook one of those creatures that we saw earlier, you had better be prepared to—"

"Yow!" cried Alonzo as the pole was nearly jerked out of his hands. The force on the line whipped Alonzo around and dragged him several yards across the sand on his stomach.

"Help!" he screamed.

Danziger was sprinting alongside him, and when the pilot finally lost his grip on the pole, the mechanic leapt for it. He caught the antenna and tried to pull it in to his chest, but it felt as if he had ahold of a cyclone. He was jerked one way, then another, and ended up being dragged across the wet sand on his back.

"Help!" hollered Danziger.

The others were racing along beside him, screaming with a combination of concern and excitement. Devon leapt directly on top of his chest and gripped the pole with both of her hands. Four hands barely made a difference, however, and the two of them were dragged downstream together, Devon squealing with delight.

Just as all seemed lost and it was impossible for either one of them to hold on a moment longer, Morgan joined the fray. He dove for the pole and got a good grip on the top of it. Then it became a free-for-all, with Bess, Julia, and the children piling on. With a dozen hands on the pole, their nemesis was finally slowed down.

Thankfully, Yale and Zero had kept their feet, and the twosome soon took control of the pole and the situation. They actually began to drag the fish out of the water, as the others tried to collect themselves.

Morgan sat up in the sand and dazedly shook his head. "I didn't realize fishing was a team sport."

Bess hung on his back and kissed him. "You were wonderful," she cooed.

Danziger helped Devon up. "I should thank you," he panted. "I was about to lose it."

"It happens to the best of us." She winked at him. "Let's see what we've caught."

With the rain still pelting them, the band gathered eagerly around the riverbank to see what all their effort had wrought. Baines and Danziger lifted Alonzo up and carried him over to the gathering, so that he could see the result of his fishing expedition.

True, Uly, and Julia gasped when the catch was dragged out of the water. It was the first fish many of them had ever seen, and a bigger, uglier specimen would have been hard to imagine. Even Danziger whistled with admiration at the five-foot-long aquatic vertebrate, thinking that it looked prehistoric—a black, walleyed, leathery thing with a dozen sharp fins and spines encircling its stubby body. Its mouth was the most gruesome part of its anatomy—barbed, with long, curling feelers, and lined with sharp teeth.

After being still for a moment, it flopped around like a thing possessed, and several of the observers jumped away screaming. The fish rolled over on its stomach and began to crawl toward them, using its fins as prehensile legs. Now everyone shrieked and stumbled to get away.

Bess stood her ground and looked right at the creature. "I'm sorry, fish," she said, "but we've got to eat something else besides emergency rations." With those words, she brought a pipe down on the thing's head, and there was a loud, crunching sound.

By darkness, the rain had moved upriver, and they had found enough beached driftwood to make a roaring fire. The ugly fish, christened an alonzo for the man who had first spotted it, was roasted on a spit over the open flame. Despite eating around bones, fins, and a leathery skin, no one complained about the charbroiled delicacy. The fish was unexpectedly tender and had a smoky taste, and before the night was over, some of the brave diners were nibbling on its tail and head.

"Who would have thought that something so ugly could taste so good?" marveled Morgan. "Do you think we could catch a bunch of alonzos and export them?"

"I don't know," said Julia. "The closest restaurant is twenty-two light-years away. That would take a lot of ice."

While everyone laughed, Morgan nodded seriously. "Yeah, this isn't it."

"Isn't what?" asked Devon.

The little man smiled enigmatically. "The answer to my prayers."

Alonzo rubbed his stomach. "Well, it's the answer to *my* prayers."

"Mine too," agreed Danziger.

True nestled into the crook of her father's arm and said, "Me too."

The way this evening was going, the girl decided, was almost too good to be real. The shared hardships, and now the shared reward, were making them all feel like a family. Who would have thought that they would relax and laugh at each other's jokes at the bottom of this gigantic canyon? Yesterday, it was their biggest headache—tonight it was like home.

Home, she thought curiously. What must that be like to actually have a home, a place you left but always came back to? She and her dad had shipped around so much that she was used to the vagabond life, but she never felt deprived. She could see that life was a lot worse for other children, like Uly, before his transformation into a healthy kid. Or the orphans, or the ones who grew up in foster homes while their parents were away on long missions, in cold sleep. She looked at Alonzo, thinking that if he'd had children as a young man, they would be old enough to be *his* parents by now.

She molded herself into her father's chest and thought about stories she had read in her last day of school, stories by a man named Mark Twain. The children in those stories grew up and spent all their lives in the same small town. That hardly seemed possible, although she guessed that some people spent a long time on far-off colonies. It was like having both a mom and a dad, something that only seemed to happen in storybooks. But one thing about those stories had been true, True remembered.

"Dad," she said softly, "they lived along a river."

"What, darlin'?" he asked.

"Those children Mark Twain wrote about. They lived on a big river like this one, and it was home to them."

"That's true," said Danziger with a smile. "A river is sort of like a . . . a spaceship. It offers water, food, transportation—everything people need."

She snuggled into him. "I like the river better than a spaceship."

"So do I," he admitted wistfully. "But a river is wild and dangerous, beyond our control, like the Kobas."

True frowned.

"What's the matter? Do the Kobas scare you?"

"No," she said forcefully. "They're not wild and dangerous."

Danziger whispered, "Are you forgetting what they did to Commander O'Neill?"

"He shot his gun at them. He tried to kill them."

"Yes," conceded Danziger, "that was a mistake. We have to learn to live alongside wild things, like this river, not try to kill them."

"I want to have a home," said True with heartrending sincerity.

She felt her father's arms tighten around her scrawny shoulder. "So do I, honey. Maybe this will be it."

"The river?"

He shook his head. "Uly's mom wants to go to New Pacifica. Maybe that will be our home."

"Is it as nice as this?"

"I don't know, honey." He shook his head and stared at the camp fire. "None of us have ever been there." He gave her an encouraging hug. "If it's not, we'll come back to the river. Okay?"

"Okay," she said happily.

"Besides," said Danziger, "anyplace where *you* are is home to me."

She returned his hug. "That's true, isn't it, Daddy? I love you."

"I love you too, sweetheart."

True tried to stay awake, but the warmth of her dad's arm, the crackling fire, and the gentle rushing noise of the river lulled her to sleep. She was inhabiting the netherworld between dreams and reality when her father carried her to her tent and wrapped her within her sleeping bag.

"Good night, Daddy," she murmured.

"Good night, sweetheart." He kissed her.

True was alone in the darkness, but she didn't quite feel alone. Something was wrong, and she was about to get out of her sleeping bag and go look for her father, when a smooth, little body snuggled against her chest.

"Kitty!" she gasped with excitement.

The Koba chirped a contented hello and squirmed under her chin. She could never understand how scales could feel soft, but they did.

"Kitty," she cooed, "I knew you'd come back."

She hugged her pet, and it hugged her, and the two of them drifted off to a dream of life along the river.

The morning was glorious. A golden light crept down the canyon walls and turned them into stained-glass mosaics of every color in the spectrum. Most amazing of all, thought Devon Adair, was that the colors leapt out in relief—they seemed to be so close that she could touch them. Through this jumble of colors and shapes flowed the turquoise river, a solid presence that anchored the jagged buttes and gave them a magical base, like rocks in a fishbowl. In this wonderland, the humans seemed as insignificant as the breeze, just insubstantial ghosts drifting through a time and space where they didn't belong.

Would the stones remember them after they left? wondered Devon. Would a single footprint remain? No, was the answer. For all their grandiose ideas and plans, they were nothing to the endless flow of the river and the monumental life span of the buttes, plateaus, and archways. She had never been a spiritual person, or much given to mysticism, but the silent grandeur of the canyon made her feel as if forces were at work that she didn't understand. That she could never understand, or control. She could accept them, or fight them, but in the end it wouldn't make any difference.

Devon tried to shake off her reverie and concentrate on all the things she had to do that day. Unfortunately, all of her plans involved finding ways to leave this place, and she was not thrilled with the idea of getting back to a forced march across the wilderness. So far, they had seen nothing as beautiful as this canyon, nor did she expect to see anything as beautiful. So what was their hurry?

With horror, Devon shook her head at her own laziness. If *she* felt this way, what must the others be thinking? She glanced around and saw them, laughing and joking as if they hadn't a care in the world. Despite weeks of breaking camp at first light, no one was taking down a tent, or even thinking about it. Several of them were trying to make fishing poles. Bess was devising a net in which they could wash, or at least rinse, their clothes in the river. True and Uly were building sandcastles—actual buildings, not space stations. Julia and Alonzo were playing tic-tac-toe in the sand, while Yale and Zero argued over a game of checkers.

Only Danziger was doing any work—he was lazily digging a hole in which to bury the remains of their fish dinner from the night before. More fish dinners were probably on his mind.

Everyone was taking the day off quite seriously, thought Devon with alarm. She decided that she had to get them out of here fast—to continue their journey—or they might never leave. Unfortunately, the turquoise waterway was like a baited trap, imprisoning them and offering sanctuary at the same time.

Devon sighed and went to make sure that the ATV was charged and ready to go. She had some concern that not enough sunlight reached into the bottom of the canyon to keep the solar-powered vehicles ready, but the ATV purred when she touched the ignition. Even the vehicles seemed to like the pleasant climate by the river. She had geared herself to fight a mutiny, should it arise, but she had never thought that contentment and happiness would be her most dangerous enemies.

How could she convince them to leave this paradise? Devon gazed up at the sky, as if looking for a sign, and lo and behold, she found it. There was her giant bird again, soaring among the distant plateaus. She almost called to the others to look, but then it glided out of sight. Better keep quiet, thought Devon, or not only would they think she was a cruel, heartless leader but that she was daft too! Giant birds, indeed. No one else had seen them, had they?

Although she would have preferred to keep the giant birds secret, two of them appeared over a crest, gliding down the center of the canyon in perfect unison. Well, maybe it wasn't a figment of her imagination after all. But what was it? Devon looked around the campground, only to see that everyone else was still engaged in their leisure pursuits. No one paid the slightest attention to her or her giant birds.

She peered again into the distance and could see that the pair had been joined by a third. As she watched in amazement, two more winged creatures launched themselves from the cliff, forming a tiny squadron of flyers. At this distance, it was impossible to say exactly how large they were, but she saw no reason to revise her initial impression. Their wingspan looked to be about twelve feet, if that was possible. That would put them in the class of California's giant condors, extinct on Earth for about a century.

So, she thought to herself, why shouldn't there be condors in this canyon? It was a logical place for a condor to want to live. But, as the flying creatures drew closer and she studied them more intently, she had the disturbing impression that they weren't birds. There was something about their elongated limbs and their color—a solid, drab brown from head to toe—that was eerily familiar, yet strange. Very strange.

Not wishing to panic anybody, she jogged over to where John Danziger was pounding down the sand in the hole he had dug.

"Danziger," she said. "Remember I told you about a giant bird I saw?"

He wiped the sweat from his brow and nodded. "Yeah?"

"Take a look at that." She pointed toward the squadron in the sky, which was clearly, if unhurriedly, gliding toward them.

"Whoa," muttered Danziger. "You weren't kidding. And they're headed this way."

"What do they look like to you?" she asked.

"Harpies."

She frowned. "Harpies? What are those?"

"You aren't up on your Greek mythology, I see. If Harpies were real, you wouldn't want to meet one."

"Well, those things *are* real," Devon insisted, "and I'm not sure I want to meet one."

Danziger cupped his hands to his mouth and shouted, "Everyone! We have visitors—from the air! Can somebody grab some jumpers?"

Instead of grabbing jumpers, everyone froze where they were and stared into the easterly sky. Two more winged beings leapt off the plateaus that dotted the canyon and glided into formation with the others. The squadron now numbered seven. With a start, Devon realized that the creatures could have taken up positions all along the canyon walls during the night. Who knew how many there were? They had seen enough strangeness on G889 to expect almost anything.

The flyers came inexorably closer. With a few lazy flaps of their wings, they began to make tremendous time and close the gap considerably.

"Oh, no," muttered Alonzo, as if he recognized them.

"What are they?" Devon demanded.

"Pterodactyls!" screamed Morgan. He dropped his fishing pole and ducked for cover in one of the tents.

Devon doubted they were really pterodactyls, but Morgan's guess got everyone moving. Julia started to drag

Alonzo to safety, and everyone rushed to hide or grab a weapon. Suddenly paradise was turned into chaos.

Even John Danziger was backing away. "Perhaps we should take cover until we find out what they want."

"These Harpies," asked Devon, "what do they do?"

"They're a myth," said Danziger.

"Yes, but what do they do!"

"They tear people apart and eat them," answered the mechanic.

"No kidding," said Devon, backing toward the TransRover.

Baines rushed past them. He glanced worriedly over his shoulder and grumbled, "So much for our day off!"

As panic was in full swing, Devon saw no reason to issue orders and complicate matters. Even Yale and Zero were moving to a position behind the TransRover. The seven flying creatures—they were definitely *not* birds—were swooping over the water now. It was certain they were headed toward the camp. They moved with such swiftness that it was still impossible to get a good look at them, even though they were barely fifty yards away and closing.

At least, thought Devon with satisfaction, she had seen the attackers in plenty of time to warn everyone. They were all under cover, weren't they?

She looked around, hoping to make a quick head count, but some, like Morgan, had taken refuge in the tents. Most were crouched behind the TransRover, and Julia and Alonzo had taken cover under the DuneRail. Everyone was accounted for, except. . . .

Uly!

The boy, alone, was standing his ground on the beach. In fact, he was walking toward the incoming creatures.

Chapter 8

• • • • • • • •

"Uly!" screamed Devon.

She rushed out of hiding, and Danziger lunged for her but missed. Devon sprinted across the sand, praying she could reach them before they reached Uly. But the sand was no good for running, only plodding, and the boy was walking away from her.

She gasped and fell headfirst into the sand as the first creature swooped over her head and landed just behind her. Devon picked herself up and watched with amazement as all seven glided to the ground on their outstretched wings. The winged beings flew with the grace and agility of eagles—remarkable for creatures that were seven feet tall. She gasped again when she realized what they really were:

Terrians!

There was no mistaking their slim, leathery bodies;

sunken faces; lean, scaly limbs; and the claws on their feet and hands. Terrians with wings! They had stolen her son once, and they weren't going to do it again! She rushed forward and virtually tackled Uly.

"Mom!" he protested. "What are you doing?"

"Saving you," she panted.

"They're not doing anything but looking at us," the boy insisted.

She gazed around at the statuesque figures and had to admit that Uly was right. They had apparently landed just to get a closer look, and they looked with interest at the tents and vehicles. As Devon inspected them more closely, she realized that their wings weren't attached to their bodies, except by straps on their arms, chests, and shoulders. As if it weren't disconcerting enough to see Terrians pop out of the ground, now they were zooming in from the sky.

"Baines!" she heard Danziger bark. "Put that rifle down!"

"But what do they want?" the man growled.

"I don't know, but they're just standing there."

Reluctantly, Baines lowered the rifle and waited along with the others. One of the winged Terrians pointed to the DuneRail, under which Julia and Alonzo had taken cover.

"They want our DuneRail!" insisted Baines.

"No," said Uly with certainty. "They know Alonzo."

"Yes," admitted the pilot, crawling out from under the DuneRail. Julia crawled out with him and hovered protectively near the pilot.

"I dreamt of flying with them," said Alonzo with wonder. "When I first saw the canyon." The young man nodded to the Terrian in recognition, and it nodded back.

Another Terrian stepped forward to stroke Uly's brown hair, and Devon smothered the boy. When she saw the crestfallen look on the creature's face, she let Uly reach out and touch it. The Terrian made a facial expression that might have been a smile.

Danziger walked forward slowly, holding out his hands. "Let's not spook them, okay? They seem to be friendlier, or at least more trusting, than the other Terrians we've met."

"This tribe is very remote down here," said Alonzo. "They don't have much contact with other Terrians. Or anybody, for that matter. I think they're honestly glad to see us."

Yale strode forward and remarked, "With the composition of this canyon, and the close proximity to water, it's possible that they can't live underground like the other Terrians. But they've compensated for it by making wings and learning how to fly. Amazing!"

"Doesn't water bloat the Terrians?" asked True.

"Yes," answered Alonzo. "But you notice, they keep their distance from it."

Devon still clung tightly to Uly. "Do you suppose," she asked hopefully, "they could show us how to cross the river?"

Alonzo closed his eyes for several moments and seemed to be in a trance. When he opened his eyes, the Terrian who had communicated with him in his dream nodded to him again. Then it started to remove the wings from its lean, muscular torso.

Devon watched with fascination as the Terrian undid the elaborate straps and drew the pair of six-foot-long wings off its arms. It walked calmly toward her and set them at her feet. She reached down and picked up the surprisingly lightweight sails. With a start, she realized that they were made from the same tough skin as the fish they had eaten the night before.

Alonzo smiled. "This is quite an honor. They will loan us their wings so that we can *fly* across the river, as they do."

"I wouldn't try it," cautioned Yale. "Despite their height, they are substantially lighter in weight than humans. And they probably have centuries of practice using those gliders."

Devon nodded and smiled at the Terrian who had offered his wings. "I'm not going to try it," she said, "but it's a wonderful offer, nevertheless. Even if some of us managed to fly across, what would we do about the vehicles, Alonzo, and the children?"

With reluctance, she handed the wings back to the Terrian and made a walking motion with her fingers. Then she pointed to the river.

The Terrian nodded and seemed to understand. It motioned to its fellows, and those six began to climb up the steep hillside the climbers had slid down the day before. The Terrians took long strides, oblivious to the heights they were scaling, until they were about a hundred feet overhead. One by one, they stretched their remarkable wings and took a flying leap off the incline.

Devon and the others watched in astonishment as the Terrians angled their wings to catch the drafts, flapping gracefully when needed, until they had obtained enough height to cross the river. They looked like a squadron of dark angels as they soared over the turquoise river, then swerved down the center of the canyon. Some of them had better luck catching thermals than others, and the unlucky ones had to alight occasionally onto nooks and crannies where it appeared only a Koba could tred. Then they became accomplished climbers, moving upward to better angles for new assaults at the air. In this unhurried fashion, the six made their way back down the canyon, in the direction from which they had come.

The lone remaining Terrian held up its wings in a manner that was reminiscent of the way the ground-based Terrians held their staffs. Using the wings, it pointed in the direction its comrades were flying, then set off at a brisk walk.

Uly broke out of Devon's arms to follow the Terrian, and she hesitated just long enough to call out, "Danziger! Can you break camp and get the vehicles moving?"

"Sure!" he called back. "But I don't want the two of you going with them alone!"

"I'll go!" Said Bess, charging after them.

"Keep in touch," said Danziger, handing her some Gear as she passed him.

"Thanks!"

Morgan timidly poked his head out of his tent. "Is it safe to come out now?"

Devon, Uly, and Bess followed their taciturn guide for the better part of an hour before Devon began to notice any difference in the river. Along this part of the canyon, the colossal walls were no less imposing, but the slopes leading down to the river were wider and not as steep. The river seemed to take advantage of this elbow room, and it widened substantially, curling into pools and eddies along the rocky bank. The once-broad beach was little more than a narrow strip, as if the river had decided to reclaim it too.

Devon was no expert on rivers, but she would have bet that John Danziger was correct—the current did appear to be calmer here. Perhaps the vehicles could have crossed at this spot, but there was no reason to try it. Not only might it offend their hosts, but the river might get even more manageable farther up.

She could hear the purring of the ATV in the distance, and she was glad that Danziger and his party had caught up with them but were keeping a respectful distance, so as not to frighten their guide. The Terrian stopped occasionally to make sure they were still following, but otherwise seemed oblivious to them. Perhaps he was enjoying the novelty of his stroll along the riverbank, thought Devon.

Uly tugged on her sleeve and pointed up toward the rim of the canyon. She followed his finger to see three more Terrians, drifting lazily along at nosebleed altitudes. She had known space jockeys and explorers, deep-hole miners and oceanographers, but she had never known daredevils like these. How many lives had they lost perfecting their amazing gliders and techniques? How long did it take to master those thin slips of fish skin? She shuddered at the thought.

After another hour of walking, the figures sailing across the sky became commonplace. The flyers seemed less an escort, however, than a disorganized band of curiosity seekers. They would buzz the newcomers—with special interest in the lumbering vehicles—then fly off to be replaced by new flyers. Still, it was disconcerting to be inspected from above, as if by a human watching a stream of ants march across his patio.

"Mom!" cried Uly, again tugging her sleeve and pointing excitedly into the distance.

Along with the disappearance of his illness, Uly's eyesight had gone from being the worst in the band of survivors to being the best. Devon could barely make out what he was pointing at. It seemed like just another awesome stretch of canyon and water ahead of them.

"A village!" said Bess with amazement.

Devon stepped up her pace, and before long she could see the settlement too. On the far side of the river, there were mounds dotting the hillside leading up the canyon. Only they weren't mounds, as they had at first appeared, but low-slung lodges fashioned from the grasses that grew on the hillside. The lodges looked like anthills more than anything else, and she wondered how deep into the earth they extended.

As they drew closer, they could see more evidence of civilization, including extensive plots of salt fruit and, strung across the river, what looked like clotheslines made from fish gut. Devon could also see steps and stairways dug into the rock face at various intervals, leading up to small plateaus. As one flyer alighted on a plateau, and another took off, Devon realized that the Terrians had made themselves launchpads from which to start their aerial journeys.

The river itself was remarkable in this part of the canyon. It was framed on both sides by lovely waterfalls, which, Devon realized, must have actually been some distance from the village. Instead of surging along in a deep crevice, here the blue-green water cascaded over hundreds of descending ledges, each no more than a foot tall. Trees sprouted in small islands among the swirling eddies, and the shade made the water look cool and becalmed, even as it rushed along on its inexorable journey.

Devon had once hired an architect to design a fountain that would create a mood like this. The fountain had been constructed in a parklike setting in front of one of her corporate buildings. It had been a tremendous extravagance, for which she was justly criticized, but she had judged it a success. Until now. That fountain, she realized, was a pale substitute for this—a shady glen filled with hundreds of miniature waterfalls, and swirls of blue-green water that looked like icing on a cake.

"My gosh!" exclaimed Bess, stopping to admire the view. "It's beautiful, isn't it?"

"Yeah!" said Uly. "Can I go swimming, Mom?"

"Yes," muttered Devon, as if in a trance. Then she quickly shook her head. "I meant, yes, it's beautiful. *No,* you can't go swimming."

"Aw, Mom!"

"Are you forgetting the fish that live in that river? We made a meal of one, but one could make a meal of you too." She touched his nose with her fingertip.

The boy frowned seriously at the thought.

"Speaking of fish," said Bess, "look at that!"

Devon looked back at the system of pools and waterfalls to see half a dozen of the big, ugly fish suddenly leap through the air, like salmon fighting their way upstream. They flopped from ledge to ledge in a mad rush to get over the natural obstacle course and back into open water. At once, their guide took off at a dead run toward the nearest line strung across the river, and Devon could see other Terrians moving just as swiftly on the opposite bank. They discarded their wings and grabbed spears.

Weapons in hand, the Terrians clambered up the rocks to where the clotheslines originated. The first one up grabbed a loop device with one hand and went rappeling down the rope and sailing across the river. With its free hand, the being aimed its deadly spear but didn't throw it. Instead, it's weight dipped it low enough over the water that it speared one of the great fish in mid-leap. The Terrian's momentum carried it over to the other side, and it dropped its prize onto the narrow beach just before reaching safety in the rocks. Another Terrian was there, waiting to catch the fisherman and loop, then set off in the other direction.

It was like a three-ring circus, thought Devon, with Terrians swooping back and forth across the river. Not all were successful. Some missed the thrashing fish by inches; others speared them in the tail or fin, where the spears wouldn't hold. A fish might escape one rappeler, only to be stabbed by the next one. Some Terrians rushed down to the beach to club the fish before they could squirm back into the water. Despite the daredevil nature of this work, none of the Terrians whooped with joy or excitement. Instead, there was a solemnity about the occasion, as if they were professional athletes who had to do this for a living.

Devon, Uly, and Bess had stopped dead in their tracks to witness this strange fishing expedition. Alonzo, in the ATV, stopped a few feet behind them and killed his engine.

"Wow!" he said. "Is there going to be a fish fry tonight?"

"Looks like it!" Bess agreed cheerfully.

Devon heard footsteps crunching in the sand, and she turned to see John Danziger striding up to watch the show. He arrived just in time to see one of the Terrians lose its grip on the loop and tumble into the water.

Several Terrians shrieked when this happened, and the children turned to watch with morbid curiosity. But no one made an effort to save the unlucky fisherman. The school of fish was dwindling down to a handful, and everyone was trying to spear the last of them.

"He'll drown!" said Bess with alarm.

Before she knew what she was doing, Devon was running toward the miniature waterfalls, and she heard Danziger pounding the sand right behind her. Already the poor Terrian's body was beginning to bloat as it absorbed water through its porous skin. The shock was too much for it, and the being quit struggling and fell into unconsciousness.

Danziger rushed past Devon, his long legs carrying him into the swift turquoise water. She waited to see how he fared in the current. He stumbled a few times, but he was able to plod steadily toward the bloated Terrian. Then he fell down when one of the ugly fish made a desperate escape from the spears and went sailing over his head.

That was when Devon waded in after him. The coldness of the water was more shocking than the current, and she struggled just to stay on her feet. She gathered her strength and plunged forward, and she was able to lend a hand when

Danziger finally reached the unfortunate fisherman. The Terrian looked like a man made out of inner tubes, and Devon had to suppress her repulsion as she grabbed ahold of a rubbery arm. Together, she and Danziger lugged the Terrian's swollen body toward the riverbank.

As they dragged the body out of the water, it was the Terrians' turn to stare at them in frank amazement. Even the flopping fish on the bank were ignored as the tribe gathered to watch something they had apparently never seen before: a person enter the water and emerge wet but unharmed. Devon jerked away as one of the Terrians reached out to touch her shoulder. Then she realized that it was merely touching her to make sure that its eyes weren't deceiving it.

"Yes," she panted. "We're fine, but what about your friend?"

Julia rushed into the throng, and she bent down to take the swollen Terrian's pulse. "Well, it's alive," she finally said. "I don't know what I can do for this patient, except to let him rest—out here in the sun."

The bloated Terrian suddenly shuddered and rolled over on its back. It gazed gratefully at the humans, moving its mouth but saying nothing, then it closed its eyes and slept. Another Terrian brought a pair of wings and laid them over the sleeping body. Whether it was for warmth or symbolism, Devon didn't know, although she could imagine that this had happened many times before. The wings were probably the equivalent of an old wives' cure.

Their fallen comrade safe for the moment, the Terrians went back to harvesting the catch. Yale, Morgan, and the others left the vehicles and came forward to inspect the bloated Terrian.

Morgan stood beside Devon, shaking his head distastefully. "Why do they live so close to the water, when they know how dangerous it is for them?"

"Why do so many humans live in space?" replied Devon. "Or on moons, or planets with a deadly atmosphere? Space is a totally hostile environment to us, but we're willing to take the risks in order to reap the benefits. The same with them."

"No risk, no gain," said Morgan, conceding the argument. He looked around at the simple village. "I wonder if they've got anything of value here."

Devon looked scornfully at him. "Besides a peaceful, natural existence that has probably been unchanged for thousands of years?"

"Yeah," answered Morgan, "besides that."

Devon was too busy shivering in her wet clothes to think of a suitable response, then their Terrian guide stepped in front of her and pointed to the lines strung across the river. The Terrian made the same walking motion with its fingers that she had made to it.

"Can we, Mom?" cried Uly. "Please!"

"Yes, please!" echoed True.

"I don't know." Devon turned to Danziger. "What do you think?"

The mechanic scratched his head. "The strongest of us could ford the river here, but you know how strong the current is. I don't think the kids can walk across, and I'm not sure I want to try to carry them. Maybe to rappel over the river is the best way, providing they hang on tight." He glowered meaningfully at the two children.

"What about the vehicles?" asked Devon.

"I don't know," answered Danziger. "Driving the Trans-Rover across here might destroy their fishing grounds. A hundred yards back, I saw places that would do just as well for the vehicles."

"I concur," said Yale.

"The rest of you should take the express," Alonzo piped in. "I would, if I could."

"Yeah! Yeah! All right!" exclaimed True and Uly.

"There has to be somebody to catch them on the other side," said Devon. She turned to their Terrian host and made a catching motion with her arms.

The Terrian nodded and climbed into the rocks, where the nearest line originated. True and Uly began to scamper after him, followed by Bess. The Terrian motioned to one of its comrades on the other side of the river, and it climbed into position.

"Hang on with both hands!" cautioned Devon. "That water is frigid!"

As the oldest of the children, True had already assumed first position, and the Terrian handed her a loop, fashioned from bone. As instructed, she grabbed ahold with both hands and, with a final grin, took off sailing over the water.

"Yahoo!" True screamed, lifting her legs straight out to clear the water. She didn't wait to be caught on the other side but instead let go as soon as she reached the narrow strip of beach. The loop went sailing up into rocks, where a Terrian caught it. He immediately flung it back, and the empty loop zoomed by itself over the water.

Devon held her breath as Uly took off. But she needn't have worried, as the boy was not about to spoil his fun by letting go too soon. He sailed all the way into the rocks, where the Terrian caught him with ease and set him on his feet. The being sent the loop back to where Bess stood waiting, a big grin on her face.

"Careful, honey!" called Morgan.

She gave him a dismissive wave and took off. Weighing more than the children, Bess's rear end skimmed the water and made a turquoise spray as she flew across. Danziger, Alonzo, and several of the settlers laughed at the sight of an adult having so much fun. Bess landed by herself on the bank and let the loop continue on its own.

"It's fun!" she called back.

"Yeah," said Danziger, "but anyone who's much heavier than Bess ought to go across on the vehicles." He glanced at Morgan, Yale, Baines, and most of the men.

"Fine with me," said Morgan, heading back toward the TransRover. "I hate cold water."

"Aw, too bad," muttered Baines. "Women have all the fun."

Julia approached Devon and smiled. "Shall we?"

"Lead on!"

Devon watched as Julia rappeled over the water, the wind whipping her hair back. When the loop hit her hand, it tingled from the impact, but Devon gripped hard and let her feet fly off the rocks.

The wind smacked her in the face and whistled through her clothing as she breezed over the blue-green swirls. She dipped low, suppressing a scream from the exhilaration, and her rear end sent a spray of icy water shooting into the air. Her momentum abruptly carried her upward, and the water seemed to fade into the distance. Like True, she bailed out before the rocks and tumbled into the sand, ending up on her damp posterior.

She laughed aloud as she jumped up and shook off the sand. Uly, True, and Bess grinned at her.

"Come on!" she called to the other women. "It's fun!"

As they clambered up the rocks, she saw the men on the other side of the river, looking disappointed and downcast, especially Alonzo. Danziger motioned to the men, and they traipsed back to the vehicles.

"I'll meet you downriver!" she called.

"Thanks," muttered Danziger with a diffident wave.

Bess grinned. "Why shouldn't we have all the fun?"

• • •

By late in the afternoon, John Danziger and the men were a quarter of a mile downriver, and they had the vehicles lined up in the order they were to ford the waterway. First in line was the TransRover, with a steel cable connecting it to the DuneRail manned by Zero's head. Behind that, connected by another cable, was the ATV driven by Alonzo. Danziger shook his head at the odd caravan, thinking that it reminded him of a wooden pull toy he had loved as a child.

His main worry was whether the TransRover would get bogged down and stuck in the mud. That was followed by the equally serious concern of having one or both of the smaller vehicles swept away. He couldn't do much to prevent the TransRover from getting bogged down, but having the vehicles tethered together should prevent losing any of them to the current. He hoped.

Although the current wasn't as swift here as where they had first tried to cross, the river itself was considerably wider, which offered more places for treacherous mud or sinkholes.

When Danziger gazed up at the massive rock face on the other side of the river, he couldn't help but wonder if all this effort were even worth it. By the miracle of gravity and a foolhardy stunt that he was glad he hadn't witnessed, they had managed to get the vehicles *down* into the canyon. But how would they get them *up* to the opposite rim?

He could see Devon, Bess, True, Uly, and the others on the far bank. As old-fashioned as it sounded, he consoled himself with the fact that at least the women and children were safe. They still had the Gear Bess had been carrying, but they couldn't do much with it, except to root them on.

He was about to climb into the cockpit of the TransRover and give the other men the order to climb aboard, when Morgan tapped him on the shoulder.

"We've got company," he said, pointing behind him.

Danziger turned around to see a Terrian approaching slowly on foot. It was easy to think that all Terrians looked alike, but they didn't, of course. From the short topknot of seaweedlike hair on his head and his immature height of only about six-and-a-half feet, he was recognizable as the young Terrian they had saved from drowning. He still moved jerkily, like a man with arthritis, and he used his spear as a cane. But the bloating had passed, and the contours of his skin had returned to normal.

The young Terrian stopped near Alonzo's ATV, leaned on his spear, and gave Danziger what might have been a smile.

The mechanic waved politely, then climbed into the cockpit of the TransRover. "All aboard!" he called out.

Morgan, Yale, Baines, and the other men who had no vehicles to drive climbed up into the TransRover and hunkered down wherever they could. Somehow, thought Danziger, they didn't look nearly as cheerful as the women had looked when they were preparing to rappel across the river.

At the moment, the women on the far bank didn't look very cheerful either. Devon was pacing nervously, Julia was clasping and unclasping her hands, Bess was standing by tensely on the Gear, and True was chewing on her knuckles. Nevertheless, there was nothing else to do but give it a try, and Danziger pushed the starter on the TransRover. The engine roared with authority, and he shoved the vehicle into first gear and lumbered toward the water.

At once, the Terrian ran up to the vehicle, waving its spear frantically. Danziger stopped the TransRover.

"He's trying to attack us!" Morgan shouted with alarm.

"No," said Danziger, killing the engine. "But what the hell does he want?"

They waited expectantly as the young Terrian walked

cautiously to the riverbank and stuck its spear into the water. With some effort, it pulled the spear out, and it was covered with gooey mud.

"He's trying to tell us it's too muddy here," said Danziger with amazement.

"What does he know about mud?" groused Morgan.

Content that he had stopped their progress, at least temporarily, the Terrian walked behind the TransRover and stepped over the cable. Then it began hobbling down the riverbank.

Danziger got on the Gear to Alonzo in the ATV and asked the pilot, "What do you think he's doing?"

"Remember," said Alonzo, "these guys fly over this river all the time. From the air, they may be able to see the bottom of the river, especially along here, where it's shallow."

"Everyone wait here," ordered Danziger. He leapt down from the cockpit and began to follow the young Terrian.

Upon seeing him, the Terrian waved its spear jauntily and motioned to where some eddies swirled along the bank. It pointed its spear at one of the tiny whirlpools and shook its head.

"Gotcha," said Danziger. "Go on."

Finally, about a hundred yards downriver, the young Terrian stopped and again walked cautiously to the bank. Without hesitation, it plunged its spear into the water and brought it up quickly, with no mud on it. Danziger could see nothing in the rushing stream, so he began to put his leg in. The Terrian shook its head vigorously and pulled him back from the water. Then it offered Danziger its spear.

Danziger nodded his thanks and plunged the spear into the water in the same spot the Terrian had. It struck rock, as if there were an invisible bed of slate under the frothy water.

Now it was Danziger's turn to smile gratefully. "Thank you, thank you," he said, returning the spear.

The Terrian took its spear and drove it into the sand. It left it there to mark the place, and the two walked slowly back to the vehicles.

"What was that all about?" asked Morgan.

"About saving us a lot of trouble," replied Danziger, as he climbed back into the cockpit. "I'm convinced these Terrians know everything there is to know about this canyon."

"Is that a fact?" said Morgan thoughtfully.

The Terrian was about to go sit on a rock to watch the crossing, when Morgan shouted at it and waved. "Hey, you! Come on! Ride with us!"

"I wonder if that's wise," muttered Yale.

"Why not?" said Morgan. "Never hurts to be friendly. Let's show him what we have to offer."

Morgan kept waving insistently until the young Terrian finally got the idea and climbed aboard the TransRover. Without being told where to go, it scrambled to the highest roll bar and perched there, clinging for dear life even before Danziger started the engine.

Morgan chuckled. "That guy flies on a kite half a mile in the air, and he's afraid to ride on a TransRover." He turned to the Terrian and gave him a thumbs-up. "You'll be fine!"

"Okay," said Danziger into the Gear. "Zero, Alonzo—let's go at a steady five miles an hour down to where you see the spear in the sand. That's where we'll cross."

"Roger," they answered in unison.

Danziger put the TransRover into gear, and they lumbered down the riverbank once more. He turned back to look at his unusual passenger, and he had to stop himself from laughing. He had seen numerous Terrians before, but they had always looked stoic, confident, mysterious. He had never seen one look at him in wide-eyed terror before. He almost stopped the TransRover to make the Terrian get off, but he was afraid that such an action might be taken as an insult. The Terrian was high enough up on the roll bar that only a tidal wave would get it wet.

The mechanic held his breath as the TransRover hit the rushing current. Frigid blue-green water splashed and swirled all around them, but they plunged ahead. The passengers got tossed around as the big tires rolled over a few submerged rocks, but the tires kept churning. There was no listing this time, because there was no mud to speak of. Bless those Terrians and their keen eyesight, Danziger thought to himself.

The only problem occurred when Alonzo's ATV, at the rear, took on a lot of water and the engine died. The ATV shifted around as the current battered it, and Alonzo was momentarily up to his chest in water. But he was solidly strapped in, and he didn't panic. He had the presence of mind to put the vehicle into neutral immediately, and Zero speeded up in the DuneRail ahead of him. The cable pulled taut, and the ATV was jerked out of trouble. Like a child's toy splashing through a mud puddle, all three of the vehicles rolled up the riverbank.

They were met by cheers and handshakes. Danziger jumped down and got a kiss and a hug from True, and Morgan got similar treatment from Bess. Julia didn't exactly hug and kiss Alonzo, but she did rush to check his splint, which was soaking wet. She looked at it unhappily, knowing she would have to change it. Yale congratulated Zero on his driving, then helped to return the robot's head to his body. Baines and most of the others slumped into the sand with relief.

Even Devon Adair had a smile on her face as she strolled up to Danziger. "Not bad," she acknowledged. "After three days of trying, we're two-thirds of the way across this canyon. I wasn't sure we'd get this far."

"We've got to thank our guide," said Danziger. He looked

back at the TransRover to see the terrified Terrian still clinging to the roll bar.

"It's okay," he said, coaxing him down. "Come on."

The young Terrian leapt clear to avoid the dripping wet sides of the vehicle. Morgan gave it a thumbs-up, and it held up a clawed hand in a poor imitation. Then it stood quietly and proudly, as if waiting for another opportunity to be of assistance to the people who had saved its life.

"I like that fellow," said Morgan. "I'm going to get to know him."

"In your dreams," said Danziger.

Morgan bristled. "No, I mean it."

"So do I," answered the mechanic. "That's how Alonzo does it—in his dreams."

"Yeah," said Morgan thoughtfully. "I should listen to my dreams, shouldn't I? Say, Devon, we're not in any rush to leave here, are we? Our day off got sort of eaten up by all this excitement. What say we take tomorrow off?"

There were murmurs of agreement, and Devon looked around at her happy but weary band. "All right," she answered, "although some of us might spend tomorrow looking for a way up. Should we make camp here, or closer to the village?"

"Closer to the fish fry," answered Alonzo with a grin.

Chapter 9

After making camp and pitching their tents, the bedraggled band of colonists spent the rest of the waning daylight watching the tribe of Terrians remanufacture their harvest of fish. "Remanufacturing" was the only term that Morgan Martin could apply to what they did to the ugly fish. The Terrians accepted the visitors without comment and let them observe all they wanted. As Morgan was looking for whatever it was in the canyon that would make him rich, according to his dream, he observed most carefully.

First the Terrians painstakingly stripped the skin off the fish with their stone knives, and hung the skins to dry on the gut lines stretched across the river. Then they filleted the meat off the fish into thin strips, but they didn't cook them. In fact, they didn't eat the fish at all. They dried the meat in the sun, chopped it, and spread it on their crops as a fertilizer.

The Terrians took the guts of the fish, stretched them, and wove them into thick threads, a process that reminded him of a wool-carding demonstration he had once witnessed. This left only the bones, the larger of which were used to make tools and rappeling loops, the smaller of which were used for jewelry, needles, and precision tools. He noticed that each activity had its specialists. When the workers were finished, there was virtually nothing left of the fish to be thrown away. It was all used.

Morgan saw all of these products in different stages of manufacture, but he couldn't imagine that fish fertilizer, fish gut ropes, or fish skins would make him rich. It had to be something else, but what? As Julia had pointed out, G889 was too far away from anywhere to make a fish exporting business feasible.

To Morgan, the villagers were nothing but a bunch of primitives making the most of their meager resources, a prospect he wished to avoid for himself if at all possible. Unfortunately, except for the vehicles, there wasn't much difference in circumstances between the survivors and the Terrians.

"So, no fish fry?" asked Alonzo with disappointment when Morgan returned to the camp.

"'Fraid not," answered Morgan. "Although I imagine the dried fish is edible."

"They don't seem to think so," Alonzo pointed out.

Morgan rubbed his hands and shivered. "It's getting dark. When are we going to build a fire?"

"Not tonight," answered Alonzo, shifting in his hammock to get more comfortable. "Devon is afraid that a fire will spook the Leather Wings."

"Leather Wings?"

Alonzo smiled. "Yeah, that's what they call themselves."

"How do you know that?" asked Morgan.

The young pilot shook his head in wonderment. "Ever since we got to this planet, I've known things about the Terrians. It's usually through my dreams, or by concentrating. Sometimes, it's just an insight that comes out of the blue. Did you notice that the Terrians never talk to each other?"

"Well, yeah," answered Morgan, casting a wary glance over his shoulder. "I thought they were just quiet."

"No," said Alonzo. "On the face of it, they look primitive, but they communicate through some kind of telepathy. I'm sure of it. Occasionally, when they're excited or trying to talk to us, they will deign to use a gesture, but that's rare."

Alonzo paused to look back at the peaceful village, now almost totally obscured in shadows. "I think the Terrians are a much older race than humans. These Terrians are particularly old—hundreds of years old, some of them."

"How do you know that?"

Again, the pilot shrugged. "There's just something about them. That one who's their leader, who guided us to the village, is about four hundred years old, I think. It's not an accident that they live down here, isolated, next to what is a deadly environment for them. These Terrians are special."

"Hundreds of years old," mused Morgan. "Now, that's something special."

Alonzo lay back in his hammock and smiled. "I no longer fear my dreams so much. Maybe I'll try to learn something about the tribe's history tonight."

"How do you contact them, like in your dreams?"

"Well," said the pilot, "I figure it's a little like what they used to call astral projection. It sounds strange, but you sort of leave your body and meet them in a special place, reserved for that kind of meeting. Because we have no other way to relate to a mental state like that, we interpret it as a dream. Anyway, you just know each other's thoughts, and you see with each other's eyes. Sorry, I can't explain it any better than that."

Morgan waved his hands. "Yeah, but *how*?"

"You've become friends with the one that Adair and Danziger saved from drowning. Just sort of concentrate on him. Let him know you're available."

The bureaucrat frowned at this particular choice of words, and Alonzo laughed. "Think about it. As Danziger says, they're connected to this planet like the rocks and the trees. I have a feeling they know if you're open to communication."

"I will," said Morgan with determination. "Yeah, I will."

"What's this?" asked Alonzo, peering over Morgan's shoulder.

From the deepening shadows came a small contingent of Terrians, led by their original guide and the adolescent they had saved from drowning. In their scaly hands, they carried strips of dried fish, saved from an earlier store of fertilizer. The way they carried the fish made it clear that they offered it as food. Morgan thought about what Alonzo had just said. These creatures had shared their thoughts—they knew humans ate fish, even if they didn't.

Morgan, Devon, Danziger, Julia, and the others stopped what they were doing to meet the welcoming party. True and Uly, as always braver than the adults, were the first to grab the shriveled strips. Morgan saw their parents look doubtfully at the dried morsels, but they couldn't say anything without appearing rude.

Wanting to appear friendly, Morgan reached for a strip of the fish too. It looked as colorless as a bone and felt like a piece of bark. He sniffed it—it still smelled fishy. How bad could it be? he wondered.

"This is great," he said. "Thanks!"

Uly put the fish to his lips. "Can we, Mom?" he asked hopefully.

She shrugged. "Sure. Take small bites, until we see what effect it has on your stomach."

Morgan, Bess, the children, and a few of the others took tentative bites. Actually, the fish couldn't be bitten—it had to be gnawed off with the back molars.

"Hmm, chewy," Morgan mumbled, trying to unstick his teeth.

"I like it!" crowed Uly, chomping cheerfully.

"Easy does it," his mother cautioned again.

Still chewing, Morgan went up to the young Terrian and looked him in his pale, almond-shaped eyes. "We need to get to know each other better, if you know what I mean." He winked. "You know what I mean."

The Terrian cocked his head in a puzzled way and held up another strip of fish.

"I'm Morgan," said the bureaucrat. "I'll be your buddy. Okay?"

Devon asked, "What are you up to?"

"Hey, can't a guy get to know the locals? They brought us food, got us across the river, and gave us the run of the place. We owe them. Well, maybe my new friend owes *us* a little, too."

John Danziger went up to the leader of the Terrians and said with sincerity and a note of finality, "Thank you. We appreciate everything."

As if he understood, the Terrian nodded and turned to go, the rest of his party following in silence. Morgan's new friend hung back a moment to take a curious look at the human. It seemed to have gotten the message.

Morgan gave it a thumbs-up sign. "See you later!"

The Terrian held up a scaly thumb, then strode off.

Devon gnawed thoughtfully on a fish strip. "I don't know what you're up to Morgan, but you had better respect these beings."

"What'd I do?" asked the bureaucrat, appealing to the others. He pointed to the shriveled fish in Julia's hand. "If you're not going to eat that, Alonzo might like it."

She frowned at the dried morsel. "I hate to poison a patient, but you're probably right. He would like it."

As Julia walked off, Devon patted Uly on the back. "As soon as you finish your snack, I want you to buzz your teeth."

"Okay," the boy agreed. He popped the last bit of fish into his mouth and worked his jaws on it.

"The fish is okay," said True, sounding as if she wanted to mean it, but it wasn't really true. The ten-year-old looked distracted, thought Morgan, glancing into the shadows at every opportunity.

"What's the plan for tomorrow?" asked Danziger, more for conversation than anything else.

"Well," answered Devon, "all of you have the day off. Yale and I are going to scout upstream for a way to get the vehicles up to the rim. Unless we find a rock slide or something, I'm not optimistic."

"If we can't get across," said Danziger softly, "are we going to stay down here?"

"No," Devon responded sharply. "We'll find a way to get them up."

Morgan chuckled. "Devon, did anybody ever tell you that you worry too much? Got a problem—sleep on it. That's what I'm going to do. Good night."

"Wait, honey!" said Bess, hurrying after him.

When they were out of earshot, Bess whispered to her husband, "What *are* you up to?"

He shook his head with sadness. "Don't tell me you're suspicious too."

"I'm not suspicious," she said, "I just know you."

Morgan lowered his voice. "There's something in this canyon that's priceless. I can *feel* it! So far, it's been all bad luck since we got to this stupid planet, but I'm going to find a way to turn our luck around."

"It hasn't been so bad," said Bess, giving his arm a hug. "On the stations, it was always business—this deal, that deal—trying to climb the corporate ladder. Here, I feel like I have you all to myself."

"I'm still thinking about the corporate ladder," Morgan insisted. "But maybe I can do even better than that. I've got plans, Bess. Big plans!"

She gave him a wink and pulled him into their tent. "Me too."

There was a smile on youthful Alonzo Solace's face as he swayed in his hammock, rocked by the cool breezes at the bottom of the canyon. The aroma of the tiny red flowers wafted about his nose, and the sound of the cascading water lulled him into dreamland. It was a blissful sleep from the start, one that took the wounded pilot on a random access journey through time and history. History was etched on every inch of towering rock all around him, and it seemed to press against him, much as the wind, rain, sun, and animals had forced their way into the canyon's life story.

His journey was not linear, he knew instantly. It started with a fire, a horrendous blaze that scorched the walls of the canyon and turned them blood red. Something great had perished in this fire, but it was so long ago that it swiftly disappeared from Alonzo's view, fading into the distance like the dying ember of a campfire.

His dream devolved into an even older image of a vast

river, monstrous in its grandeur. Like a tidal wave, the river swept across the plains, the greatest force on the entire planet two billion years ago. This epoch lasted for millions of years after the ground started to move and the oceans receded. Alonzo flowed with the river, through the passage of time, and he saw the rising of the rim to the west, the lowering of the rim to the east. There were abrupt changes in climate, accompanied by drops and rises in the water table.

The canyon felt each of these changes intimately, and it adjusted. Half-a-billion years ago, still mighty at half its previous flow, the turquoise water gave birth to a cathedral of buttes and cliffs that strained toward the sky. In the present era, the river was little more than a ghost of its former self, but it had learned to display its awesome accomplishments. Alonzo gaped at the ravages and beauty formed by two billion years of free-form sculpture.

As if he were looking at a mass exodus through time, Alonzo could see the migration of millions of animals into the canyon. Strange creatures that were long extinct—Kobas, Terrians, Grendlers—flowed through the vast crevice. These visitors came and went, staying for a month or a millennium, but no one probed the secrets of the canyon more than the Terrians. They studied it from the air, while living in its depths. One foot on the ground and one foot in Heaven, thought Alonzo as he envisioned the Leather Wings.

Terrians did not express time in any format that Alonzo could interpret, so he didn't know how long the Leather Wings had made the gorge their home. A million years or more was the sense that he got. Every season they remained, the tribe planted themselves deeper in the bosom of the canyon. They trained for the rigors of life down here, learning how to harvest the fish and the salt fruit, learning both to soar above the river and to alight among the plateaus like windblown leaves. Then he could see the elders, enjoying their ripe old age. It was a very ripe old age for some of them.

In his lifetime, a Leather Wing might witness a hundred thousand moons crossing the canyon. It could participate in thousands of fish hunts and aerial expeditions. It would feel the chill of winter and the rebirth of spring hundreds of times. When overpopulation became a problem, the tribe was accustomed to breaking up, sending offshoots flying away to distant parts of the canyon. He could see some of the river-born Terrians trekking off into the wilderness to discover and join other Terrian tribes, most of them never to return.

They were intelligent enough to lead more complicated lives, thought Alonzo, but why should they? For the fortunate Leather Wings, there were centuries of quiet contemplation of the ever-changing tapestry of life in the canyon. For the unlucky ones, there were early deaths, drownings, and fatal falls. The canyon provided amply for death, as it provided for life. At fourteen or four hundred years of age, death was accepted as another gift, like the fish and the sacred grotto.

At the thought of the sacred grotto, a term which he didn't understand, Alonzo felt himself flying. He could feel it more than see it, as the wind pressed his body even while it lifted him higher. This flight was not as clear as his first vivid dream of the canyon; perhaps it was taking place at night, he thought with a start. Would the Leather Wings be foolhardy enough to fly at night?

He knew they would, after taking the proper precautions. As if operating by a sixth sense, a type of spatial radar, he could feel the flyers sticking to the center of the canyon. This allowed them to make the split-second adjustments needed to control their flight, even on the darkest nights.

Landing was the most dangerous part of flying by night, he realized. To reach the sacred place without having to land to get a better thermal, the Leather Wings needed a certain type of wind that only occurred on nights when the crack of sky at the top of the canyon was obscured by slabs of luminous clouds. Tonight was one such night, and they were flying at a medium altitude, allowing considerable distance between flyers. Alonzo could sense the camaraderie of the pilgrims and their holy mission: to prolong life and health.

Alonzo suddenly realized that wisdom was the ultimate goal of this effort to thwart the aging process. The tribe kept a telepathic history that was handed down through its dreams, as it was being handed to him. So a Terrian had to live a long time to compile enough dreams to absorb the entire history—the teachings, the stories, the accounts, and the wisdom. If you lived hundreds of years, you grew very wise, wise enough to know that some strangers were harmless. Others weren't. Alonzo felt this very clearly in his dream—the certainty that there were enemies in this idyllic landscape. And some of them were a threat to the sacred pool!

But what was the pool? That part was blocked from him. This dream was only a fraction of what there was to know, like flipping quickly through the pages of a book. However, Alonzo knew without a doubt that the secret pool was the kernel of the Leather Wings' knowledge, the mystery that held the tribe together. They took it as their sacred duty to live as long as the pool allowed them, and the pool was part of the canyon.

The flyers finally circled around to land, and everyone tensed because it was the most harrowing part of the flight. There were no landing lights in the canyon, no strings of pulsing blue beacons. To land in the darkness took all the instincts, reflexes, and skills at a flyer's command. It was a test of worthiness, and some of the unworthy never returned from the night flights. The river claimed them, or the rocks.

Alonzo could feel that he was under the protection of a powerful flyer, probably the Leather Wings' venerable leader. Its wisdom and its undiminished skills made Alonzo feel comfortable even as he swirled toward the rocky plateau, the outline of which was barely visible in the light from the luminescent clouds. This plateau had been used for centuries by the night flyers, and some ancient memory took over and guided Alonzo down.

Alonzo staggered to keep his balance on the rock, without toppling over, and he finally had to crouch to get his bearings. Peering into the rugged crags surrounding the plateau, he was relieved to spot a narrow footpath. It was not much wider than the Koba trail Devon and the others had followed, but it frightened him at first. He sensed the risk, an overwhelming feeling of tampering with fate. Overriding the fear was a sense of duty—a duty to live long and dream to remember.

So Alonzo floated down to the path about six feet below him. Bladder bushes, bottle plants, and vines grew in splendor, but they curved away from the narrow path, clearly tracing its outline through the rocks. Alonzo moved swiftly for a man unaccustomed to this place or the darkness, and he heard other pilgrims shuffling along before him. He knew there were a myriad of plateaus in this section of the canyon, and they all had paths leading this way, toward the sacred place.

The mouth of the cave was so large that he was inside it before he realized it was indeed a cave. It was the dusty smell that alerted him, the accumulation of millennia. Then the layers of clouds overhead were gone, replaced by jagged rock that loomed in his senses, if not his sight. Alonzo felt the fish skins sliding off his arms, and he knew without being told that he would have to leave his wings in this outer chamber if he wanted to pass—along with dozens of other pairs of wings stacked at the mouth of the cave.

With the passageway narrowing, Alonzo crouched down and felt his way along. If this hadn't been a dream, he thought ruefully, he wasn't sure he would have been able to go on.

With the passage of time, the pilot began to feel the presence of another visitor, one who was not Terrian. His first thought was that it had to be Uly! Ever since the boy's abduction, rescue, and miraculous recovery, Uly had shared a special connection with the Terrians. It was a different connection from Alonzo's, physical rather than mental, but there was the same intensity.

"Uly?" he spoke. His voice sounded hollow, but whether that was caused by the cave or the dream, he didn't know.

"No," said a disembodied voice. "Where are we?"

"Morgan, you made it," said Alonzo, not really surprised at the bureaucrat's presence. Morgan did not seem real, more like a voice on the Gear, someone monitoring his progress.

"We're underground," explained the pilot, "in a cave in the canyon. How did you get here?"

"My buddy," said Morgan with amazement. "It was in my dream, just like you told me it would be. It motioned for me to follow it. Is this real?"

"I've always heard that while they last, dreams are as real as life."

"Where is my Terrian?" wailed Morgan. "It led me here, down the path. But I lost it inside here when it got dark."

"We should stop talking and concentrate on the Terrians," suggested Alonzo. "We need them to guide us."

"They are very old, aren't they?" said Morgan, excitement rising in his voice.

"Just watch and wait," remarked Alonzo. "The goal is wisdom."

With that thought, his tenuous contact with Morgan was broken, and he could see a trace of phosphorescent minerals glowing on the walls of the cave. It didn't offer light, exactly, but it split the darkness with glowing fibers, enough to lead him to believe that his destination was near. Perhaps the phosphors were part of his dream state. Alonzo didn't know, but he was thankful for them. His pilgrimage was almost over, the secret about to be revealed . . .

For a price.

The Terrians were not greedy; they had no money. But they expected a yin and yang to life, a give and take, an understanding. Alonzo was more prepared to give now than when the Terrians had first invaded his dreams, but he didn't feel as if they wanted anything more from *him*. His smashed leg was his ticket to their dream world, and it was up to others to pay their own freight. The account was accruing, and he wondered when the bill would come due.

Suddenly, the phosphorescent markings along the cave walls became much more pronounced, and they led downward. Alonzo crouched low and followed, his fear being swept away by curiosity and a growing sense of awe. In this vast mosaic of time's secrets, he was going to be shown the greatest secret of all.

A strong smell assaulted his nose—it was an acrid odor—sulfurous, laced with burning and boiling substances that he could never identify. Alonzo forced himself to breathe through his mouth as he plunged deeper into the cavern.

"We're here!" said Morgan excitedly. Once again, the bureaucrat was just a disembodied voice in the darkness, but he sounded closer this time, more real.

Alonzo felt a twinge of resentment, as if this secret should be for his dream-eyes only. Was Morgan the right one to share this secret? That decision was not up to him, he told himself curtly, but to the Leather Wings. If Morgan's Terrian wanted to take that scoundrel into their confidence, that was their decision. There was no doubt in his mind that Morgan could stand to learn a few things.

Rounding a corner, he felt the presence of the pilgrims, the Leather Wings. Some were here on this very night; others were here in the slipstream of time, thousand of years in the past or the future, their memories and discoveries helping to guide the others.

Alonzo could see the Leather Wings clearly now, because the entire floor was aglow with a phosphorescent pool. It bubbled like a cauldron, casting acrid smoke and fumes into the sweltering atmosphere. If this hadn't been a dream, Alonzo wasn't even sure he would even have been able to breathe in this place. Every time a bubble burst in the pool, a muted star glimmered for a second on the roof of the cavern.

Inexplicably, Alonzo felt frozen in place, as if he were not allowed to walk any farther into the holy place or get any closer to the pool. This bothered him for only a moment, because the sight was so amazing. One by one, the solemn Terrians immersed themselves in the glowing grotto, but Alonzo could tell it wasn't a pleasant experience. They moaned with pain, and some of them fainted and sunk beneath the surface. Or maybe they were in ecstasy; it was hard to tell. There was somber chanting all around him, although no Terrian raised its voice. It was all in the mind, thought Alonzo.

He wondered what Morgan was seeing, whether it was anything like this. The mere thought of the bureaucrat seemed to drive his dream vision away, and Alonzo grasped to get it back. But the vision, the connection, was broken—his eyelids were fluttering awake.

Alonzo bolted upright in his hammock and looked around the camp. Except for the fact that a river roared only a few feet away, it was much like their camp on many other nights when they had done without a fire for whatever reason. Should he tell Devon, or anyone, about this dream? If that place really existed and wasn't a metaphor his mind dreamed up, it could be a boon to all the creatures of the planet! It could relieve so much suffering and, perhaps, even work greater miracles with the children who were coming, the ones with The Syndrome.

Hell, thought Alonzo, maybe it would even cure his busted leg! But it was a secret, and to reveal it might harm the Leather Wings and the core of their existence. All this time, he had thought that nothing could be more magnificent than the flying aspect of their existence, but he had been wrong. They traveled in the air, but they were of the ground, tethered in mysterious ways.

No, the pilot decided, he would not blow the whistle on their fountain of youth. Something was already threatening the security and sanctity of the holy place, and he didn't want to further endanger it. Besides, Alonzo was less interested in the prospect of greater longevity than most people would be. He had his own fountain of youth, of sorts, in the numerous cold sleeps he had taken on long space flights. He was already like the Terrians in one respect: If he kept up the same line of work for a couple hundred years, he could still look good.

However, Alonzo thought glumly, his present condition testified as to why three-hundred-year-old space jockeys were rare, even if they were theoretically possible. Nobody had that much luck. Some close call or accident eventually drove every pilot out of the business, or put him six feet under.

Bitterly, Alonzo realized that his time spent in cold sleep was a cipher, a nothing. It was just time that had been robbed from him. It hadn't affected his body negatively, which was good, but it hadn't affected his mind positively, which was not so good. The time spent in cold sleep hadn't given him anything, except new calendars to look at when he woke up.

He contrasted that with the sacred pool, which gave the Leather Wings the greatest gift of all—the gift of time. They had all the time they needed to pass on their history in dreams, and to buzz the canyon on their fish-skin gliders.

No, thought Alonzo, he wouldn't blow the whistle on them. But, unfortunately, he wasn't the only one who knew the secret.

Morgan's heart was still pounding like the pistons in the vehicles. Could he believe what he had actually seen? A genuine Fountain of Youth! It hadn't been said in so many words, but that was the impression he had gotten—healing waters that made one live longer. Real long! He could imagine all the wealthy people—industrialists, presidents, artists—all the ones who would have to curry his favor in order to try out his sacred grotto. Invitation only, he told himself, and priced to the max.

Hold on, Morgan reminded himself. It was only a dream. Maybe his buddy was a practical joker in the dream world, and this was a Terrian's idea of a laugh. Or maybe it was just his own subconscious, telling him what he wanted to hear. But this dream sure fit in well with the other dream, during that cold night on the plateau. Besides, he couldn't imagine anyone taking a dip in that horrid stuff if there weren't something to gain.

Alonzo would be his liaison with the Terrians; Danziger would be a high-level manager, the get-it-done guy. Bess and he could do the sales. Although, thought Morgan with a smile, increasing a person's life span by four or five times shouldn't be a hard sell anywhere in the universe! The fly in the ointment was that everybody who counted was twenty-two light-years away. But the rich could afford the fare to G889, and they would gladly give up twenty-two years of cold sleep for near immortality! In the beginning, thought Morgan, the rich were bound to live longer than the poor, but it would even out. And so what if it didn't?

He chuckled to himself and snuggled back into his sleeping bag. Bess thought he was trying to get closer to her, and she snuggled in return.

"You know," she murmured, "I was just thinking about how we're going to get rich here."

"You were!" whispered Morgan excitedly. "So was I!"

"Yeah, I think it's pretty clear," Bess yawned.

"Yeah, me too!"

She smiled and nestled under his chin. "We sell that dried fish as an aphrodisiac."

Morgan scowled. "Wait a minute. Are you serious? We're sitting on a gold mine here, but it ain't dried fish."

"What is it?" she asked doubtfully.

He whispered, "A Fountain of Youth."

Bess snorted a laugh. "You can get arrested for making claims like that."

"No, it's serious," he insisted. "I saw it."

"Yeah? Where?"

"In a dream," he said with wonderment.

She smiled. "Okay. Good night, honey."

Hmmm, thought Morgan. Without proof, a Fountain of Youth might be a very tough sell. He needed the proof.

Chapter 10

"Come on," Morgan whispered to Alonzo. "It's real, and you know it is."

The pilot sighed and leaned so far back in his hammock that his head hung over the top rope. Upside down, he could see the morning sunlight drifting into the canyon from just over his chin. "I don't want to talk about it," he replied.

"You've got to talk about it," insisted Morgan. "You were *there* with me! We were fated to work on this *together*."

"Work on what? We don't own anything in that cave. For whatever reason, we were given a glimpse into a special ceremony that doesn't involve us. Other than that, it's not our concern."

Morgan nearly swallowed his tongue, and he looked around to make sure that no one was close enough to Alonzo's hammock to overhear him.

"Are you kidding me?" he gasped. "That's the Fountain of Youth, we're talking about! We've got to claim it before somebody else does! Don't you want to live to be four or five hundred years old?"

"I might live to be that old, anyway," answered the pilot smugly.

"Yeah, but it won't be as easy as taking a bath. And you'll get to *live* all those years, not *sleep* them away."

Alonzo decided that Morgan wasn't likely to leave him alone, not while he had this potential gold mine in his greedy claws. Unfortunately, the pilot couldn't think of anything to say that would discourage Morgan and make him forget about the wonders of the sacred grotto.

"You can't go there," he muttered. "You don't know where it is."

"This second, I don't. I plan to change that. It did look to be some distance. I mean, they have to fly there, don't they?"

"Yeah," muttered Alonzo. He immediately cursed himself for giving even the slightest aid to this sleazebag and his selfish plans. At one time in his life, the pilot might have joined Morgan in a dash for the cash, not caring whether anyone suffered in the process. But he was a different person since crash-landing on G889. He was a person who cared about the land and its native beings; he wanted to guard their way of life, not exploit it.

He knew that Morgan was only interested in stealing the sacred pool away from the Leather Wings, and he couldn't let that happen.

"If I know Devon Adair," Alonzo said finally, "we're pulling out tomorrow. But the canyon, the pool, and the tribe of Terrians will be here long after we're gone. I want to leave it the way it is. That was a sacred trust they showed us, not a scheme to get *you* rich!"

Morgan stepped back with a sneer on his face. "How do you know that? Maybe these Terrians would *like* to live in the penthouse of a big apartment building. They could jump off the balcony and fly as far as they wanted. They could have somebody else farm for them, using real chemical fertilizer. It's a small tribe—this could be a real windfall for these Terrians."

"But they wouldn't be Terrians anymore!" growled Alonzo, balling his hands into fists. He instantly regretted his anger, because it gave him a spasm of pain in his lower back. "Ow!" he groaned.

"Ssshhh!" cautioned Morgan.

Alonzo glanced around the camp and could see the other members of their party, moving lazily this morning because it was their official day off. Most of them hadn't even bothered to get themselves breakfast yet. Even so, they weren't too lazy to stop and look when two people started shouting and groaning at each other. Alonzo lowered his voice and tried to ignore the onlookers.

He whispered through clenched teeth, "Don't you understand that I don't want to have anything to do with exploiting the sacred pool? Leave it to the Terrians—they need it more than we do. If you tell the others about the dream, I'll deny it. I won't back you up, and I won't help you."

Morgan crossed his arms angrily but kept his voice low. "So that's how it is? Fine! You're just slitting your own throat, Solace. I'll do all the communicating with the Terrians by myself—I don't need you."

He stormed away, leaving Alonzo muttering to himself. So that was why Morgan wanted him to be a part of his greedy scheme—to be his interpreter to the Leather Wings! To get them to sign some ungodly contract or other. The pilot didn't like this turn of events one bit, because he had been enjoying their pleasant sojourn at the bottom of the canyon. Now he had to hope that Devon Adair cracked the whip and drove them to continue their journey up the other side as soon as possible.

What would Morgan do with his knowledge? That was the main question.

A few yards away, Devon Adair finished packing the DuneRail so that she and Yale could scout upstream along the bank. The cyborg was several yards away, filling two water bottles from the tanks on the TransRover. Devon looked back at the camp, finding it remarkably tranquil and unhurried this morning. That was in contrast with the usual bumbling rush to break down the equipment and load the vehicles. They needed the day off, there was no question about it, but she hoped that a day of laziness didn't seem too attractive to them.

Life along the turquoise river, protected by the canyon—it had enormous attractions—but this wasn't where they were supposed to be! Their home, where they were needed, was thousands of miles away. It was a daunting thought even to Devon that they had to leave this idyllic natural wonder in exchange for mile after mile of hardship and danger. They had to give up the glorious canyon to risk their lives to reach a land they had never seen. But they couldn't rest, and Devon knew it. They just couldn't.

She was about to climb into her seat when she saw John Danziger striding toward her, a satisfied smile on his face. Yeah, he looked like he was taking a day off. He waved cheerfully.

"Hi, Devon!"

She jumped into her seat as planned, then tried to ignore him. No matter how many of them she would have to fight when it came time to leave the canyon, John Danziger would be the one she would have to defeat. If he insisted on staying, it would be a war.

"Are you deaf?" he asked pleasantly. "I said, hi!"

"Hi," she muttered.

"I've come to talk you out of this madness that says you have to work on a beautiful day like this, when you've given everyone else the day off." He motioned around at the glory of the riverbed and the cathedral of copper and rose-colored cliffs rising into a crystalline sky.

"How I choose to spend my day off is my business," she snapped.

"Okay," conceded Danziger, holding up his hands to surrender. "You two have a great time. What exactly are you looking for?"

Devon was thankful that Yale came strolling up at that moment, carrying two water bottles, which he stored in the DuneRail. "You know," he said to Devon, "tonight we should build a fire, get the kettles out, and boil some of this river water. We could stand to replenish the water in our tanks."

"I'll take care of that," promised Danziger. "I'll get volunteers to collect wood for a big fire. I'll just tell them it's to roast all the fish they're going to catch."

Before Devon could thank him, her attention was captured by one of the Leather Wings. It leapt off a plateau about halfway up the canyon wall and soared gracefully over their heads.

She sighed. "It's too bad we can't fly like them, or we could scout twenty miles in a day. To answer your question, Danziger, we're looking for a way up. It'll probably be a footpath for the humans, although we need something wider for the vehicles."

She tapped the steering wheel of the DuneRail. "You know, once we got some people on the rim, we could probably rig a pulley system to haul the DuneRail and ATV up the canyon. I don't know about the TransRover, though, and I'd hate to abandon it."

Devon didn't mention her fear that if they left the TransRover at the bottom of the canyon, some of the survivors would probably want to stay with it.

Danziger shrugged. "If you did rig up a pulley system, you could disassemble the TransRover and haul it up in pieces."

Yale pointed out, "You're talking about several days', maybe weeks', worth of work. There may be another way."

"I'm listening," said Devon.

"Even if we found a very steep incline, the TransRover could use its own power to climb up, while we kept it from slipping back with the pulleys and cable. You might call it an aided ascent under its own power."

"Let's look for the incline," said Devon, firing up the DuneRail. Yale hustled into the seat beside her.

Danziger stepped back and waved. "Have a good time. Watch out for that waterfall!"

Devon spun the wheel, and the DuneRail bounced along the riverbank, spitting up chunks of mud and sand.

They drove very slowly past the Terrians' village, sticking close to the water, where there were no huts. The tall, dignified Terrians watched them with interest but from a considerable distance, most having scrambled into the rocks at the first sound of their approach. The Terrian they had rescued was the only one who came right down to the water's edge to greet them. Several Leather Wings glided high overhead, keeping an even greater distance than their brethren on the ground.

Devon tried to ignore all of these distractions and concentrate on the job at hand. She had to look for two things: a footpath and an incline up the canyon wall. Steepness of the incline wasn't an issue.

In some odd way, it felt good to be free from the others and traveling alone with her trusted companion, Yale. Although most of the colonists were talented people, they *were* useless for this kind of wilderness trek, as Danziger had pointed out. They would be making their real contributions later on at New Pacifica. But how could she get them there, if they weren't suited for the journey?

"Yale," she said, "since I'm driving, you look for a footpath. I'll look for the incline. Don't hesitate to tell me to stop if anything looks promising."

"Understood," answered the cyborg, scanning the canyon wall earnestly. "May I suggest you drive behind the waterfall?"

Devon nodded gamely and angled the vehicle farther up the bank toward what looked like an enormous skyscraper made out of blue-green water. As they entered the mist, she once again became completely drenched and had to breathe through her mouth in order to keep from drowning. On the side of the canyon, a smaller waterfall graced the cliff, and these twin falls flooded the valley with so much water that they formed the intricate system of ledges and minifalls that framed the beauty of the Terrian village.

Directly behind the waterfall, it was muddy and slippery, and she had to concentrate to keep the balloon tires on a muddy ledge that was about four feet wide. She didn't even turn to look at Yale, who was sitting closest to the drop-off. If they fell into the roiling waters, they would be shoved to the bottom, possibly never to be seen again. The thunder of the cascading water was so intense that it completely wiped out the sound of the DuneRail as it sloshed through a patch of mud.

Devon slowed to concentrate on keeping the wheels straight. To get her bearings, she stole a glance at the wall of water; with the sun behind it, the waterfall gleamed like a thousand layers of turquoise silk, all of it drenching her to the bone. If she had any sense, thought Devon, she would abandon the DuneRail right here and now and save their lives! But she didn't have any sense, and she plowed ahead, knowing that a miscue with the wheel could plunge them into tons of water that had fallen a mile.

Finally, a glimmer of sunlight broke through at the end of the liquid curtain. A minute after that, they came out of the thick mist. Sopping wet, Devon immediately steered the DuneRail into the sunshine to dry them off, even as she picked up speed. She shook her head like a Labrador retriever.

"Whew!" she exclaimed.

"Quite exhilarating," echoed Yale.

"There's another impossible place to get the TransRover through," muttered Devon. "It doesn't look good for the big guy."

"Devon, I have never known you to get discouraged," said Yale with disapproval. "Come on, we didn't think we'd get this far, but we have! And we're none the worse for wear."

"Yale," she began, never taking her eyes off the riverbank, "I have a hypothetical question. Do you think the two of us could get to New Pacifica by ourselves? Say, for example, we got over the top and just took off in this little DuneRail."

"That's a long joy ride," Yale remarked with a chuckle.

But Devon was serious. "What do you think?"

The cyborg cocked his head thoughtfully, as he kept his eyes on the canyon, searching for a possible trail. "It would certainly be easier on the *others* if we left them here, in relative comfort, while you and I completed the journey to New Pacifica. I presume you would return for them at your earliest convenience?"

"Yes."

"And they wouldn't be hard to find," noted Yale. "Just descend anywhere in the canyon, and you are bound to locate them sooner or later. Yes, that is workable and comfortable from *their* point of view, but you and I might have a very difficult time of it."

She started to interrupt him, and Yale held up his hand to silence her. "For example, if injury or death befell either of us, the other one would have to carry on alone. I don't need to tell you how vulnerable that person would be when he slept. There would be no one we could turn to, no one to rescue us. If we didn't make it, the people in the canyon would likely stay in the canyon forever, never connecting up with the children and the other colonists."

Devon muttered, "That could happen to us, anyway. I admit it, I'm impatient—I want to get to New Pacifica, and I know you and I could get there faster without dragging along the others."

"Yes," said Yale with a smile. "You are impatient, always have been. I remember when I used to promise you a cookie for doing your homework, and you would jump up and down, and scream—"

"Please!" begged Devon, nearly screaming now. "Just consider this as a possible course. In case the others refuse to leave the canyon, which could happen."

"If they want to stay, you must talk them out of it," said Yale with concern. "There is strength in numbers, and all of history has borne that maxim out. When people band together, they accomplish things; when they drift apart, they don't. If you're asking my opinion, I say that we find a way to keep our wretched band together. In fact, I remember another saying: United we stand; divided we fall!"

"Enough slogans," muttered Devon. "These are real people we're talking about, as Danziger likes to remind me. We cannot ignore their safety. If I could leave them in a safe place like this, I would feel okay about it, knowing they would probably be there when I came back."

"But," protested Yale, "we have no idea what lies at the top of this rim, or over the next rise. It could be a crisis that needs the very person you have left behind. And what about the children? Do you want to leave Uly here?"

She took her eyes off the canyon to glare at him. "Do I want him to be somewhere that's safe? You're damn right, I do! This place looks pretty safe to me right now, after all we've been through."

Devon paused for a moment to reflect on her outburst, then she admitted, "For all I know, *none* of us will get out of this canyon, and this conversation will be moot. We'll all grow old here, eating fertilizer, and zipping around the canyon on gliders."

"I don't think so," said Yale, peering into the distance. ."Stop us, please."

She braked immediately and tried to follow his line of sight. "What do you see?"

"Kobas," answered Yale. "A few of them leaping over there in that tall grass."

"We've got to be careful," she cautioned, pulling her gloves farther up her wrists. "I know it would be great to find another Koba path, but those things can be dangerous."

"I'm pretty sure they'll run off when we get close enough," said Yale, climbing out of the DuneRail. Devon hurried after him, wondering if she had been stupid not to bring a weapon.

A few seconds later, they were surrounded by thigh-high grasses in a sort of miniature meadow that graced this part of the canyon. Yale strode ahead, and the Kobas did indeed take off at his approach. He stopped to inspect something they had left behind in the grass.

Yale held up a girl's hair barrette. "I think this belongs to True," he remarked with a puzzled expression.

Devon shuddered. "I know at night the Kobas get closer to us than I want to imagine. Let's look for that trail."

It didn't take long to find a matted trail in the high grass that wound into the rocks and presumably higher. Devon was certainly glad that the Kobas had to come down to the river for water. As expected, their trail was suitable only for pedestrians of a very cautious nature. She assumed it would take at least two days to scale this side of the canyon. Going uphill was going to be harder, she reminded herself.

Devon craned her neck to survey the striated cliff side, stretching a mile into the distant sky. She couldn't see the rim of the canyon for the incoming gray clouds.

"Okay," declared Devon, "we've found our footpath. Let's keep going, because it looks like it might rain."

Julia gazed up at the clouds, thinking that it might rain. Darn it. Her plan had been to sneak off and get a bath somewhere in one of the eddies or pools that played at the water's edge. She had seen them downstream, where the river widened. She didn't know if she would find the ideal spot, or if the water would be too cold, but she figured that taking a bath was a worthy goal for a day off.

Failing that, she would go for a shower near the waterfall. She had just watched the spray from the crashing falls swallow up Devon, Yale, and the DuneRail, so it ought to be able to get the trail dust off.

Julia unpacked an old pillowcase that she had been saving to use as a towel, slung it over her shoulder, and tried to sneak away from camp without being noticed.

When no one seemed to notice her escape, Julia quickened her pace and was almost running down the beach—when she heard footsteps thudding after her.

She looked around and groaned. Of all the people she didn't want traipsing along on a bath, it was Morgan Martin.

"Julia! Julia!" he called, seeing he had her attention. "Can I talk to you for a minute?"

She turned on her heel but kept moving away from him. "You can walk with me for a minute or so, if you promise to leave me alone when you're done. Today is my day off too, you know."

"Oh!" exclaimed Morgan. "You're going to get primitive and take a bath? Well, that's the kind of thing I want to talk to you about!"

"About taking baths? I recommend it. Nice to talk to you, Morgan."

"No, wait! What if I told you there was something here in this canyon that would cure any illness and conquer old age? And this is no joke!"

She slowed down a bit. "A wonder drug?"

"Not a drug," he said in a whisper, even though they were fifty feet beyond camp. "This is a pool, in a grotto. You immerse yourself in it. The Terrians showed the pool to me in a dream last night. Alonzo had the same dream. This place could cure him in a flash."

Now Julia stopped and looked askance at Morgan. "Are you talking about a native medicine? Something homeopathic?"

"All of those," answered Morgan excitedly. "If you get a chance, examine one of these flying Terrians. Make a guess as to how old they are. Some of them are hundreds of years old. Alonzo knows about that too."

"If Alonzo knows so much, then why don't we talk to him?"

"He'll deny it," answered Morgan. "He doesn't think anybody should know about the pool but the two of us, like it was revealed to us special. I suppose that's true, but the humanitarian in me keeps insisting that a discovery of this magnitude should be available to *everyone*. This is the real thing, Doctor. It's something civilization has searched thousands of years to find."

"Are you talking about a Fountain of Youth?" asked Julia skeptically.

"You are the medical expert," said Morgan graciously. "I leave it up to you to evaluate the finding. I just wanted to make sure you were aware of it."

"Can you take me there?" asked Julia. "Show this miracle to me."

"Not yet," admitted Morgan. "But I'm working on that end of it. It's possible other people have dreamt about this healing pool. I would ask around, if I were you. Remember, if you ask Alonzo directly, he'll deny it. He likes you—I'm sure you could find a way to get to the heart of the matter."

Julia nodded "Maybe. Morgan, if this is some kind of scheme of yours, and there's nothing to it—"

"You'll have every right to be mad at me," he interjected. "All I'm asking is that you check into it. Alonzo and I saw this place in a dream—it was as real as you are, standing in front of me right now. It's a place these Terrians fly to in the dead of night, to immerse themselves. I can't explain it, but it stops the aging process."

"Right," said Julia doubtfully.

Morgan started backing away, but he motioned around the incredible canyon as if he were the gnome guarding the kingdom of Faerie. "Take a look around, Doctor. You can feel it—you just know there's something amazing down here."

He walked away chuckling, which disturbed Julia more than his strange claim. A Fountain of Youth? Right. But something had been affecting Morgan the last couple of days, turning him into this cheerful gnome instead of his usual surly self. It was an improvement, certainly, but it couldn't have come out of nowhere. Was there any germ of truth in this strange explanation?

Suddenly her bath didn't seem all that important. A quick shower near the waterfall would probably banish the trail dust just as well. If Morgan and Alonzo had really experienced a shared dream about the Terrians, that was important on its own. Morgan had never been a dream conduit before. At least he had never mentioned it, and she didn't think he would keep this to himself. If he and Alonzo had both shared a dream, others might have shared it too, she reasoned.

It was worth prodding Alonzo with this information just to get a reaction out of him. Julia often worried that the injured pilot was becoming *too* introspective, especially for a young man who has used to being active and outgoing. Anything that got a rise out of him, even a bit of anger, was worth a few minutes of her time. If it turned out to be a fantasy, then so what?

Julia didn't want to sneak up on him in his hammock, and she could tell that he was dozing. So she stopped behind a row of drying clothes that somebody had strung up under the TransRover and observed Alonzo for a few seconds. Doctors were allowed to observe, she told herself, and it couldn't be helped if their patients were young and handsome. You had to have a handsome one every now and then, just by the law of averages.

"Something I can do for you, Julia?" he asked, never opening his eyes.

"Uh, yes," she answered, stepping under the clothesline. "Before I abandon you for the day, I just wanted to make sure you didn't need anything. Have you got water within reach? Somebody who can help you if you need to get up?"

"Yeah, yeah," he muttered. "I'm covered. Baines is just sleeping all day in the sand. Where are you going?"

"Going to try to find a place to get clean," she said matter-of-factly. "I thought maybe the waterfall."

Alonzo sighed. "Yeah, that looks inviting, doesn't it? I wish I could enjoy this day off, but I can't. Would you believe, this is more boring for me than a day on the trail, when we're just trying to eke out the miles? At least then I've got the responsibility of the ATV."

Julia stepped closer to his hammock and squeezed the splint on his right leg, checking for water damage. "So are you sure you don't want a new splint? This would be a good time to do it, while we're stopped."

"Just when I'm getting used to this one?" he asked in mock horror. "It's almost all dried out, I think. Hard to tell, because it always feels clammy and sweaty. The way I figure it, Doc, when I get this splint off, it's going to be for good."

"I hope so," she said with an encouraging smile. "There's one other small thing I want to ask you. Have you been having dreams about a healing pool where the Terrians go? I believe they fly there at night."

Alonzo squinted his eyes at her, then lay back in his hammock. She knew she had struck paydirt, even though he was trying to look disinterested. "I can't recall a dream like that. What about it?"

Julia regretted having to use a small ruse, but she knew how stubborn Alonzo could be once he made up his mind. "A couple others in the group have been telling me about a shared dream they had. I figured if *they* had this dream, you must have had it too."

"Who told you about the dream?" he asked suspiciously.

Julia smiled. "Can't tell you that. Doctor-patient confidentiality, you know. But don't worry, Alonzo, you would know this place if you saw it. Apparently, it was quite spectacular. You shouldn't be spooked by it, if you saw it, because others saw it too."

"It didn't spook me!" said the pilot defensively. "I thought it was beautiful, an extraordinary place. Even now I can't believe it was real—except that I really saw it! What's the most amazing thing to me is that the Terrians are so trusting they actually *showed* it to us. I hope they don't live to regret doing that."

Julia swallowed. "Is it really the Fountain of Youth, like they're saying? Are these flying Terrians really hundreds of years old?"

Alonzo nodded somberly. "Yes, but I think we should leave their sacred pool alone. If we get involved with it, it could destroy the Leather Wings and their way of life."

"Even if it would help *you*?" asked Julia.

He shook his head and gave a hollow laugh. "I'm not so important. None of us are. You know, I'm not so naive to think that we can land on this planet, colonize it, and not change anything about it. I hope we have some consideration when we make changes—we want to blend in, not take over—but there are some things on this planet that are too important to change. They must be left the way they are. That's how I feel about the Leather Wings."

He swept his arm toward the vast grandeur of the chasm, where a herd of gray clouds was swallowing the jagged buttes in the distance. "See this? It's not just people like Morgan who might destroy this place—it's regular people, like you and me.

"Morgan is only after the money, and you can get rid of him by taking away the money. But the do-gooders, the ones who want to heal the universe, how can we stop them? How do we keep ourselves from *becoming* them? No matter how useless some people are, they all think they deserve to live forever. Julia, do you want to possess the power to decide who gets to live forever, and who doesn't?

"It would come down to somebody having that power. If it became known that we had a Fountain of Youth in this canyon, how long would it take before people flocked here from all over the universe?"

"We could keep it a secret," insisted Julia.

Alonzo snorted a laugh. "Right. We only had the dream last night, and already everybody knows about it."

"But that was the Terrians' choice to show it to you," Julia pointed out. "They must have had a reason. What was it?"

Alonzo sighed. "That's what I'm trying to figure out. I know somebody is threatening the sacred pool, but I don't know who. Normally, I would think that *we* would be the biggest threat. But then why show it to us?"

"Why don't you tell me about the dream?" suggested the doctor. "Perhaps I can interpret it differently."

"I will," Alonzo answered gravely. "But it won't change my mind about stealing the pool from them."

Chapter 11

The rains came by mid-afternoon, drenching the band of survivors and forcing them into the shelter of their tents, or under the axles of the TransRover. So much for their day off, thought John Danziger. He gazed forlornly at the pile of driftwood he, True, and Bess had collected to build a fire. Although they had thrown a tarpaulin over it, the wood was undoubtedly soaked. He noticed that the Terrians had disappeared from the sky with the first drops, and now all of them had crawled into their anthill-like homes. Only the surging river seemed happy to frolic in the rain.

Danziger was lying on his stomach under the left rear tire of the TransRover, wondering if there were anything he should be doing. Or could be doing. He felt for Devon and Yale, who were still upriver somewhere, and he hoped they weren't getting too soaked.

He could see True and Uly, sticking their small hands out of one of the tents. As children will, they couldn't resist getting wet and then squealing with laughter over it. He wouldn't mind getting wet himself, thought the mechanic, if he had clean, dry clothes to change into.

He saw a slim figure dash through the rain, stopping just long enough to call out, "John Danziger!"

"Over here!" he yelled. He risked the downpour long enough to lean around the big tire and wave.

A moment later, Julia Heller scooted under the Trans-Rover to join him in comparative dryness. She, of course, was sopping wet.

"I'd offer you a towel," he said, "but I haven't got one."

"Tell me about it," she replied. "Listen, since Devon isn't here, I need to ask you for advice."

"Go ahead."

"Did you hear about the Fountain of Youth that Morgan and Alonzo dreamt about last night?"

Danziger smiled. "A Fountain of Youth?"

"Don't laugh. They both swear they took a dream journey with the Leather Wings last night. They went to a sacred grotto, where there's a luminescent pool. You immerse yourself in the pool—and you're healed and can live almost forever. Alonzo is so adamant that we should make no effort to find this pool, or use it for ourselves, that I can't imagine he would be making it up. He feels that way even though it was the Terrians who showed it to him. Morgan, of course, wants to share the pool with everyone."

"For a price, I'm sure," remarked Danziger. "What advice can I offer you? I'm not much of an interpreter of dreams."

The doctor frowned with indecision. "I have conflicting ethics on this. I'm sworn to heal people, and healing the children is the whole reason we came to this planet. We know Uly was healed by the Terrians, although that was hundreds of miles from here. But it could be related. Then I've got Alonzo, telling me to stay away from the pool, or it will destroy the Leather Wings! Part of me knows he may be right, but I can't just give up on it, not if there's any chance this pool could be for real."

As he was thinking, Danziger stuck his hand out and felt for the rain, but it had let up considerably. "Well, I'm just a mechanic, but the first thing a mechanic does is to make sure the thing in question is worth the trouble of fixing it. Before you drive yourself crazy with the ethical questions, is there any way you can prove this Fountain of Youth exists?"

She nodded. "If I had two Terrians to examine, an older one and a younger one, I could run a few comparative tests. That would at least tell me if they do live to be hundreds of years old."

"We know both a young one and an old one," said Danziger. "There's Morgan's friend and our guide, who looks ancient but is still very spry. Come on, the rain's letting up. Go get your medikit."

"Thanks," said Julia with a brilliant smile. She jumped up and jogged away into the light sprinkle.

Within the next seconds, rays of sunlight blasted through the fast-moving clouds on the rim, unleashing shafts of light that raced down the buttes and flowed across the turquoise river. For a few glorious seconds, there were rainbows extending the entire length of the canyon. They looked like magical slides that one could ride up and down as if on a flying carpet.

By rain or shine, the canyon was an extraordinary place, thought Danziger. It was filled with a beauty and agelessness that made talk of a Fountain of Youth sound almost plausible. At any rate, this new development was another good reason to spend a few more days in the canyon, as if they needed another reason. The prospect of scaling the canyon and hitting the rugged trail again, probably without vehicles, made his teeth ache.

He had to figure out a way to talk to Devon about this, thought the mechanic, as he slithered out from under the TransRover and into the sunlight.

Devon shivered. Even though the sun was temporarily shining again, she was soaking wet, and she'd been soaking wet and traveling in an open vehicle the entire day. The rain had cut short their exploration and forced them back about noon. Except for the Koba path they had found just beyond the waterfall, the day had been a total loss. They had seen lots of gorgeous rock formations, including two spectacular arches. They had seen no part of the canyon that even one of the vehicles could ascend, aided or otherwise.

Devon was still freezing and about to get another drenching from the waterfall on their return pass. The wall of turquoise water loomed a hundred yards ahead of them, and a mile straight up.

More to keep her teeth from chattering than anything else, she remarked to Yale, "I think we should stay another day, and scout in the other direction. In those few miles we traveled to get to the village, I think we passed some inclines that might do."

Yale smiled wistfully. "Even you want to stay."

"No, I don't," she argued. "We're not going to save any time by trying to get out of this canyon the wrong way. I've just about made up my mind on a course of action for the group. We have to keep moving, or we will be tempted to stay. So we'll take one more day to scout, then you and Zero and most of the band will go up by foot on the path we just discovered. You will get the pulley system together. The small vehicles are light, I'm not worried about getting them up."

"You know," said Yale, "why should we try to scout in this dangerous manner, when the Leather Wings have surveyed everything for hundreds of miles around? Let's find some way to ask them how to get out."

"Be my guest." Devon shivered again with the first blast of spray from the turquoise waterfall. "If we have to, we'll take the TransRover apart, like Danziger suggested, and haul it up piece by piece. The important thing is that we keep moving toward our objective. Better to lose a few days to hard work that pays off than lose several months to indecisiveness."

Yale smiled. "Devon, you've never been accused of being indecisive. What do you think the others will say about this?"

She shrugged. "What can they say? There's no reason to stay here, other than laziness."

Yale shielded his eyes from the pounding water. "This time you get to look into the basin of the waterfall. That is an impressive sight, but I don't want to see it from too close."

But Devon Adair kept her eyes straight ahead on the muddy ledge, following the tracks she had left in the morning. She didn't need to look at the falls, because she could hear the deafening roar of the water plunging back to G889 after a long drop. In fact, she would hear it for weeks to come as a ringing in her ears.

Having once navigated the ledge behind the waterfall, she was less nervous this time, and she guided the DuneRail through without a mishap. She saw two flyers take off from the plateaus in the distance, and her gaze drifted down to the Terrian village and the sparkling miniature waterfalls. At the sight of their own tents beyond, Devon felt as if she were coming home.

There was a strange familiarity about this isolated spot of G889, as if there were no point in looking further. Reluctantly, she told herself that she couldn't afford to think like that. Her home was elsewhere, and they were just passing through.

Then she saw a smaller figure come tearing down the beach, through the Terrian village, and bounding toward her. As she needed to dry off a bit before seeing fellow humans, Devon steered the DuneRail into the sunlight, stopped, and cut off the engine. She stood to stretch her legs and shake the water and mud off, while she waited for little Uly to catch up with them.

He wasn't so little anymore, she reminded herself. When he was ill, she had grown accustomed to caring for him as if he were still a baby. Now he had turned into a little person beyond her control, especially in a constantly changing environment where danger was everywhere. Even wearing his immuno-suit, he had been growing, she realized. Now his clothes looked two sizes too small.

"Mom, have you heard?" shouted Uly. "Have you heard?"

She laughed. "Heard what? We've been gone all day. But we did find another Koba path, just like the one you and True found."

"Forget about that," said Uly importantly. "Do you know about the Fountain of Youth?"

Yale nodded. "Of course, we do. The Spanish conquistador, Ponce de León, searched for it in Southern North America, but it turned out to be a myth."

Uly shook his head as if the cyborg were hopelessly out of touch. "Not *that* one, the one here in the canyon. Morgan, Alonzo, and Julia know all about it. In fact, Julia was testing the Terrians to see if it's true, and it is! There's a Fountain of Youth right here in the canyon. Julia thinks it could be the same thing that cured me."

Devon took a deep breath and looked at Yale. "I guess that news beats a Koba path."

The cyborg looked thoughtful. "Perhaps Zero and I could make it to New Pacifica by ourselves, if you wanted to stay here and investigate. Although I will remind everyone how much time Ponce de León wasted."

"I want to shake Dr. Vasquez's hand when he lands," vowed Devon Adair. "And I want him to see Uly, as proof that he was right. Nothing has changed those goals for me. Climb in, Uly, and let's see what this is all about."

Half an hour later, Devon had been briefed by Julia, Morgan, Danziger, and a gloomy Alonzo Solace. Others in the band listened intently, including the two children. As well as Devon could piece it together, Alonzo and Morgan had shared a dream in which they had flown with the Leather Wings to a sacred pool. They had witnessed the devotees immersing themselves in the pool, and known without hearing it spoken that the pool restored health and retarded aging.

Dreams were one thing, thought Devon, but Julia's findings were something else. According to the doctor's examination of its blood, X rays, and tissue samples, the young Terrian was about twenty years old, as expected. By comparative analysis, the Terrian who had led them to the village tested out at over four hundred years of age!

Alonzo was upset that Julia had even examined the two Terrians. "I can't believe you did that," he growled. "Have you no respect for their way of life?"

Julia glared at the injured man. "You're awfully holier than thou, aren't you, Alonzo? You don't mind inserting yourself in their dreams, exploring their inner thoughts, and learning secrets you don't want the rest of us to know! In fact, it didn't sound like you had to be dragged to the sacred pool last night."

"I didn't ask to go there," countered Alonzo. "They *showed* it to me."

"They showed it to me too!" announced Morgan. "But I never got the feeling that we had to keep it a secret."

"Some secret," muttered Alonzo.

Julia insisted, "I don't see any harm in giving them an examination. They consented. I don't know how long Terrians normally live, but their leader has *scars* that are three hundred years old! He's ancient by any measure, but he's still in excellent physical condition. If there's something around here that retards aging and cures The Syndrome, I want to see it. At least to take samples of its chemical makeup."

Alonzo scowled and motioned at the grandeur all around them. "Do you think you can duplicate *this* in a test tube? The pool is an intregal part of the canyon, and you can't take it out, or make the Terrians give it up."

Julia looked about to explode, and Devon held up her hands to quell the argument. "That's enough. You both make good points, but I have a point to make. Yale, will you tell these people what happened to Ponce de León?"

Yale cleared his throat in a professorial manner. "I would be delighted."

"Aw, we don't need a history lesson," groaned Morgan.

"Yes, you do," answered Devon. "I listened to all of you and your arguments, and now you're going to listen to Yale for a moment."

"Thank you," said the cyborg. He projected a holographic image of a studious-looking Spaniard with a long, narrow goatee. "Juan Ponce de León," he began, "was one of the most successful and respected Spanish governors in the Caribbean. Then, later in his life, he became obsessed with finding the mythical Fountain of Youth. His search led him to discover Florida and claim it for Spain, but he searched for years of utter failure until he was badly wounded by native people. He died old and penniless."

The cyborg turned off the image. "Are there any questions?"

Danziger raised his hand. "Are you trying to tell us we're idiots for looking for this thing?"

"Not exactly," said Devon, "but looking for a Fountain of Youth is not our primary mission. We have a colony to establish, *then* some of us can return to the canyon and look for the sacred pool, if there is such a thing."

She glanced at Alonzo and added, "Maybe we can find the same curative powers elsewhere, without disrupting a thriving society of Terrians."

Morgan shook his hands helplessly at the sky. "I can't believe you people! At the very least, you've got the answer to all of humankind's health problems right in your hands! More than likely, you've got a way to get stinking rich, and you can't be bothered to look for it! Are you crazy?"

Bess gently massaged his shoulders. "Better calm down, honey. You know getting angry isn't good for your blood pressure."

"That's just it!" wailed Morgan. "I *need* the Fountain of Youth! We all need it!"

Alonzo shouted back, "That's why we can't have it! Everyone will want it, and we'll steal if from the Terrians even if we don't mean to. Even if we have the best of intentions, we'll betray them. Ask Yale—we've done it throughout history."

"He's right," admitted the cyborg. "The record of humans is dismal in this regard. This pool, if it exists, is a natural resource—no different than coal, oil, gold, or any of the other resources we've plundered all over the galaxy."

Julia turned to Devon and appealed to her directly. "Can't we stay for a few days to check it out?" she begged. "For the sake of the children."

Devon's lips thinned. There was no right answer to this question, no way to please everyone, not even herself. The last thing she wanted was to exploit the property of the

Terrians, but if this pool had a connection to Uly's mysterious healing—how could they fail to check it out? She also had to worry that if they made a dramatic discovery in the canyon, it would only prolong their stay and make it harder to leave.

Devon knew, even before all this talk of a Fountain of Youth, that it wouldn't be easy to get the colonists out of the canyon, physically or emotionally. They were drained from the crash landing, the journey across the plains, then the rugged descent into the canyon. Every one of them knew there was a harder climb and a longer journey ahead of them, and an excuse to stay was perhaps all they needed to give up their goal of reaching New Pacifica. Sensing her quandary, Danziger suggested, "I don't see the harm in staying one or two more days. Besides, we don't really have a plan to get out of here, do we?"

"Yes, we do," said Devon, bristling. "Yale and I found a Koba footpath up the canyon. We can get the people up right away."

"Real smart," scoffed Morgan. "We continue on foot, leaving all the vehicles *and* the Fountain of Youth down here! Well, I for one am *not* leaving."

There were murmurs of assent, especially from Baines and Julia. This was it, thought Devon, the clear mutiny she had been waiting for. But she had always thought it would occur on the trail, after a day of sacrifice and hardship. If she had thought about it, she should have realized the mutiny would come after a day off, in a lush valley surrounded by fresh seafood, friendly Terrians, and a Fountain of Youth.

"All right," she sighed. "We're going to stay at least one more day, while we try to find an incline that will help us get the vehicles up."

There was a cheer, even though this was really a

nondecision, a delaying tactic that didn't appease anybody or solve anything, and Devon knew it.

Alonzo scowled, closed his eyes, and sank back into his hammock. "I'm not going to help you," he said. "Whatever I learn about the pool, I'm keeping it to myself."

"You do that," crowed Morgan. "See if we need you." He jerked his thumb downriver. "My buddy is going to show me how to get there tonight. Right?"

Devon followed his gaze and saw the young Terrian, who was indeed standing on the bank, watching them, as it had ever since they rescued it from the river. It was difficult to say if the young Terrian was eager to help Morgan, because its scaly, fanged face wasn't very expressive. But it did seem to be looking at them with an intense interest.

In fact, the Terrian began running toward them, pointing excitedly toward the sky. The creature was so excited that it actually made a few audible clicks.

Devon turned to look in the direction the Terrian was pointing, and she saw a huge squadron of Leather Wings, perhaps a dozen or more. They were at a considerable distance, still on the other side of the waterfall. They were beautiful, flying in formation on what had turned into a sunny afternoon. She wondered why so many of them were traveling together.

Then she heard it—a whistling sound—and she turned to see another Terrian standing on a large plateau, swinging a chunk of bone round and round. The whistle the bone made wasn't very loud, but the alarm galvanized the village, and Leather Wings came pouring out of their huts. Some of them were already strapping on their wings; a few grabbed spears. Morgan's Terrian rushed past them, and another Terrian handed it some wings.

As soon as a Terrian's wings were secured, it scrambled into the rocks to find the closest plateau. They moved swiftly, efficiently, as they had when the school of fish burst out of the water yesterday. Devon glanced at the river, but it was calm—no rampaging fish. Those adult Terrians who didn't grab their wings and take to the sky waited in the village, spears in hand.

"What's going on?" asked Morgan worriedly.

"You know so much about them," sneered Alonzo "You tell us."

Danziger had the right idea, as he went to the equipment locker on the TransRover and pulled out a pair of jumpers. Devon was distracted by the sight of a nearby Leather Wing launching itself from the cliff face. It pumped its arms and struggled for altitude, working feverishly and with a desperation she hadn't seen the flyers exhibit before. She turned to see the incoming flyers in the distance—they were pumping their wings hard, as if they were in a race.

"Something is wrong," said Bess with concern.

True grabbed her father's waist and hung on. "Daddy, I counted the flyers leaving today, and there weren't that many of them."

Danziger squinted into the jumpers. "Yeah, you could be right. And I don't remember that the Terrians who live in this village tie reeds around their chests. It looks ornamental, like a sash. I'm no expert on Terrians, but these look different to me."

"I'm scared," said True, hugging him tighter.

Julia instinctively grabbed her medikit. "Should we get closer?"

"Not yet," answered Devon. "Let's see what happens." Uly ran over to her and gripped one of her hands.

"Hey, I know!" said Morgan hopefully. "Maybe this bunch went out a few days ago and are just coming home. This is the welcoming committee, going out to greet them!"

Devon glanced at one of the spear-bearers, who stationed

itself at the entrance to a hut full of harvested salt fruit. "This doesn't look like a welcoming committee," she said glumly.

The incoming squadron of Terrians was forced into a double file as they swooped wide of the giant waterfall. This spread them out across the canyon walls, like a string of charms on a necklace. Most of them maintained their high altitude, but a few broke off and dived downward to meet the first of the flyers launched from the village. Devon stared, because the opposing flyers were headed directly toward one another!

She swallowed hard and took a step forward, hoping that this was some sort of intramural sport, a Terrian form of chicken. Because if it weren't, those two groups of flyers were going to crash into each other! She watched with dread, like a person who sees an accident happening but can't prevent it, as the two groups of flyers dived at each other. They connected and twisted momentarily into grotesque beings with four frantic wings.

Then one of them went tumbling toward the blue-green water, and another Terrian spun out of control toward the rocks. Miraculously, it gained some command over its damaged wings, enough to crash-land on the beach, much to Devon's relief. She couldn't see what had happened to the Terrian who fell into the water, but she suspected the worst.

"That was weird," she said as if in a daze. "It looked like they crashed into each other on purpose."

"They did," said Danziger, lowering his jumpers. "They tried to break each other's wings. Devon, this is warfare."

Chapter 12

• • • • • • • •

A bizarre battle took place, in which the flyers swooped through the air and plowed into one another, trying to knock their enemies out of the sky. Through his jumpers, Danziger was able to watch individual combatants. He saw one invading flyer zoom down to hit a defender, only to miss the enemy completely. This put the attacker in a nose dive toward the river, and it struggled valiantly to pull out of the dive. Just as it righted itself and regained command of its wings, another flyer streaked over it and kicked one of its wing tips with its foot. That was enough to send the unlucky Terrian spinning into the water, which the being hit with a spume.

Danziger jerked the jumpers back toward the sky and caught a dogfight in progress. One flyer was swiftly flapping its wings to overtake another. The prey Terrian made a number of brilliant evasive maneuvers, but its pursuer adjusted cagily to every desperate move. Knowing it would never escape, the pursued flyer angled upward without warning and crashed into the chest of its enemy. After the initial flurry of wings, the two Terrians dropped like crumpled leaves to the beach.

A moment later, Danziger was relieved to see that both of them were moving. One of them even staggered to its feet and lumbered toward the rocks to try another launch.

The mechanic pointed the jumpers back into the air just in time to see two flyers zooming toward a head-on collision. He nearly averted his eyes, but at the last moment, one flyer angled upward and cracked the other in the head with a knee. While it righted itself, the dazed flyer went sailing like an arrow toward the cliff. It sheared off a thin spire of rock before crashing into some bushes that covered a ledge. Maybe it wasn't a fatal crash, through Danziger, but it sure looked painful.

Devon and Julia ran past him, shouting for the warriors to stop. What good would that do? thought Danziger. You couldn't separate combatants who were a quarter of a mile over your head!

Against his better judgment, he found himself slogging through the sand toward the battle zone. Bess, Baines, and a few others were trudging along him beside him, and he marveled at the dazed expressions on their faces. None of them could believe that this peaceful canyon would erupt in bloodshed like this.

The mechanic glanced over his shoulder to see True dashing after him, her little arms working like a steam locomotive. He had told her to stay back, but of course she couldn't resist the sight of war. Who could?

He slowed down long enough to let her catch up. "I told you to stay back!"

"Dad!" she shrieked, jogging past him. "They're hurting each other!"

He caught her up in his arms and tried to distract her from the bizarre spectacle in the sky. "Sometimes people do hurt each other."

"Even humans?" she asked with alarm.

"Especially humans."

True craned her neck to look past his shoulder, and he finally gave up and turned to watch. From a distance, without jumpers, it looked like a swarm of flies zooming around a chunk of garbage. The line of the invaders was in a shambles, as each of them had been contested by a defender from the village. The fact that no invaders had broken through to attack the village allowed the spear-bearers to leave their defensive positions and move forward. Danziger supposed that meant that the Leather Wings were repelling the attack.

He was reluctant to get closer to the battle, but True wriggled out of his grasp and ran after Julia and Devon. When he glanced around, he saw Yale with his arms wrapped around a struggling Uly, and he dashed after True.

He caught his daughter and tackled her in the sand. "Dad!" she shrieked.

"Quiet! You don't know how people get when they're in a war. It's called bloodlust. They could just as easily kill you or one of their own comrades as the enemy. We don't have any idea what the invaders think of *us*. Maybe they consider us to be the enemy too. If you want to watch, you'll have to do it where it's safe, meaning right here."

"Okay, Dad," she said and nodded somberly.

When Danziger staggered to his feet and turned to survey the battle zone, fewer than half a dozen flyers were still in the air. He blew the sand off the jumpers and put them to his eyes. He could see the invaders on the riverbank, limping away; most of them were injured from falls or bloated from contact with the water. A handful of defenders who weren't injured chased the invaders, prodding them with their spears when they got close enough to do so. But there wasn't much fight left in anyone, and the disorganized retreat continued successfully, with most of the invaders escaping.

"Come on," said Danziger, touching his daughter's shoulder. "You can see the results of war."

Just beyond the village, they came upon Devon, who had pulled a bloated Terrian out of the water. She dragged it into the sunlight, and one of the villagers covered it with mats. Nevertheless, the Terrian kept shivering and jerking around from the pain of its distended skin.

They left her and kept walking until they found Julia, who was setting a compound fracture on a Terrian's leg. The tall, scaly creature bore the pain stoically, but the anguish on Julia's face was anything but stoic. "Worse than Alonzo's break," she told them. "Get any of them you can find out of the water!"

"You stay here," Danziger ordered True. "Help the doctor."

"I will," she answered.

Danziger saw a bloated body float into the shallows and become marooned on one of the ledges. He splashed through the icy water to get to the victim before it drowned, and he was stunned to recognize the Terrian's distinctive topknot. It was the leader of the tribe, the one who had guided them to the village! He gripped the elder Terrian under his slippery arms and dragged it through the shallow water to the bank.

After dragging the Terrian ashore, Danziger lay panting in the sand for a moment, wondering if he had been too late. The Terrian was barely recognizable in its waterlogged condition, and it was lying very still, either in shock or dead.

After a moment, the Terrian's hand moved and slithered across the sand to touch Danziger's hand. It was a feeble grip, but he squeezed back.

"You live, old fella," he said. "But that air battle is a crazy thing for you to be doing. I'm going to help some others."

Danziger stood up and saw two more Terrians struggling ashore under their own power. Bess waded in to help one of them, and Danziger grabbed the other one. After he got the Terrian to the safety of the beach, he noticed twin sashes made of reeds tied like an X across its chest. He looked around nervously, afraid the enemy flyer would be attacked, but no one showed any interest. The foe was allowed to lie peacefully in the sun and recover, the same as the villagers. As soon as the enemy flyer was able to move, it staggered to its feet and lumbered off, and no one prevented its escape.

For all the fury of their aerial combat, the Terrians were surprisingly compassionate about the enemy, Danziger decided. They apparently let them live to fight another day, unless they perished in the actual combat. In a strange way, they reminded him of World War I pilots he had read about. Those gallant pilots from early in the twentieth century often refused to fire on downed enemy airmen, and they usually exchanged captured airmen. All of these niceties were forgotten by the time World War II came around, when it was common to shoot pilots in their parachutes after they had ejected from their aircraft.

The mechanic shook off these troubling thoughts of war and jogged toward the canyon wall, where Julia and True were helping injured Terrians. Julia was putting a sling around a flyer's arm, while her young nurse applied an antibiotic ointment to a nasty wound on its forehead. The patient took all of this unusual attention in stride and sat staring at the upper regions of the canyon. Was it thinking about its narrow escape? wondered Danziger, or was it gauging the possibility of there being another attack?

As Julia and True didn't need him, Danziger wandered back toward the village. In front of a hut, he found Morgan nursing his young friend, who had obviously taken a tumble into some bramble bushes. It had cuts and scratches all over it, and Morgan was going through a tube of ointment from the first-aid kit to patch it up. The Terrian's wings lay crumpled beside it.

"You'll be okay," Danziger heard Morgan say to the young Terrian. "You'll have to go to the sacred pool tonight, won't you? To get well."

"Morgan," Danziger said with disapproval, "don't you ever stop thinking of yourself?"

"I'm not thinking of myself," said Morgan with outrage. "Look at him. Look at all of them. They'll be going to that wonderful place, you can bet on it."

The bureaucrat patted his friend on the back. "If you can't go by wing, you'll go in your dreams, right? You need to get well, and so do we. All you have to do is show me where it is, and I'll take good care of you."

Danziger looked up at the patch of sky by the blue-green waterfall. A few minutes earlier, that sky had been filled with warriors trying to knock one another out of the air.

"Morgan," he scowled, "there happens to be a war going on here. Don't you think that sheds a different light on things?"

"Well, of course we'll help *them,*" said Morgan, motioning to the dazed Terrian. "These interlopers are obviously trying to steal the pool from us."

"Us?" asked Danziger.

Morgan shrugged. "Figure of speech. Although I told Devon, and I'm telling you—Bess and I live here now.

Martin Canyon is our home, and we're going to protect our investment."

Danziger shook his head and just walked away. The sight of injured Terrians, wounded in war, was bad enough, but Morgan tending to them from the goodness of his greed was too much. He strolled toward the camp, where Yale had finally managed to calm Uly and the two of them were watching the proceedings through jumpers. Zero and Alonzo were the only other members of the band who had remained in camp—all of the others were helping with the injured Terrians, or just gaping. Alonzo was lying in his hammock, apparently asleep, and Zero stood at attention, awaiting orders.

"Do they need our help?" asked Yale with concern.

Danziger looked back at the battle zone. "I think things are under control. Zero, you might want to go to the village and see if you can be useful."

"Not a bad idea," said the robot, clanking away.

"Is it over?" muttered Alonzo, his eyes remaining shut.

Danziger shrugged. "All over but the shouting. And the patching up, and the burying. You know what, guys, this place isn't paradise."

"No place is paradise," answered Yale, redirecting Uly's jumpers. "Look toward the huts, and see what the doctor is doing."

Uly firmly kept the jumpers focused on the sky. "But when are they going to fight again?"

"Hopefully, never," answered Yale. The aged cyborg looked back at Danziger and frowned. "What do we do? Do we try to help them? Could we possibly end this conflict?"

"That's a good question," conceded Danziger. "I don't know the answer."

Alonzo spoke as if he were thinking aloud. "I knew someone was threatening them, but I thought it was *us*.

That's our payment if we want to use the sacred pool—that's what they want from us—to take care of their enemies for them. They don't have the stomach for it."

"If they've seen inside our minds, they know we do," said Danziger, gazing toward the blue-green waterfall in the distance.

Julia Heller wasn't sure she would ever get the blood off her hands, and she scrubbed them repeatedly in the cold, rushing water. Terrian blood was exceptionally sticky, like syrup, and it had turned her fingers the color of cherrywood.

She rose, darkness ending her efforts to patch them up. The wounded Terrians had seemed neither appreciative nor upset over her ministrations. They endured her care as they did everything else in their lives, with dignity and stoic acceptance. Having tended to the Terrians for several hours, she felt she knew them better. It seemed as if their beliefs welcomed death as a condition of life, a gift from the same source that brought them everything else—the canyon.

But there was a sadness about them tonight that went beyond their injuries and fatigue. She had witnessed their combat, which was both deadly and ritualistic, frightening and beautiful. She knew their weakness. They were still capable of hating and harming one another. The rival tribe of Terrians were their mirror images, no different except for the reed sashes they wore. The tribe could have been an offshoot of the Leather Wings, she thought to herself, a branch cast out of the tribe for some reason. Maybe it really was a battle over access to the sacred pool, if the pool existed.

Julia hoped the sacred pool existed, to speed the Terrians' healing, but then she was a romantic. Only an utter romantic, she decided, travels twenty-two light-years to practice frontier medicine on the wrong side of a primitive planet. Maybe this bizarre life was exactly what she deserved for being such a fool.

The doctor picked herself up from the sandy riverbank and shuffled wearily back to camp. From fifty feet away, she could hear the band's noisy discussion, and she wondered what she was going to say to them. In fact, they were arguing about several different things at once:

"We should find the Fountain of Youth and claim it under Earth law!" shouted Morgan.

"We need to help them make peace!" insisted Bess. "We can't let them keep fighting!"

Devon asserted, "We need to leave here and get to New Pacifica. That is our primary goal."

"But the Terrians—we can't let them get hurt!" True broke in.

"If we don't get out of here now," claimed Alonzo, "we'll be trapped here forever, part of a war. Do you want that?"

"History bears him out," Yale interjected.

That started the round of arguments all over again, with Morgan introducing his tired refrain: "Fountain of Youth! Fountain of Youth!" That was followed by Devon and her equally familiar chant: "New Pacifica! New Pacifica!" And the loudest chorus of all were the sensitive ones who wanted to stay and broker peace between the warring Terrians.

Julia stepped into the circle of light cast by the campfire, and the arguments began to die down. Here was their doctor, and her words about the healing pool carried more weight than anyone else's. Morgan smiled confidently, waiting for her to come down on his side, as she had earlier. Alonzo scowled and turned away. Devon looked nervous, as if she realized that if Julia wanted to stay in the canyon, search for the pool, and help the Terrians, it would be hard to get the others to leave. They might not stay to aid Morgan and his wild schemes, but Julia knew they would stay to help her.

Plus, these were urban and space-born people—they only had one doctor. If given a choice, they would rather stay with their doctor than cross three thousand miles of wilderness without one.

The choice seems to be up to me, thought Julia. She gazed from face to face, all of them somber and shadowy in the flickering firelight. The doctor cleared her throat and tried to straighten her aching shoulders.

Until the moment she said it, she didn't know what she was going to say. Then clear as the swath of stars over their heads, Julia declared, "We have to leave."

Alonzo jerked up in his hammock and stared at her in wonderment, but Julia ignored him and addressed her remarks to everyone. "Sure, I'd like to find a Fountain of Youth, a healing pool, as much as any of you. But none of us are seriously ill. We don't need to find it right away. There are serious questions about what kind of deal we would be making with the Terrians in order to use the pool. If it exists, and if we can find it."

She glanced at Yale. "We do have to think about the Ponce de León factor. A prolonged search for something that may not exist—that has only been seen in a dream—that could be a terrible way to squander our time."

She motioned to Devon. "In our hearts, we know she's right. There are millions of wonders on this planet, but we can't go tearing after each one of them. We need a base of operations. We need to *live* somewhere. And I think we should greet Dr. Vasquez and the children when they arrive. By then, think how much we'll know about G889 and her flora and fauna. Imagine how frightened they'll be of the Terrians, if we aren't there to explain."

She saw True pouting. The girl looked as if she wanted to interrupt her, but she held her tongue.

"I'm almost done," said Julia. "We don't know how long

these rival tribes have been fighting in this fashion—it could be centuries! I'd like to stop it, but I don't want to devote the rest of my life to stopping it. That's what it could take."

Julia sighed, and her shoulders slumped. "That's it. I'm with Devon and Alonzo—I want to move on. But I want to come back here someday, and I will."

"Everything Julia says makes sense," concluded Danziger. He put his arm around True's scrawny shoulders. "But let's not split the group up again. Let's just pick one direction or the other—up or downriver—and we'll walk until we find a place to go up. We'll find a way up for everything and everyone."

"Yeah!" said Alonzo in agreement. "This is a dangerous place—what happened to me could happen to anybody. If you got hurt, wouldn't you want all of us to be there to help you? I say we stay together."

Morgan gaped at them all and sputtered like a fish. Instead of saying anything, he spun on his heel and stalked off, with Bess scurrying after him.

Devon also looked as if she had some doubts. "I just want to say that traversing the bottom of the canyon could mean going considerably out of our way, plus wasting precious time doing it."

It was Yale who stepped to her side and pointed out, "United we stand; divided we fall."

"All right," Devon acceded. "But if the Terrians have any knowledge that would help us, I'd like to know it. Alonzo, Yale, anybody who thinks they can communicate with the Terrians—see if they know of a way up. All it has to be is an incline for the vehicles—I'm guessing we can find Koba paths all over the canyon. Even if they could just point us in the right direction, that would be a big help."

"I'll work on it," promised Alonzo.

"I'm going there now," said Yale, who promptly ambled off toward the darkened village.

Devon clapped her hands and announced, "Everyone, we're pulling out tomorrow!"

Some of them groaned, and Devon waved them down. "Listen, after we establish New Pacifica, anyone who wants to organize an expedition back here has my blessings and all the support the colony can muster. But this is a stop on our journey, not our home."

She clapped her hands. "Now let's get that fish stew going. Thanks to Mr. Baines and Zero, who had a very successful day off, we have fresh fish for dinner!"

The big crewman grinned, and the robot waved bashfully.

Twenty yards away, Morgan Martin fumed. He plopped down in front of his tent and shook his head. "Those idiots! Those fools! Talk about giving up a bird in the hand for who knows what in the bushes!"

Bess sat down beside him and rubbed his shoulders. "Don't get yourself upset, honey; they just have their own set of priorities. I think we should stay in the canyon too, to stop this terrible fighting between the Terrians. You just can't ignore something like that. This canyon is too beautiful for warfare."

"At least they can cure their injuries," muttered Morgan. "We can't even do that. And I was so close to finding out where the pool was, I'm sure of it."

"Do you think your friend was going to tell you about it tonight in your dreams?"

"Sure, he was. That Terrian loves me."

"It isn't fair," pouted Bess. "The Leather Wings want you to know where it is, but Devon won't let you find it, or go there. If I knew where it was, I'd have half a mind to go there, anyway."

Morgan blinked at her in surprise and jumped up to his knees. "What did you just say?"

"I said, I have half a mind to just go there, anyway. To heck with them."

Morgan grabbed his wife and kissed her. "You're beautiful, you know that?"

The curly-haired woman snuggled into his chest. "I like it when you tell me so."

"Yeah," said Morgan with excitement, "they can't stop us if we just go there. Take a few samples, post a claim marker, try out the pool. The caravan probably won't get under way until about mid-morning, and maybe we can be back by then. Nobody will be any the wiser."

He kissed Bess again, and she kissed him back. "Is it bedtime?" she asked with a glint in her eye.

"Yeah," he said enthusiastically, "it's bedtime."

Bess clasped her hands together.

"You stay out here," Morgan added.

She looked at him puzzledly. "I stay out here? You want to go in by yourself?"

"Right," answered Morgan, crawling into the tent.

"What am I supposed to do—out here?"

"Keep watch, silly," he answered from inside the tent. "Don't let anybody disturb me. I need to get to sleep. And *dream*."

Bess shrugged and muttered, "Fine. Pleasant dreams."

She shivered a bit and watched the campfire, but that looked too warm. Instead she looked up at the sky and gasped at the amazing array of stars, framed by the blackness of the canyon walls. They looked more or less like the stars one saw from space, thought Bess, but it seemed extraordinary to look at stars when you were trapped inside the bowels of the planet. It made the stars and the places they represented look even more faraway than usual.

Bess had always pretended to be nonchalant about space travel, saying she didn't mind the travel but she didn't care for the time commitments. Now that the option of space travel had been taken away from her, she found she missed it. She didn't miss it as much as poor Morgan did, but she missed the option of going to those faraway places—cities with stores, restaurants, casinos, theaters . . .

Stop! she told herself. That was another time, another existence, and this was her life for the present. At least it isn't boring, she reminded herself, and her feelings of kinship with the land were getting stronger every day.

Bess yawned and gazed back up at the star-studded sky, and that was when she saw them—the fleeting impressions of bodies moving against the stars. They were like shadows that move across a window blind. My gosh, she thought, if those were Leather Wings, they were flying awfully high up, near the rim of the canyon.

She couldn't remember how many shapes she had seen, and she tried to find them again in the night sky. But the velvet blackness had swallowed them up, and there weren't enough stars to make them visible again.

The young woman shivered, figuring it was all her imagination. That high up, it probably was birds.

Yale was greeted in the Leather Wings' village by silent looks and one or two nods of recognition. That was about as jovial as the Terrians got, he figured, and he was glad to be treated as a friend, not an enemy. He had seen how they treated their enemies.

The cyborg couldn't help but to feel that the Leather Wings were more subdued tonight than usual, after their ferocious battle. They must not have feared an attack at night from the rival tribe, because there were no guards in evidence. The only Terrians moving about were a few who were walking off their injuries.

The cyborg waited patiently in the center of the darkened village, wondering if the leader would come out to meet him. After a few moments, the venerable one crawled out of a hut, stood with difficulty, and limped over to him. Both elders possessed more than one lifetime's worth of experience, and it shone in both their eyes.

Yale wanted to ask the Leather Wing why they fought with the rival tribe, but he had a feeling that he wouldn't understand the answer. To outsiders, war never made any sense. To the combatants themselves, peace made no sense. It had never been put into words, but he felt as if the Leather Wings were embarrassed about the fighting their visitors had witnessed. He wondered how often they had tried to make peace with the rival tribe, and failed.

Despite the best intentions, it was only a pleasant sentiment that the humans would be able to mediate an end to the conflict. They could barely keep peace among their own small band! Yale reminded himself that escape from the canyon, not peace, was the knowledge he sought.

Unlike Alonzo, the cyborg wasn't in telepathic communication with the Terrians, nor was he very adept at sign language. But he had his own means of communication. As the Terrian looked on with interest, Yale projected a holographic image into the dark space between them.

Once again, he went back to stock images of twentieth-century half-tracks, tanks, and trucks. Only this time the vehicles were not parachuting from the sky but climbing up hills. Giant vehicles surged over one hill after another, ever upward. For variety, Yale mixed in footage of motorcycles climbing hills, people on foot, hovercraft, trains—anything he could think of to convey the idea that they wanted to get machines to climb out of the canyon.

At the end of this visual question, Yale showed an aerial view of the Grand Canyon on Earth. It wasn't quite as large or impressive as the Terrians' canyon, but he hoped it would show that he was looking for a specific place inside the canyon.

"Where?" asked Yale, as he turned off the holographic image.

The Terrian nodded and knelt to the ground, with obvious pain. Yale followed suit, and his old joints ached too. The cyborg watched with amazement as the Terrian put a claw into the sand and drew a wavering line. It had to represent the canyon, Yale thought to himself. The Leather Wing lifted his finger and drew another line connecting with the first, forming a crude Y in the sand. At the end of this shorter line, the Terrian drew a circle. Then he punched his fingernail into the center of the circle, as if to say *Right here.*

Yale motioned behind him in the direction the longer line seemed to be pointing. "If we go downriver," he said, "another canyon connects up with this main canyon? We should turn up the smaller canyon, and we'll find the spot where we can climb out?"

The Terrian said no more, but he stood and ambled back to his hut, as if there were no more he could do for the strangers.

"Thank you," said Yale. "I hope."

The cyborg started to leave, but he turned to look back at the primitive village. He wanted to do something for the Terrians, to give them something valuable in return for their help. But what could he do for them?

Yale looked down at the crude map scrawled in the sand

and shook his head. "I hope that will be good enough for Devon," he said.

Morgan waved to his Terrian friend in his dream, but the young Terrian didn't wave back. The being seemed preoccupied, saddened. It lifted off the ground, pumping with its great wings, but its energy seemed to be down. The light in the dream was all wrong too. It was daylight, in fact, when the dream should have been taking place at night. But Morgan told himself to relax and not to question the visions too deeply. His buddy would show him what he needed to know. He also had to remember that the Terrian had been shaken up in the fighting and might not be at its best.

By daylight, he could look for landmarks better, Morgan decided, and he needed to have landmarks. After the human came to that conclusion, his dream vision became clearer, but it still had the fuzzy feeling of a memory, not the sense of an immediate happening, as on the night before.

They were flying low in the canyon this time, sailing downriver to the spot where the party had descended on that dreadful trail. That gave Morgan a whole raft of landmarks to look for, and he giggled happily when he spotted each one. He could see the tracks on the beach where they had unsuccessfully tried to ford the river, only to get surprised by the Leather Wings. Then came the hill they had slid down on their butts, and the spires where that clumsy doctor had nearly killed them all.

After that, he was in virgin territory, and he tried to find new landmarks. He saw a small crater on the beach that might have been the spot where the others parachuted down in the TransRover. Farther along there was a distinctive archway on one side of the canyon, and a small but lovely meadow on the other side.

Then a major landmark yawned on his right: a second

canyon with a churning river that emptied into Martin River, causing riotous rapids. Curiously this river was all blue, not turquoise. He flew quickly by the gaping canyon, although something down that tributary exerted a strong tug on him.

Now he was angling toward the ground, the flight almost over. He certainly understood why the Leather Wings couldn't make this flight at night, except on special nights when the air currents were with them. He had a feeling that the Leather Wings came to the pool at night to prevent others from finding the way. At least, that's how he would work it, Morgan figured. That made it doubly special to be given the privilege of seeing the way to the grotto by daylight. Grudgingly, he realized he had to cut his Terrian friend in for a larger piece of the pie, but fair was fair. Besides, it wouldn't hurt to have an inside man with the Terrians.

He swooped down toward a small plateau, and he tried to remember every detail of it—its shape, color, even the bushes that grew around it. In the crisp daylight, he landed without complication, but the vision began to fade almost immediately. Before it left his mind, he scrambled down to a narrow but well-trod path, and he knew he could find the grotto from there. At that thought, the vision faded completely, and he was deep in normal sleep.

"Thanks, friend," his dream voice said.

He moved up to that restful state between sleep and wakefulness, and it was tempting to stay there. But Morgan knew he couldn't afford any more sleep—not when there was fame and fortune to be won!—so he forced himself awake. He rolled over and grabbed his flashlight, canteen, and the provisions he had packed the night before. Then he cautiously stuck his head out of the tent.

There was a definite nip in the night air, and it tickled the hair in his nose. A huge mound of blankets lay off to one side of the tent flap, with geysers of steam shooting out of one corner of it. There wasn't anything left of the campfire but a sparkling echo. Carefully he shook Bess's shoulder, trying not to startle her too much. She was prepared to be rousted, however, and she blinked at him with a game smile.

"Did it happen?" she asked.

"You bet it did." He gave her a wink. "We're gonna be rich, and live forever."

"And save the Terrians."

"And save the Terrians," he grumbled under his breath. "I've got everything we need right here. We'd better get going—it may be a long walk. Is anybody awake to spot us leaving?"

"Just Zero. The last time I looked, Devon had posted him way over there, toward the village." Bess yawned and cast off the blankets in favor of her jacket.

"Great," whispered Morgan. "I don't see him coming. Let's go." He squirmed out of the tent.

"Should we just leave everything?"

"Sure. We'll have a good head start. So what if they know we're gone?"

It was easy to be noiseless in the sand along the river, and Morgan chuckled to himself as he and Bess made a clean escape from the camp along Martin River.

Chapter 13

Ah, thought Devon Adair, splashing some cool river water onto her face, it was a glorious morning! The red sun was just reaching down through the buttes to touch the river, and the morning held the promise of new discoveries, new ways of doing things. She was even adjusted to the idea of just striking off down the canyon, hoping for the best. The vehicles had come down in an unorthodox manner, and maybe they would go up the same way. At least they would be moving out, and as long as they were moving, there was hope they would greet the children when they arrived at New Pacificia.

She took a last look around the canyon, wondering if she would ever see such unspoiled beauty again. Despite all the pleasant feelings she held for the canyon, it still felt great to be moving out. In a strange way, the aerial battle between the Terrian tribes had been a blessing for the survivors. It reminded them of two things: No place was paradise, and if you want to build anything close to a paradise, you must be willing to fight for it.

They also had to remember that the Terrians were complex, mysterious creatures. There was no way they could interpret what they had seen yesterday afternoon. To become deeply involved with Terrian affairs might be a mistake that would haunt them for years. Of course, there were always people like Morgan Martin, who didn't care what effect their dealings had on native cultures. Morgan would just have to find some other way to get rich, Devon decided, because they were leaving the canyon without plundering it.

She heard footsteps crunching toward her in the brown, dew-crusted sand, and she turned to see Yale, who also looked rested and ready to hit the trail. The cyborg's creased face smiled at her.

"I think we've been pointed in the right direction," he claimed happily.

"Oh, yeah! Which way?"

The cyborg pointed. "Downriver. Past the spot where we came down, there's another canyon which joins this one. I've been told that we're supposed to go up the tributary."

Devon smiled. "Who told you this? The G889 Tourist Bureau?"

"No," he answered, "I used simple visual aids to ask my question of the Terrians. But I would say it's worth a try to go downriver, wouldn't you? Besides, this second canyon actually turns off our side of the river and heads more in the direction of New Pacifica, so we can't go wrong."

"If this other canyon exists," Devon pointed out. She finally sighed and shook her head. "I guess everyone is right—we just have to choose a direction and go. Before we make up our minds, let's see if Alonzo had any contact with the Leather Wings."

As she strode through the quiet camp with Yale at her side, Devon had a desire to shriek "Wake up!" at everybody. But the colonists needed their rest; emotionally as well as physically they were burned out. The descent had been hard enough, and then to find a serene paradise with a Fountain of Youth, only to see the serenity of the canyon marred by warfare—it had left all of them drained. So let the colonists sleep. They weren't likely to travel twelve miles today, anyway, so there was no rush.

Alonzo saw them coming and waved. He looked chipper too, Devon thought. For once, she began to think that giving them a day off had actually paid off.

"Top o' the mornin' to you," said Alonzo with a jaunty salute.

"Sleep well?" asked Devon.

"Yes, I did," yawned Alonzo. "Best sleep in weeks—no dreams."

"Oh," said Devon, a bit crestfallen. "You don't know which direction we should go?"

"Haven't a clue," Alonzo said and beamed. "Why don't you ask Morgan?"

Yale broke in, "I had a conversation of sorts with the leader of the Leather Wings, and he drew me a map in the sand. I think he was trying to tell me that there's a smaller canyon downriver that intersects this one. I think we're supposed to go up the smaller canyon to find a way out."

The pilot shook his head helplessly. "I don't know anything about it." Then he snapped his fingers and squinted thoughtfully at the sky. "Wait a minute, that's not exactly true. In my very first dream about this place, the night before we actually saw it, I remember there being another canyon intersecting this one. But I couldn't tell you where it was."

"Well," said Devon, "that sounds like another vote for going downriver to look for this second canyon. I hate to ask him, but let's see what Morgan says."

"I'm ready to pull out when you are," said Alonzo encouragingly.

"Great." Devon gave him a thumbs-up.

She felt so good that she doubted if even Morgan Martin could bring her down this morning. She strode over to the tent he shared with Bess and figured they were already awake; there was a pile of blankets outside the tent.

"Morgan!" she called. "Hello, Morgan?"

When he didn't answer, she tried his better half. "Bess! Bess, are you in there?"

When no one answered, she peered inside the tent, only to find it empty and as disheveled as the pile of blankets on the ground. Now she cupped her hands and yelled loudly:

"Bess Martin! Morgan Martin! Where are you?"

Her bellow was enough to wake all those who were still trying to delay the inevitable. John Danziger, Julia Heller, True, Uly, and the others emerged sleepily from their tents and blinked at her. Devon wandered through the camp, staring into their dazed faces, wondering if, for some bizarre reason, Bess and Morgan had slept in the wrong tent. But, no, all the tents were inhabited by those who should have been inhabiting them. She saw Zero running toward them from the Terrian village.

Julia asked, "Is something wrong?"

"We've lost Morgan and Bess. Anybody seen them?"

John Danziger was still tucking in his shirt and buttoning his pants when he ran up to her. "What do you mean you've lost them? Bess and Morgan are *missing*?"

"Let's put it this way," answered Devon through clenched teeth, "we don't know where they are."

As Zero plodded toward her, she demanded, "Have you seen Bess or Morgan Martin?"

"No, sir," the robot answered, cocking his oblong head puzzledly.

"They didn't go to the village?" she asked. "To look around, or take a shower in the waterfall?"

"They did not pass my way," the robot reported. "Trust me."

Devon was getting a feeling in her stomach as if she had spent too much time at zero gravity. "You don't suppose they went to look for the sacred pool?"

"Oh, no," muttered Yale, putting his hand on his head.

"Damn!" growled Danziger.

From afar, Alonzo shouted, "Look on the bright side—maybe they were kidnapped!"

Devon was seething inside, but she rubbed her face and tried to compose herself. "All right," she said calmly, "they didn't go toward the village, which is upriver, so they must have gone downriver. We have no idea how much head start they got, but it could be considerable."

She ran back to Morgan and Bess's tent and began to look for tracks in the crunchy sand. "Stay back," she ordered the others, not wanting a rush of misguided helpers to obliterate the tracks. Recent rains and heavy dew had left the sand wet enough still to hold footprints, and she quickly found some likely candidates—shod feet, a small set and a large set.

Devon kept following the footprints all the way down the beach, and they showed no sign of disappearing quickly. She put her hands on her slim hips and headed back toward the others.

"We're going after them," she vowed. "They may have a head start, but we've got the smaller vehicles. Yale, you and

Zero take the ATV. Danziger, you and I will go in the DuneRail."

The three of them nodded and ran off to get the vehicles, while Devon turned her attention to the doctor. "Julia, I'm putting you in charge of breaking camp and loading the TransRover. We'll be in Gear contact, but since we're all going the same direction, I would suggest you pack up and follow us as soon as you're ready."

"Fine," nodded Julia. "What about saying good-bye to the Terrians?"

Devon looked toward the TransRover to see Alonzo, who was watching them from his hammock with a disgusted but knowing look on his face. She took several steps in his direction and stopped. "Alonzo, we have to leave. Can you find a way to say good-bye to our friends?"

The injured pilot nodded. "I'll try."

"Tell them that we appreciate all their help, but we must go. Tell them, if we can manage it at all, we'll find a way to return here someday."

"I'll tell them," promised Alonzo.

Devon heard one of the vehicles roar to life, and she turned to see Danziger in the driver's seat, waiting expectantly for her. She saw Yale position Zero's head on the controls of the other ATV, then the cyborg took a seat beside the headless robot.

As Devon strode to the DuneRail, she slammed her fist into her palm with determination. "All right, people!" she shouted. "Get something to eat, get packed, then get moving! Leave Morgan and Bess to *us*!"

Morgan Martin was whistling a cheery song as he strolled along the riverbank. He gazed up to admire the lovely morning sun glimmering off the jagged peaks and the fanciful, striped bluffs of the canyon. Then he looked down to admire his wife, who was strolling leisurely about ten yards ahead of him. Somehow, striking out on their own had made him feel like a new man! No longer was he dependent on those ungrateful and unrealistic do-gooders. Walk three thousand miles, indeed, when the miracle of the ages was right at hand! I am done suffering fools, thought Morgan confidently.

Of course, there were some problems to be solved with the Fountain of Youth, mainly marketing. How could he get word back to the people who counted? How on earth do you advertise something when you can't even get a message out? He had discovered the Fountain of Youth, or would in due course, but for him to return, somebody would have to rescue him off this planet.

That was it, Morgan decided, he had to take the secret of the pool's whereabouts away with him, and hold onto it until he was rescued. Then he would reveal it to the right people and return with the equipment, scientists, and funding needed to make it happen. Scientists were needed to write those glowing articles for medical journals—articles he could point to when people questioned his claims about the pool. Yes, it would all work out, he assured himself, given patience and the proper long-term planning. But it wasn't a bad deal—until the money started rolling in, he and Bess could look forward to living forever!

These pleasant thoughts were augmented by a memory of his dream from the night before: There he was, sailing above the canyon once again, picking out the landmarks he had seen from the ground the first time. From the ground, he ought to be able to pick them out again. He expected to see the first of the landmarks, the spot where they had met the Leather Wings, any moment. That would be on the other side of the river, he reminded himself, so he would have to look a bit harder for it.

After that, he would begin to look for the area they had climbed down, then the place where the vehicles had parachuted down, then the meadow, and the archway. He would really know he was close when he saw the second canyon empty into Martin River. That would be on this side of the river. Then he could start to look for the plateau on the other side of the river, where he had landed in his dream. From there, he would find the path, the grotto, and the pool . . .

Morgan stopped, stricken, and let his mouth hang open. "Oh, no," he groaned with sudden realization.

"What's the matter?" asked Bess, not sounding too worried as she twirled on her heel and began skipping through the sand.

"The river," Morgan moaned. "The river! We're on the *wrong side* of the river!"

Bess stopped and peered at him. "What are you talking about?"

Morgan motioned desperately at the raging expanse of turquoise water. "Don't you see, the second river joins the big river on *this* side, and we're going to get stuck at the confluence! We can't cross there—it's nothing but ferocious rapids. The only place we know we can cross safely is miles away, back at the village!"

"Okay, okay, calm down," said Bess. "What do you want to do? Go back?"

"No!" shrieked Morgan. "Not after we've come this far. The others must know we're gone by now, and they'd never let us just go back there, cross the river, and head on our merry way. If they had their way, we'd never get another chance to find the pool!"

Bess put her hand over her eyes and peered at the river. "Well, there's only the two of us—no kids or vehicles to worry about. Can't we just swim across?"

"I don't know," said Morgan thoughtfully. He looked back and saw the clear-cut line of footprints he and Bess had been leaving without giving it a second thought. "You know, if they came after us, crossing the river would be a good way to lose them."

"And a good way to get a bath," Bess added.

Morgan frowned miserably. "It still was a dumb thing to forget."

Bess put her arm around her husband and smiled encouragingly. "What else could we have done, honey? We wouldn't have wanted to get all wet in the middle of the night—we would've froze to death! It's much better to get wet now, while the sun is out and will dry us off."

"Yeah," answered Morgan, beginning to feel better about what still seemed a bone-headed mistake. What he didn't want to do was to compound that dumb mistake with an even bigger one. He looked warily at the river and saw a large piece of driftwood whiz by. The swift current bobbled the wood like a juggler for twenty yards and finally pushed it under, never to be seen again.

He gulped. "Do you really think we could do it? You're a good swimmer, but I'm not."

Bess looked around and picked up a piece of sun-baked driftwood. "If we collect enough of this stuff, we can be sure you'll float."

"Yeah," said Morgan. "And I brought some rope. Let's rope ourselves together, so we won't be separated."

"How romantic," replied Bess.

With Bess's unerring instincts for finding good wood, Morgan soon had a veritable life preserver made out of big chunks of driftwood and tied together with rope. He tied the bundle of wood to his chest, leaving just enough rope for Bess to tie one end around her waist. She would only be about ten feet away from him, Morgan told himself, and she would always be in contact.

"Listen," said Bess, tiptoeing to the edge of the river and peering into its turquoise depths, "we've got to jump in together. I'll be swimming hard, and you'll have to do as well as you can to keep up. If either one of us makes it to the other side, we'll be fine."

Morgan gulped. "And if we don't?"

She shrugged. "You're the one who wants to find the fountain, not me."

"Okay," growled Morgan, stiffening his shoulders. "Bess, sweetheart, I love you."

She gave him a warm hug. "I wouldn't do this for a man I only liked."

With Morgan holding his nose, they jumped into the freezing water.

It numbed Morgan's entire body, and he had no idea how he was supposed to move, or even know he was moving, let alone swim for shore. A wave splashed over his head, completely drenching him, and he became vaguely aware of how fast they were moving in the current—the bank was a blur! To keep from getting sick, he looked up and tried to focus on the towering buttes of the canyon.

With his body numb and tied securely to a life vest made of driftwood, Morgan just floated along. He found himself getting into the rhythms of the current, which carried him along like a bullet train. He was gazing up at the bright blue of the sky when he felt a tug on the rope tied to his waist. When he didn't respond, the tug came harder, pulling him under for a moment.

"Hey!" he sputtered. "Watch it!"

"We're going to die, you idiot!" Bess shouted back. "Start swimming! Got to make the other side!"

"It's cold!"

"I know!" she shrieked. "Try to think about the rapids up ahead, and the rocks!" When Morgan moved sluggishly, she added, "And the fish!"

He recalled their first day in the canyon, when that horrible, scaly behemoth had come flopping toward them, its jaws snapping ferociously. That image got Morgan's arms and legs pumping. He was amazed to find that there was some feeling left in his limbs, and he was soon slapping the water in an imitation of swimming. After a few minutes, he looked back at the near bank and noticed that they were almost halfway across the river. That gave him heart, until he realized it was more a function of the runaway current, rather than anything they were doing.

He tried to find Bess, and he saw her swimming gamely for the other side. Although she looked very determined as she plowed through the water, she couldn't get out of the center of the river. The current pushed everything to the center, and they bumped up against more driftwood and clumps of sodden reeds. He saw a black shadow move briefly beside him in the water, then it was gone. He tried to hold still so as not to alert the creature, although he felt guilty when he wasn't at least trying to swim.

It didn't matter, anyway. Bess was swimming her heart out, but she had stopped making progress toward the other shore. The current was just too insistent on taking everything straight down the middle.

Morgan suddenly knew that they were going to die. They were going to get crushed on some rocks, eaten by fish, or shoved so far under by rapids that they wouldn't be found for centuries! By then this whole area would be built up as the Fountain of Youth Health Spa, probably owned by Devon Adair! He would be left out once again. If he had nothing else to show for his life, at least he wanted to die with Bess in his arms. He was awfully proud of her.

"Bess!" he called. "Give it up! Come back, and hang onto this wood with me!"

"We'll die!" she screamed.

"That was bound to happen on this stupid planet!" he yelled back. "I love you!"

"I love you too!" Wearily, she started swimming toward him, but she had only gotten a few strokes when something abruptly yanked at the ropes and snapped Morgan backward like a rubber band.

"Whaaa!" he screamed, thinking a fish had gotten him, but he plowed into a rock a moment later and was saved only by the bundle of driftwood tied to his chest. It splintered and cracked away from his body as he gripped desperately onto the rock. When he realized he wasn't dead yet, he started screaming.

"Bess! Bess! Where are we? Bess!"

"Morgan!" He heard her voice, shrill and surprised. "I'm on the other side! Over here!"

He looked up and realized that their rope had become entangled with a boulder in the center of the river. Bess had shot past one side of the rock, and he had gone down the other. Only the rope was holding them to the boulder. He could touch the top of the rock, but he couldn't see over it. He was glad to hear that Bess sounded all right.

This had to be a break for them, he figured, because where there was one rock, there were usually more rocks. If they had hit this boulder head-on instead of slipping to the side, the ride would've been over. If only he could get a handhold and climb over the top, Morgan told himself, then he could rescue Bess. And then what?

He struggled against his ropes, but he was effectively pinned against the rock by the stiff current and the remains of his life vest. He didn't want to scream for help, but he didn't know how the heck he was going to get Bess out of this scrape. He wanted to calm her at least, to tell her . . . to tell her what? That he'd been a damn fool? That he and Ponce De León had been a couple of saps!

He started to snivel. "Bess, Bess, I'm sorry! I'm sorry! Forgive me!"

"It's okay," her voice said quite plainly. He craned his neck backward to look up, and he gaped with amazement. Bess was standing on the top of the rock, looking down at him!

She was drenched to the bone and had several cuts and scrapes on her, but nothing serious. She wasn't smiling as much as he was, maybe because she could see how much of a mess *he* was in.

"I was lucky," she said over the rushing water. "I got pushed around into a depression in the rock, and I had room to move. But I don't know what I'm going to do with you."

Morgan groaned and struggled against his ropes. "If only I could move around . . ." Suddenly his efforts had an effect, and he started to shift. In fact, he started to float away! Bess dived to her stomach and grabbed the collar of his jacket.

She screamed, "I can't hold you! Get around to the back of the rock and hold on!"

Morgan didn't need to be told to move quickly. At that moment he was in desperate fear of leaving Bess a young widow with people like Alonzo and Danziger around. He clutched for all he was worth the tiny pockmarks carved into the rock by erosion, and Bess was finally able to release him. He caught his breath, expecting to be swept away, but his fingers held their grip on the boulder. He grunted with exertion as he pawed his way to the rear of the rock, where the rapid flow of water slackened somewhat in its rush to get around the rock. Bess was in front of him, extending a hand, and he crawled up on the rock like a prehistoric fish crawling out of the water for first time, gasping and slobbering.

That's about what he looked like too, and Bess howled with laughter and relief. "Wow!" she exclaimed. "When we go on an adventure, we go on an *adventure*!"

Morgan lay clinging to the rock, gasping for breath, for several moments before he was able to feel the rest of his body. Lord, it felt good to be in the sun instead of the water, and he could slowly feel the nerves awakening in his legs. They were howling with pain, and his legs felt like accordions when he tried to stand up on them. Bess had to steady him.

"Are you okay?" she asked.

"Yeah," he croaked. "Now what?" He looked around and nearly passed out when he saw where they were. By almost total accident they had gotten marooned at a bend in the river, where the river jackknifed away from the rock. It positioned them almost two-thirds of the way across! There was only about another thirty feet to go before the water swhirled into eddies and little pools along the bank. Only thirty feet, he thought to himself, but it might as well be *three hundred* feet.

"What do we do?" he moaned.

"Well, you don't want to live on this rock the rest of your life, do you? I think we can make it to the shore now, but we've got to jump as far off the rock as we can, and swim like crazy for it."

He gulped. "Swim for it?"

She took his shoulders in her firm hands. "The rope is gone, the driftwood is gone—you've got nothing but your arms and legs. But you can do it! I have faith in you, honey, that's why I've followed you this far."

He wanted to match her bravery, but he didn't really feel brave anymore. He felt sick and exhausted. Then he looked back in the other direction and saw a hundred feet of icy, careening water. Even if someone came along to rescue them, an unlikely prospect, how could they attempt a rescue without equipment that just plain didn't exist on G889? No, it really was just his two arms and legs, as Bess had said.

"Can you go first?" he asked sheepishly.

"I will," she said with a smile. "But once I jump off this rock, I'm not coming back. Not even for you, sweetie. Once we jump off this rock, it's the other side, or nowhere."

"I know," he said. "I would just feel better seeing you do it first."

"Okay," she said, rubbing her arms together. "The secret is to jump as far as you can, because that's a lot of distance you don't have to swim. You will be watching me, right?"

"I'm watching." He gave her one final kiss. "I love you."

"I love you too," she assured him. "Ready?"

"Ready."

Without a moment's hesitation, Bess leapt off the rock like an Olympic swimmer and hit the water almost in a belly flop. At once her arms and legs churned, and her momentum carried her a few more feet. The swift current whisked her far downriver, even as she kept making progress toward the bank. Morgan could barely see her now in the distance, but she never let up. She did a sweeping butterfly stroke over a curl in the water, and that seemed to be the last hurdle. He cheered himself hoarse as she staggered into one of the small eddies and dragged herself out of the water.

After a moment, she stood to look back at him, and she shook her head in disbelief, surprised at how far the current had carried her.

"Come on!" she yelled. "You can do it!"

"Riches, fame, living forever," Morgan chanted to himself. "Riches, fame, living forever. Don't forget Bess. There's a lot to live for, dammit!"

With that thought, he hurled himself off the rock. When he struck the icy water, he didn't wait to let it numb him—he grabbed a big lungful of air and paddled and kicked like a fish in frenzy. He thought he heard Bess's voice, cheering him on, but with water pounding in his ears he couldn't tell for sure. He just kicked his feet and slapped his arms as fast as he could, trying to envision championship swimmers churning down the home stretch.

Morgan didn't even stop to look where he was, figuring that if he didn't make it, it didn't matter. His lifeless body was probably going to flow all the way to some ocean. He kept pounding the water long after his endurance was spent, until a miraculous thing happened—his madly kicking foot hit something hard. It was the bank! The bank!

He stopped swimming, thinking he could stand up, and that was a mistake. The current tried to suck him back into the center of the river. He started to panic, but then he felt a firm grip on his arm and the sensation of being pulled.

"Thank you!" he moaned. He rolled over to look at Bess, who he assumed was rescuing him, and he came face-to-face with one of those monstrous fish—its slobbery, barbed mouth was wrapped around his forearm! The fish was pulling him all right—into a shallow pool where it could have its way with him. To keep from getting his arm shredded to pieces, he stumbled along with the fish, all the time shrieking:

"Bess! Bess!"

"I'm coming!" she called. He saw her running along the bank, kicking up sand. With a murderous gleam in her eyes, she drew a small knife and leapt into the swirling water. Morgan was close to fainting, but he tried to hold the fish's head up. Bess didn't disappoint him—she stabbed the big fish right behind its gills, and blood swirled in the water. He could feel a loosening of the grip on his arm as she ripped into the fish again and again. Finally, the monstrous creature slapped the water with its tail and rose up like a Leviathan, but Bess smashed it in the jaw with her fist.

Morgan was bleeding from his arm, but he was free! He was also in a place where the current was weak enough that he could find his footing. So he staggered and stumbled toward the bank and dragged himself ashore. He looked back to make sure Bess was coming after him, although he didn't know what he would do if she needed rescuing. He could hardly hold his head off the sand.

She staggered ashore behind him and slumped to the beach beside him, her arm draped across his back. For what seemed like hours, they lay there, panting, not thinking of anything. The warm sun had a salutary effect, and Morgan was actually able to lift his head and gaze at her.

"Did I ever tell you I love you?" he asked.

"All the time," she said and tousled his wet hair. "How's your arm?"

He held it up to look at it. His shirtsleeve was bloody and torn, but it had given him some protection. When he rolled up the sleeve, he could see a neat arc of teeth marks on both the top and bottom of his forearm, and he thought he was going to faint again.

"It doesn't look too bad," Bess observed. "Clean wounds, not too deep. I think they should scab by themselves, and I don't think you need a tourniquet."

"My God, Bess!" he moaned. "I need a *hospital*!"

"I guess those things feed in the shallows," she said thoughtfully. "They drag their prey to the quieter pools to feed. It makes sense."

"Please," groaned Morgan. "Do you have to talk about them like you *admire* them?"

"I do admire them," she said pleasantly. "They're perfectly suited to their environment. Do you think the sacred pool would help you?"

"Yes, yes!" he shouted, staggering to his feet. "Nothing can stop us now. Let's go!"

Anger drove Devon Adair on as she plowed the DuneRail through one sand drift after another, giving her passenger several severe jolts.

"Watch it!" yelled Danziger. "When I let you drive, I didn't know you would try to kill us!"

"If it's too rough for you," she answered testily, "you can go back with the others."

"Thanks, maybe I will," he grumbled. "Are you still following their tracks?"

"I don't care about their tracks. They had to have come this way."

"Wait a minute," he cautioned. "Let's stop to make sure. What if the sacred pool is around here somewhere? Maybe they went up into the rocks. You know there are caves around here."

"All right." She slammed on the brakes, giving him another bounce, and the vehicle spun to a stop in the sand. "Go take a look," she ordered.

"Okay, I will." Danziger welcomed the chance to climb out of the DuneRail, stretch his legs, and get away from that madwoman. Devon Adair was certainly not the person you wanted to cross, if you had any brains at all. He saw Yale and Zero behind them in the ATV, keeping a much more sensible pace, and he held up his arms to stop them. When they slowed to a stop, Danziger went jogging toward them.

"Have you two seen their tracks lately?" he asked.

"I don't know," answered Yale. "We've been too busy trying to keep up with *you*."

Danziger sighed. "Let's take a look for those tracks."

He and Yale got out and explored the sand along the riverbank. Unfortunately, the tracks of the vehicles had disturbed a lot of ground, so they finally ended up walking past the spot where Devon had parked the DuneRail. Danziger stared at the sand and began to worry that the sun had dried it to the point where the tracks would have been obliterated, anyway. Either that or Morgan and Bess had made a detour at some point. At any rate, the footprints were no longer there, and they had been as clear as the turquoise water when they had started out that morning.

"They're gone," he told Devon. "The tracks are gone."

"That's impossible," she said, hopping out of the DuneRail and looking around. "Where could they have gone?"

"I don't know," admitted Danziger. "I only know that we were following some tracks, and those tracks are now gone."

Yale pointed out, "Unless somebody carried Bess and Morgan off, there's only two places they could have gone—up the side of the canyon, or into the water."

"Arrgh!" screamed Devon, crumpling her hat in her hand and throwing it to the ground. "I'm going to kill them when I find them!"

"If they're not already dead," Yale pointed out. "Danziger is right—we have to backtrack and try to find the exact spot where their tracks ended."

On foot, Danziger began to retrace their steps. "Bring the vehicles up behind me." He glared at Devon and added, "Slowly."

"Look!" shouted Morgan, pointing excitedly into the distance. "White water! That could mean the second canyon!"

"All right!" echoed Bess, brushing back her curly hair. "And look up there." She pointed even higher.

In the staggering panorama of the sunlit canyon, Morgan

had difficulty spotting them at first. Finally he saw the four flyers darting about, far beyond the confluence of the two rivers. Only someone who had seen the Leather Wings swoop through the air would know they weren't birds. Plus, he was finally getting used to the weird perspectives and amazing distances of the canyon, and he realized how high up they were.

"Boy, am I glad to see them," he croaked. "Give me some of that water."

Bess handed him the canteen. "I would've thought you'd had enough water by now. What are they doing?"

"Maybe they're guarding the pool, like they're always stationed here."

"No, they haven't been here that long," said Bess. "I saw them crossing over last night. They were flying high, I can tell you."

"Last night?" asked Morgan, peering into the distance. "But they were from the village, right?"

Bess shrugged. "I don't know. I don't think if they flew from the village, they could've gotten up that high."

Morgan chuckled nervously. "Well, they wouldn't be, like, enemy Terrians, would they?"

Bess shook her head and squinted into the distance. Morgan noticed that her hand went to the hilt of the knife stuck in her belt. He turned to take a closer look for himself at the flying Terrians in the distance, and he noticed that their random flight patterns had stopped. They had decided upon a course.

They were headed directly toward him and Bess.

Chapter 14

"Okay, this is it," said Danziger, kneeling down and poking a stick into some damp impressions in the ground along the river. "Their last tracks. You can see where they stood around, probably deciding what to do. Since there are no tracks going toward the rocks, I guess they jumped in."

Devon Adair loomed over him, her hands on her slim hips. "They're braver, or crazier, than I thought they were. This couldn't be a ruse, could it? They might want to throw us off by leaving these tracks for us to find, while they cover their real tracks."

"I don't think so," said Danziger, gazing around the canyon. "They threw us off plenty by just crossing over the river. If that's what they did, and if they didn't drown."

"We could spread out and look for them in the rocks," Yale suggested.

Devon scratched her head and stared at the far bank of the river; it was not so far away as the Terrian flies, but it was a long, dangerous swim. She had underestimated how badly Morgan Martin wanted to discover that Fountain of Youth. She would try not to underestimate him again.

"The others will be along here soon," she said, "and they can look for them in the rocks. We have to get across."

"The only place we know we can cross safely is just before the village," Yale reminded her.

"Okay," said Devon, jutting her jaw. "So what do we do, go all the way back there? Or just forget about them?"

She gazed at Danziger, and then Yale, but it was Zero's head, stuck on the hood of the ATV, who spoke up: "If they were robots, you would forget about them."

Morgan rubbed the back of his hand over his dry lips and squinted into the sky. The four Terrians were gradually winging their way toward them; there was no doubt about that. He wanted to wave and greet them, but they looked to be all business as the steady, unhurried movement of their wings brought them ever closer.

"What do they want?" asked Bess.

"How do I know?" snapped Morgan.

"Well, you talk to them in your sleep. Find out what they want." She gave him a shove forward.

"What if they don't want us to go to the secret pool?" he asked.

"We'd better find that out now, shouldn't we?"

Morgan forced himself to wave. "Hello there! Hello!" he crooned like the official greeter at a funeral.

He didn't know exactly why, but he had an uneasy feeling about this. He wanted to discover the Fountain of Youth alone with Bess, not with an escort. He wouldn't mind going with his friend, but the young Terrian was still licking his wounds. None of these high-flying Terrians could be his friend, who'd barely had enough energy to dream last night. When Morgan thought about it, he couldn't imagine that any of the Terrians from the village had been in good enough shape to fly here last night. They had exhausted every flyer by repelling the attack.

Of course, he didn't know about the enemy tribe of Terrians. Perhaps they had held some flyers back in reserve. Maybe the bold, daylight attack was a subterfuge, not expected to succeed but only to exhaust the villagers who stood in their way. Maybe the real plan was for four brave flyers to pass over the village in the dead of night, extremely high up. Then they would stake out the area where they suspected the sacred pool to be, and wait for somebody to show up who was going there.

It was a good plan, like something Morgan might have thought of. That really worried him, and he began to back up toward Bess.

"Aren't you going to communicate with them?" she asked.

"I think I just did."

The flyers were about a hundred yards away and closing rapidly. There was no place to run, so Morgan drew Bess to his chest and held her protectively. He tried to remember how frightened he had been when they first saw the flying Terrians, and how wrong he had been about them. There was no difference this time, he told himself, but then he caught sight of the reed sashes stretched like X's across their bony chests.

"These aren't our Leather Wings!" he said in a panic, but it was too late. The creatures pumped their wings hard and seemed to drop from the sky. They landed at a dead run and immediately got into a defensive crouch with their wings outstretched. Forming a fence with their wings, they encircled the frightened humans, and the fence grew smaller with every step they took. Like all Terrians, their faces were a nightmarish combination of fangs, beady eyes, and sunken cheeks. More frightening, they had a wariness and hatred about their pale eyes that said they were confronting the enemy. One of them made hissing sounds, and another shook its wings menacingly as it moved closer.

Morgan laughed nervously. "We're friends! You know, *friends*!"

He lifted his arm to wave, and one Terrian jumped up and snapped a mouthful of teeth at him. Another reached out to paw Bess with its wing, and she slapped the wing away. That brought a growl that sounded like a cornered lion, and the Terrian rose to its full height of about seven feet. It prodded her again with its wing, and she pulled out her knife.

"Careful," gasped Morgan. "What are you doing?"

"We have two choices," she answered, "fight or run."

Morgan craned his neck to look over the outstretched wings of their tormentors. "The rocks are too far away—we'd never make it."

"What about the water? They won't go there."

Morgan glanced at the coursing river and shivered. He was about to say no, when one of the Terrians unstrapped its wings and set them carefully in the sand. Then it held up a monstrous, clawed hand and began to reach for Morgan's face.

"Okay, run!" shouted the bureaucrat. He slammed into a Terrian's outstretched wing and spun the creature around, and Bess lunged at another with her knife. The flyers hissed and fought back, but their wings made it difficult for them to catch the smaller humans, who slipped between them and ran toward the water.

"Just stay in the shallow parts!" Bess yelled.

Morgan was only a few feet away from safety in the water when something grabbed him from behind and wrestled him to the ground. It was the Terrian who had removed its wings, and it was amazingly strong and agile for its cadaverous appearance. It pushed Morgan's face into the sand as if to smother him.

"Bess!" he croaked.

But she had her own problems. Morgan could see her waist-deep in the water, struggling to keep her balance while three Terrians menaced her. In desperation, she began to splash them, and that sent the creatures stumbling backward. She directed a well-aimed splash at Morgan's tormentor, hitting it directly in the face. It screeched like a banshee and clutched its face, allowing Morgan to squirm out from underneath. He dashed a few feet and rolled into the water, where Bess grabbed him and tried to keep him from being swept away.

The cold numbness began to take over his body again, and Morgan wondered how long he would be able to fight the current. He was also thinking about the hideous fish, and their tendency to feed in the shallows.

The Terrians weren't seriously injured, but they were seriously angry. They regrouped on the bank, far enough away to keep from getting splashed. Apparently, thought Morgan, they were content to wait the insane humans out.

"From the f-frying pan into the fire," he said through chattering teeth.

Bess stumbled and just managed to grab some roots before she was sucked into the current. "What can we do?" she moaned.

Suddenly, a bright fireball went zipping over their heads into the midst of the Terrians, who scattered like bowling pins. They screeched and flapped their wings as they hopped toward the rocks. The one who had left its wings in the sand went back for them, and another fireball zoomed over its head and sent it scurrying.

"They're flares!" gasped Bess.

Morgan whirled around to see the ATV parked along the far bank; Yale was standing beside it, holding a flare gun. The bureaucrat shrieked with happiness, nearly losing his balance and getting sucked away with the current. Finally, it was Bess who had enough sense to climb onto the bank and grab him by the collar. For the third time that afternoon, they hauled themselves out of icy water and lay panting and drenched in the soothing sun.

Morgan looked up to see two of the Terrians hurl themselves into the sky and flap their wings as if demons pursued them. The other two were still climbing up the canyon bluffs, trying to find a suitable place from which to launch themselves.

"Hey!" shouted Yale from the other side of the river. "What's the matter with you? What do you think you're doing?"

"Going to find the Fountain of Youth!" Morgan called back. "Thanks for the assist!"

He staggered to his feet and pulled Bess to her feet. "Come on, honey, let's go. He's on the other side—what can he do to stop us?" Stealing a look back at Yale and the ATV, Morgan grabbed Bess's arm and set off downriver.

On the other side, Yale shook his head and turned on his Gear. "Devon?"

"I'm here Yale."

"We found them," reported Yale. "They're on your side of the river. You were right to send us along this side while you doubled back and crossed."

"Of course," she said, "I'm always right. Can you reason with them, tell them to come back?"

"Negative," answered the cyborg. "But we're in sight of

the confluence of the second canyon. So that part of our information is correct."

"Good," answered Devon. "You might as well stay there and wait for the others. They should be there soon."

"Be alerted," said Yale, "there are four Terrians from the rival tribe in this area. I had to chase them away from Morgan and Bess."

"Adair out."

Danziger rolled his eyes at the driver of the DuneRail as it bounced through the sand. "That's just what you need—an excuse to put the pedal to the floor."

"You just watch," said Devon, her eyes burning with determination. "I'm going to get that crazy idiot, and he's gonna wish he *had* drowned!"

"Might be he actually knows where he's going," said Danziger. "What if there is a Fountain of Youth? That is why you came here—to find natural healing methods that our sanitized culture has lost."

"That's why," she agreed. "But we need that base of operations first. I've learned something from this trip through the canyon—that we need everybody to make our colony. That means even Morgan Martin and the sick children who are on their way. Maybe one of them will turn out to be our savior, like we're saving that idiot, Morgan, right now."

She took a bump so hard it made Danziger's teeth rattle. "Just get us there, okay. We're making good time now—we just passed the hill where we slid down."

"I know," she said, kicking the DuneRail into its highest gear.

Danziger tapped her on the shoulder and pointed skyway. "Hey, look up there."

She slowed the vehicle and followed his finger to see four

dark flyers against the blue sky, way up along the rim. That high up, they certainly looked as if they were passing through with no intentions of disturbing anyone.

Morgan laughed as he passed the roaring confluence of the two rivers—one blue, one turquoise, blending into a river that was dark purple, almost like oceans he had seen. That might also have something to do with the lateness of the day, he told himself, because the mile-long shadows were already stretching across the canyon. He knew he was close to his objective now—he could feel it! And there was no way for that meddling cyborg or anyone else to stop them!

Morgan cackled some more, and Bess peered at him. "Are you all right?"

"Yes, indeed," he grinned. "You know, I'm glad they know what we're doing, because when I make my claim, their knowledge will be corroborating evidence. This is all working out perfectly!"

He held her hand as they walked. "I know I've been acting crazy about this sacred pool stuff, but the communication with the Terrians—it was so real. I had to go with it. You understand, don't you, sweetheart?"

"Of course," said Bess, gingerly touching a bruise on her upper arm. "But I'm not going back in that river for you or anyone else."

Morgan shook his finger at the offending waterway. "First thing we do," he promised, "is to build some bridges over it. The hydroelectric plants, the dams—all that other stuff will come later."

"Oh, I don't want to spoil the canyon," said Bess. "Leave it unspoiled, you know."

Morgan stroked his chin. "If you were doing a spa business, the customers might go for that unspoiled look.

We'll do some feasability studies and see what's best for business."

His eyes caught sight of something familiar, perhaps a quarter mile away. It was not the most spectacular plateau in the canyon; in fact, it was stubby and worn, as if it had sat for a long time at the bottom of a deep river a hundred times the size of this one. Morgan's heart quickened, and he began to run.

"Morgan," yelled Bess, just starting to catch up with him. "What's the matter?"

He pointed a quivering finger at his plateau. "That's *it*! The place I landed! I remember that field of flowers, do you see them? And those bulblike things on the ridge. They grow inside the grotto too. This is it, honey! *This is it!*"

Now they were both slogging through the sand, a new burst of adrenaline driving off the aches and exhaustion. Morgan had never felt so exhilarated in his entire life, because he was finally going to discover something! Instead of somebody else getting rich by being in the right place at the right time, it would be him! He was here first, out of all the humans in the universe. Nobody could dispute his claim on this one.

Morgan was so happy that he didn't hear the peculiar noise in the background until it grew rather loud. It wasn't bugs scraping their legs together, he knew that, and he glanced behind him to see Devon closing fast on the DuneRail.

"No!" he hollered, spinning around and slumping down on the sand.

"What is it?" asked Bess, dropping down beside him. Then she saw it too, and she wrapped her arms around his slender shoulders. "It's okay. Let's explain it to them."

The DuneRail roared to a stop, and Devon cut the engine. "Okay, you two, you're under arrest! Or the closest thing we've got to that. I was going to bawl you out, but I'm too tired to do it now."

Bess leapt to her feet. "Listen, Devon, we're right here—the sacred pool is just behind that plateau! Somewhere. It's only fifty yards away. At least let us check it out, since we're so close."

"No," snapped Morgan, "I don't want them to know where it is."

Devon scowled. "You know what, Morgan, I've got a good mind to really leave you here, after all the trouble you've caused!"

"Don't be dramatic, Devon," said Danziger, climbing out of the passenger seat. "You either, Morgan. You and Bess get in the DuneRail, and show us where it is. We've all made a long journey to get to this spot, and we may not be passing this way again. Don't you want to see it?"

Devon muttered something, but she didn't say no. Bess tried to pick Morgan up from the sand. "Come on, honey. Let's see if it's real."

Part of Morgan felt like crying after having been caught so close to his goal, but the curiosity was beginning to take over again. They were offering him a chance to see it!

He led them to the base of the plateau, with Danziger jogging along beside the DuneRail. Then they began to walk through the thistles and the flowers that surrounded the small plateau. The scent of the tiny red flowers brought back the dream memories. Morgan remembered the thrill of the flight, and the way he had landed here in the dark, as much by instinct as sight.

"There'll be a path on the other side," he told them as they rounded the plateau.

"Right," scoffed Devon. But she was in the lead, and she was the first one to find the narrow but well-trod path. It wasn't a Koba path. After that, no one spoke, they just followed the path through the plants to the wall of rock and the opening to the grotto.

Leaning against the walls inside the cave were a few old pairs of leather wings.

Bess was beaming with pride, and Devon looked darkly at Danziger, as if the last thing she wanted was for Morgan to be proven right. He chuckled and led them inside. The smell was even more dank and loamy than he had remembered, and it made his heart pound excitedly. The pool was real!

As before, the phosphorescent fibers along the cave walls gave them enough light to see and also led them downward through the narrow passages. Then came the second, more powerful aroma—sulfurous and molten. Devon coughed and hung back to let Morgan take the lead. He was trying to calculate how rich he was going to be, but he couldn't help but feel oppressed by the mystery and dignity of this place. The ancient Leather Wings he had seen assembled here that night were still here, at least in spirit. He swallowed dryly and wondered if they were making a mistake. No, he told himself, the Leather Wings had shown him the way here. They wanted him to be here.

Bess gasped when they rounded the corner and saw the entire floor aglow with a phosphorescent pool. It bubbled invitingly, casting acrid smoke and fumes into the sweltering atmosphere. Sweat was rolling down Morgan's neck, and he could see it glistening on Bess's forehead. But they were here.

"You doubt me now?" he asked, his voice echoing in the cloying chamber.

"No," said Devon with a cough. "It's truly amazing, but I can't breathe down here."

"The pool will fix everything," said Morgan, moving closer to it.

"Watch yourself," cautioned Danziger.

Morgan rolled up his sleeve, exposing the bite marks the fish had left on his forearm. He was excited, but he wasn't just going to jump in—he had seen the agony on some of the Terrians' faces, and he assumed the water must be hot. Best to treat a small wound first rather than go for an extra hundred years or so of life.

He crawled to the glimmering, bubbling pool and began to immerse his arm, elbow first. He got the tip of his elbow into the liquid when scorching pain bolted up his arm and threatened to short out his brain. He screamed with terror and yanked his elbow out, as Danziger and Bess dragged him away from the pool.

"What is it? What is it?" shrieked Bess, kneeling beside him.

"My elbow! My elbow!" he shrieked. "My God, it must be a third-degree burn!"

"I can't stand it in here!" shouted Devon, staggering toward the passageway that led out.

"Let's get you out into the light," said Danziger. He lifted Morgan under his arms and began to carry him out.

"But my pool!" screamed Morgan. "The Fountain of Youth!" He twisted to look behind him as Danziger and Bess helped him out. The pool looked so miraculous the way it bubbled and cast little stars on the cave of the roof. But it was not for their kind, and he suddenly knew it.

"My pool!" blubbered Morgan as they carried him out. "My pool . . ."

They set him in the sunlight outside the cave, and Danziger examined the injury the pool had inflicted upon his elbow. Bess looked on with concern, and Devon paced nervously, upset at the way she had panicked. Danziger lifted Morgan's arm and squinted at his elbow.

"Third-degree burns, I'll bet!" wailed Morgan. "That pool is useless, just useless!"

Danziger looked very pale. "I'll be damned."

"That's not a burn, is it?" asked Bess, peering over his shoulder.

"What is it?" yelled Morgan.

"Here," said Danziger, taking Morgan's hand and directing it toward his elbow. "You won't be able to see it, but you can feel it. Go ahead, it's not festering or anything."

Curiously, Morgan felt a patch of skin about the size of a coin on the tip of his elbow. Only it wasn't skin as he knew it—it was dry and scaly, lizardlike.

"If it's not a burn," he asked, "what is it? Boy, the pain was excruciating!"

"I don't know," said Danziger, shaking his head. "I know what it feels like—it feels like Terrian skin."

Devon stopped her packing to look at them. "Maybe it tried to change his molecular structure. How else would a Fountain of Youth work?"

"Or it's just for Terrians," suggested Bess. "And if you're not a Terrian . . ."

Morgan finished her thought. "It turns you into one."

Danziger swallowed and got to his feet. "This isn't something we can explore now, or probably at all without a lot of instruments we don't have. Shall we go find the others?"

Devon shivered. "Yes, let's go."

As they walked away, Morgan turned back to look at the narrow path and the entrance to the cave.

It was getting dark by the time Yale pulled the ATV to a stop and staggered out, his jaw hanging open at the unexpected sight of a giant crater that had stamped flat a section of the second canyon. It was the biggest crater he had ever seen, rivaling those he had seen on Mars. This was the circle at the end of the old Terrian's map, he realized, and what a circle it was!

In the fading light of sunset, he couldn't tell how recent the crater was, but its perfect symmetry made him fear that it had been caused by a devastating weapon of some sort. Or maybe it had been vast mining operations. Then again, the crater might be so old that it had been carved naturally by a meteor, and erosion had weathered it further. The river had long adapted to the crater's existence, forming a sparkling pool in the center of it.

More importantly, the walls of the canyon had been leveled by the impact of whatever it was, and a toddler could walk out here.

He hit the button on the Gear. "Devon! Devon! Come in?"

"I'm here, Yale," answered the familiar voice. She sounded weary and troubled.

"We're going to get out of the canyon!" he announced. "You would not believe it, but we found a vast crater in the middle of the second canyon. It'll be a Sunday drive getting out!"

"That's great," she said with obvious relief.

"Did you find Morgan and Bess?"

"Yes," she answered, "and that's also a story, but I can't tell it right now. Why don't you make camp there and wait for us? We may not catch up with you until tomorrow."

"Is everything okay?" asked Yale, who was sensitive to Devon's moods.

"It's just that this trip through the canyon has been more than I expected."

Yale smiled. "The same for all of us. Look, the others are arriving, and we'd better make camp. We'll save you some fish stew."

"Thanks," said Devon. "Out."

Yale turned off the Gear and started to walk back to greet the others. The TransRover was just arriving. Alonzo was reclining in it, not too comfortably. True and Uly were walking behind it. Most of the colonists were another forty yards back, taking their time in the deepening shadows of the canyon.

"Wow!" said Alonzo, motioning around in amazement. "Look at this. It couldn't be better if it was an escalator going up!"

"That's what I just told Devon," answered Yale with satisfaction. "And you aren't the only one who can communicate with Terrians."

The children walked by, and True was holding her backpack in a funny way and talking to it. Uly giggled. When they saw Yale looking at them, they both clammed up and walked faster.

"What are you two so cheerful about?" he asked.

"I found something I lost!" True yelled back, then the two of them ran off, giggling.

Yale shook his head and looked back at Alonzo, but the injured pilot had already fallen asleep. No need to disturb him, thought Yale, as he strode out to greet the colonists and tell them they would be making camp.

Yes, things are getting back to normal, he thought, or what passed for normal on this strange planet.

Alonzo's body was a few feet away, but his mind was soaring among the Leather Wings in the rarified air between the buttes of the canyon. They were dreaming too, he realized, as they were still nursing their wounds from the battle. They would soon be going to the sacred pool, they assured him, and all would be well.

He hadn't had a chance to say good-bye, and he really

didn't know what he could say to them. The humans had accepted and somewhat abused the Terrians' hospitality, then they had run off at the first sign of trouble. He still didn't know what it meant for him and Morgan to be shown the sacred pool, and he tried to ask why they had been shown. How could he ever repay such a solemn trust?

The Terrians' answer surprised him, and he felt it more than heard it—the relief, the freedom from years of anxiety. Something the humans had done during their visit had actually helped the Terrians settle matters with their enemies. Their presence had counted for something.

Although he couldn't understand it, Alonzo did not question their gratitude. He knew they were grateful for everything that life in the canyon brought them, including enemies, visitors, floods, and death. So he soared with them for the rest of his dream, enjoying the magnificent views of the canyon and the dignified company.

With his last thought before waking, he assured them that the humans would return someday.